Scorched Earth

Christopher Cartwright

Chapter One

The girl on the train didn't belong there.

Paxton West's piercing green eyes studied the diesel locomotive as it snaked along the mountain half a mile away through the scope of his McMillan TAC-50 sniper rifle. The landscape was a majestic and rugged expanse, blanketed in thick snow. Tall pine trees stood like sentinels, their branches heavy with the weight of winter. The train made its slow, laborious way along the snow-covered tracks, a serpentine line of rusted metal cars – each one filled to the top with iron ore – the clatter of its progress muted by the snow.

High on the Ural Mountains, laying on the ground, hidden in the snow in winter camouflage, Paxton adjusted his Schmidt & Bender 5-25×56 PMII telescopic sight, focusing in on the young child.

She looked about six years old.

Bundled in snow-white arctic clothing that blended with the icy backdrop, the girl looked happy in her fur-lined hood. The child wore a bright pink scarf, a jarring contrast to her otherwise harsh and dull surroundings.

Her blue eyes were lively and curious.

She pressed her tiny, gloved hands against the window, her breath fogging the glass as she gazed out, entranced by the passing landscape.

The train engineer was a burly man, his face weathered and rough. He had a thick, graying beard peeking out from beneath a worn cap pulled low against the cold. Paxton figured he might have been the girl's father, or possibly grandfather. His broad shoulders filled out his heavy coat, and his hands, large and calloused, gripped the controls with the confidence of someone who had spent years in the cab of a diesel train. The engineer kept his eyes on the tracks ahead, occasionally glancing at the gauges and levers, carefully adjusting the throttle to ease the train's slow approach toward the foundry.

Alarm bells fired in the back of Paxton's lizard brain.

If he had a conscience, he would abort the mission on those reservations alone.

His 2IC – Second in Command – Alicia looked at him.

A wary expression froze on her hardened face. She went by the call-sign "Raven" and was the best sniper shot in Paxton's six-person team of Ghosts. She looked like an angel with blonde hair, pale blue eyes, and white skin wrapped in a shroud of white snow clothes. But that's where any resemblance to an angel ended. Alicia Yeager was one of the best assassins Paxton had ever met. A large backpack rested next to her, and she stared through the optical scope of a Barrett M82A1 sniper rifle.

They exchanged a quick, silent glance.

"What's wrong?" Alicia mouthed quietly.

Paxton said, "There's a little girl on the train."

"So?" Alicia replied, without concern. "Maybe her dad's taking her out for the day?"

"Here?" Paxton asked, his voice incredulous. "I don't buy it. Intel's wrong. No way would someone take their daughter to a terrorist cell camouflaged as a steel foundry."

"Why not?" Alicia continued her train of thought. "If the steel works is a cover for a terrorist operation, there's no reason for the train's engineer to be concerned. Hell, there's a good chance it's just a cover. Maybe the engineer has no idea what's really happening here. As far as he's concerned, he takes iron ore to the foundry, steel slabs and ingots back."

Paxton frowned. "Maybe."

It was a possibility.

But his gut told him it was unlikely.

And besides, he didn't like to work with maybes.

Again, he thought, if he had a conscience, he'd pull the plug and abort the mission right now. Something was wrong, but it wasn't quite bad enough that he wanted to cut his losses and walk away – yet.

Paxton shifted his weight carefully.

His imposing six-foot-six frame moved with surprising grace as he adjusted his position in the snow. Blending seamlessly into the rugged landscape, his broad shoulders filled out his lightweight, waterproof camo jacket. He brushed a layer of frost from his sleeve, revealing a forearm corded with muscle, honed by years of grueling missions in hostile environments.

Paxton adjusted the sleek earpiece of his **TEA Invisio V60**, fitting it snugly beneath the edge of his snow camo hood. The headset was nearly invisible, designed with a low profile that blended seamlessly with his gear, its black matte finish disappearing against the shadowed contours of his face. The bone conduction microphone rested comfortably against his jawline, allowing him to communicate with his team without a word escaping into the frozen air.

His face was partially obscured by a snow hood, but his eyes – a cold, calculating green –narrowed with intense focus as he angled his body to reduce his profile against the icy wind. Lowering himself just enough to peer through the scope, he steadied the rifle against his shoulder, zeroing in on the foundry below. His breath was barely visible in the freezing air as he became one with the mountain's cold, unforgiving presence.

"This is Rembrandt," Paxton said through his radio. "Does anyone have eyes on any armed guards?"

"Negative," came Bulldog's reply. AKA Cole Knight. He specialized in heavy weapons and explosives. What's more, he was Paxton's oldest friend. They had been together a long time, going all the way back to the Naval Special Warfare Center in Coronado, California – where they had completed their Basic Underwater Demolition/SEAL training. It was Cole who had taught Paxton to swim. As an orphan, nobody had ever taught him much, and with his unique bone density and muscle composition, he was heavy in the water, and unable to float. Without Cole, he never would have become a Navy SEAL or a Ghost.

Below him, the steel works sprawled like a sleeping giant in the heart of the Ural Mountains. It was a maze of monolithic structures, with smokestacks reaching up like fingers into the gray sky. The buildings, a patchwork of aging brick and rusted metal, bore the scars of time and the unforgiving Russian winters. Cargo trains, heavy with their burdens, chugged along the intricate networks of railway tracks that cut through the facility.

"Negative," came Echo's reply. "No sign of guards." Her real name was Sherylaine Ocampo, and she was the communications and infiltration master. She was a five-foot tall, Asian woman whose grandparents immigrated from the Philippines after World War II. Despite her meek appearance, Paxton considered her a close runner-up for the title of best assassin next to Raven.

Paxton's eyes narrowed on the maze of monolithic structures, smokestacks reaching up like fingers into the gray sky, belching plumes of white steam and dark fumes. The buildings were a patchwork of aging brick and rusted metal, bearing witness to decades of wear and relentless Russian winters. Stretching across the landscape were intricate networks of railway tracks, with cargo trains laden with iron ore and coal making their slow journey into the facility.

Falcon, AKA Dennis Carter, who, as a 22-year-old man was the youngest in the team, said, "Nothing from the sky." He was highly skilled in reconnaissance and aerial support, with an array of surveillance drones, which only a kid might know how to use.

To Paxton's left, a large reservoir shimmered, its surface occasionally disrupted by bursts of steam from nearby cooling towers. He noticed the artificial water channels that ran parallel to the steel works, essential for the cooling and processing of molten metal. Large furnaces gave off an otherworldly orange glow that contrasted sharply with the surrounding snow.

"I've got nothing," Hammer said. His name was Tyler Briggs. At 56, he was the grandfather of the team. He was a career Green Beret who had given more than thirty years to the United States Army Special Forces. When a mission went wrong, and he lost the rest of his team, he submitted his resignation. Paxton read his file and offered him an alternative. How would he like to join a crew that might be able to provide justice to the men he'd lost?

Revenge was a popular motivator, and Briggs had taken the deal.

Paxton frowned and kept searching the landscape. Something was off about their entire mission.

Last to reply was Raven. Paxton heard her crisp voice over the radio, despite being close by. "Negative."

Paxton frowned.

There was only so much one could ignore, and currently the sixth sense in his gut was screaming.

The Intel was looking wrong.

Despite the looming presence of icy mountains and the omnipresent snow, the heat emanating from the furnaces was palpable, even from his distant perch.

As he adjusted the focus on his scope, Paxton could see workers, their faces smeared with soot and sweat, moving busily between the structures.

His eyes landed on two workers close to the roaring furnace, their bodies almost swallowed by the immense, heat-resistant suits they wore. The thick, metallic fabric gleamed under the harsh orange glow, reflecting the fire's fury. He knew that each suit was layered and reinforced, bulkier than any standard protective gear. Their helmets were sealed tight, with large, mirrored visors that caught light, giving them an alien, featureless look. Tubes and wires extended from the back of their suits, feeding in fresh air.

They resembled astronauts more than steelworkers.

Each movement was cautious, measured. It was like they were moving underwater, as if even the slightest misstep could mean the end – which was entirely possible.

One of the workers paused to adjust a piece of equipment, and Paxton caught a glimpse of the slow, deliberate movements of the worker's gloved hands. The furnace's roar drowned out anything else, but he could imagine the pounding heat that radiated from it, beating down on them even through the layers of protection.

His gaze swept across the foundry, noting the sparse presence of a workforce. It wasn't surprising – modern steel foundries were almost entirely automated these days.

"There's no guards at all," Paxton said, almost to himself.

Raven shrugged. "Kind of hard to steal much from a foundry. Everything's heavy. You'd need a train to get anything off the mountain. The foundry runs twenty-four hours a day. The laborers probably double up as all the security they need."

"Maybe," Paxton said, hating the word as he said it.

His gaze returned to the girl in the diesel train as it slowed to a stop partially inside the steel foundry.

The little girl jumped down from the train.

She seemed only too eager to get out and play in the snow after her long train journey. One of the foremen seemed to give her a high-five.

That was too much for Paxton.

He shook his head. "I don't buy this. Not one bit."

The Intel was wrong.

If that was the case, he and his team were about to commit a serious War Crime, an act of foreign terrorism that would have him tried and sentenced to death.

The Russian government would have a field day having captured American agents so clearly in the wrong. Of course, the CIA, along with the rest of the US government would deny everything.

Paxton and his men were Ghosts.

Members of an elite team, ordained by the CIA to perform clandestine operations that needed to be performed, but nobody in this modern world was willing to accept responsibility for.

Their former lives had ended.

There had been burials at Arlington, along with posthumous awards, and some purple hearts thrown in for good measure.

They were already dead.

No records of their existence.

Which meant, if things went wrong, they would disappear forever – and nobody would ever acknowledge they had existed at all.

Paxton's lips formed a grim line.

He looked at Alicia. "Okay, give the order to the rest of the team, Raven – abort."

She pressed her lips together. "Are you sure?"

He nodded.

If they were still in the military, she would be bordering on insubordination by now. But they were Ghosts, a long way from their former military lives, and he respected her views.

Alicia said, "We could wait until that little girl climbs back onto the train and it departs?"

"No," Paxton said, his voice emphatic. "Everything's wrong here. The train, the ore carts, and especially the girl. It looks like nothing more than a Russian steel foundry."

Alicia said, "That's what it's supposed to be. Intel says the terrorist cell is hidden in plain sight within the foundry."

"Sure. But if that's the case. Where are the guards?"

"Why do they need guards? They're in the middle of nowhere, and their product – being steel, and nuclear weapons – are heavy. It's not like they have to worry about snatch and grab attacks."

"Right. But that's where things don't make sense. If it's just for show, they would still want cover for their terrorist operation. If they are indeed processing miniature nuclear weapons inside, they're going to want to keep them safe somehow."

"Maybe they think outstanding camouflage is enough? If so, it's working right now."

Paxton trusted Alicia with his life. She was an excellent operator. Smart as they come. Tough, and a more than capable killing machine. But something in his gut told him this was wrong. Really wrong. This wasn't a terrorist cell, this was a legitimate steel foundry housed high in the Ural Mountains, miles from anywhere.

And if he killed these people, it would be illegal.

Alicia said, "It's your call."

Paxton nodded.

He'd thought about the situation long enough.

Without hesitation, he said, "Tell the team to abort."

Alicia gave a curt nod of her head. She pressed her Push to Talk radio mic. "This is Raven…"

No other words came out.

Instead, a sniper bullet ripped through her skull, killing her instantly – leaving a misted spray of blood, brain, and bone fragments scattered in the snow.

Paxton swore.

He pushed himself backward, sliding all the way down the ravine, until he was certain he was no longer visible or targetable.

The sniper rifle must have been equipped with a suppressor, and even though the crack of the shot was audible, its direction seemed to be blurred across the mountain range, its source, indistinguishable.

Paxton's brain kicked into gear.

Computing every possibility.

Someone knew they were here.

Which meant, right or wrong, if they wanted to get out of Russia alive, they were going to have to complete their mission…

Paxton depressed the mic. "Rembrandt to all Ghosts – Raven's down, sniper shot in the head. Falcon, we need eyes above to find the shooter! Everyone else, it's time to go to work."

Chapter Two

Number One Observatory Circle, Washington, D.C.

The grand Queen Anne-style residence was located on the northeast grounds of the U.S. Naval Observatory in Washington, D.C. It exuded both historical charm and quiet elegance. Built in 1893, it was initially intended as the home for the observatory's superintendent before being repurposed in 1974 as the official residence of the Vice President of the United States.

The house, painted a soft cream color with white trim, stood out with its steeply pitched roof and ornate gables, hallmarks of Queen Anne architecture. Its wraparound porch, with a series of graceful columns and wooden balustrades, invited guests to linger and enjoy the surrounding views. Large bay windows punctuated the façade, allowing sunlight to pour into the interior, providing glimpses of the lush greenery that surrounded the residence.

The grounds were meticulously maintained, with expansive lawns stretching out in every direction. Carefully manicured gardens framed the house, bursting with seasonal flowers that added vibrant splashes of color throughout the year. Mature oak and maple trees stood tall around the property, offering shade and privacy while creating a tranquil oasis within the bustling capital. Pathways of red brick meandered through the gardens, leading to secluded benches where one could sit and reflect in the peaceful surroundings.

Behind the residence, a spacious lawn extended toward the observatory buildings, linking the house to its historic origins. A charming gazebo nestled among the trees provided an intimate spot for quiet conversation or relaxation. The air was often filled with the sound of birdsong, as the gardens were a haven for local wildlife.

Despite its grandeur, the house maintained a sense of warm homeliness, adapted by each Vice President to reflect their family's unique personality and needs. Over the years, subtle additions and renovations had been made to modernize the residence while preserving its historic character. It was both a symbol of tradition and an inviting home for the nation's second family.

Vice President Daniel Hawthorne sat in the deep leather chair behind his desk, the scent of aged wood and faint cigar smoke lingering in the air. He ran a hand over the smooth mahogany surface of the desk, custom-built to mimic the resolute authority of the Oval Office's iconic centerpiece. It was a behemoth of a desk, its surface adorned with only a brass lamp, a few carefully chosen photographs, and a leather blotter – every item placed deliberately to exude both gravitas and purpose.

Hawthorne leaned back, the chair creaking under his weight, a reminder of the years that had transformed his once-athletic frame. In his prime, he had been a formidable football player, a tight end known for his explosive power and unrelenting drive. Though much of that muscle had softened with age, his broad shoulders and imposing frame still carried an undeniable strength. At sixty-two, Hawthorne was no longer a young man, but he prided himself on retaining the grit and tenacity of his athletic days, even if his knees occasionally protested when he stood for too long.

His study at Number One Observatory Circle was his pride and joy – a powerful statement of his vision and his presence. Unlike the rest of the home, which bore the charm of a historic residence, this room was Hawthorne's unique addition.

Each Vice President, it was said, left their mark on the residence, and this was his. Designed to reflect his personal style and political standing, it combined the old-world charm of richly paneled walls and brass fixtures with the practicality of modern security. The room was soundproofed and reinforced, more akin to a secure bunker than a cozy home office. This was a deliberate choice for the sensitive, off-the-record meetings he often hosted here – where the real plays for power were made.

Bookshelves lined the walls, filled with volumes that showcased his interests and aspirations—political treatises, historical accounts, and the occasional football memoir. A large globe stood to the side, its polished brass base gleaming softly in the low light. The heavy curtains were drawn, shutting out the world outside, as the room hummed faintly with the sound of its hidden ventilation system.

He sighed with pride and satisfaction. This was a space of domination and total control. A location where tough decisions were made and strategies formed.

Hawthorne stared at the leather-bound notebook open on the desk in front of him. It was filled with his own cramped handwriting – notes from the day's meetings, thoughts on the upcoming budget negotiations, and reminders to follow up on a delicate diplomatic matter. He rested his elbows on the armrests, his large hands steepled before him, and considered the weight of the choices he faced. This room, this fortress of his own making, was where he felt most at home, where he could speak freely, argue fiercely, and craft the moves that would define his legacy.

He leaned back in his leather chair, staring into the flames licking at the logs in the large stone fireplace. The steady crackle filled the room, a comforting backdrop to the storm brewing in his mind.

He had been expecting them for hours, and when the firm knock came at the heavy oak door, he wasn't startled. Instead, he folded his hands on the massive mahogany desk before him and called out, "Come in."

The door opened to reveal Agent Walker, a member of his personal security detail, standing crisply at attention. "Sir, Marcus Voss, Dr. Alan Kepler, and Dylan Frost have arrived."

"Send them in," Hawthorne ordered, his expression betraying neither surprise nor urgency.

Walker stepped aside and the three men entered, each distinct yet unified by the weight of their shared purpose. Hawthorne rose, gesturing toward the pair of opposing leather lounges positioned in front of the fire. At the center of the arrangement lay a large bear skin rug, its dark fur reflecting the flickering firelight.

Agent Walker closed the heavy door, leaving them alone.

"Gentlemen," Hawthorne said warmly, motioning for them to sit. "Let's get started."

Marcus Voss was the first to step forward, his tailored suit impeccable, his demeanor as sharp as the angles of his clean-shaven jawline. The man exuded authority, his silver-streaked hair and intense gray eyes giving him the air of a corporate predator. Hawthorne knew him well as the CEO of Obsidian Sentinel Systems, a leader in advanced military technology. Voss had spent decades perfecting the art of merging innovation with power, and his reputation for ruthless efficiency preceded him.

Voss sat down with a smooth, deliberate motion, one leg crossing over the other as if claiming the room as part of his domain.

Dr. Alan Kepler, a quiet but commanding presence, followed, lowering himself into the lounge with deliberate movements. At seventy-six, he was the elder statesman of the group, his silver hair combed neatly back, his lined face a map of decades spent in the shadowy world of intelligence. His gaze, sharp and calculating, missed nothing as he took in the study's old-world charm.

Although little was known about Dr. Kepler officially, he had been employed by the CIA for nearly forty-five years. The man was a polymath with a background in neurology, global politics, intelligence analysis, and espionage. He went by the codename Peregrine, earned for his ability to see the broader picture while remaining swift and decisive when the moment demanded action. Currently, he was both the architect and the Director of the Ghosts – a clandestine organization operating in the unseen crevices of international conflict.

Finally, Dylan Frost sauntered in with the casual, almost careless gait of someone who lived in a world of ideas rather than appearances. His long hair, tied loosely at the nape of his neck, and his wire-rimmed glasses gave him the look of a guy who could have walked straight out of a tech startup – or a hacker movie. Dylan's graphic T-shirt, emblazoned with a neon-green skull over crossed keyboards, clashed with the formal surroundings, but he seemed entirely unfazed.

The youngest of the group by far, Dylan was the Ghosts' digital architect, responsible for crafting fictional lives for the Ghost operatives, including their illusory relationships, children, careers, universities, social clubs, and volunteer work. He flopped onto the lounge opposite Kepler, slouching into the cushions as though he owned them.

Hawthorne allowed himself a brief glance at the fire.

These were the men he'd aligned his fate with – a narcissistic tech CEO, an erudite academic, and a man who thrived in the digital ether. They were here to discuss matters few in the world even knew existed. As the flames danced behind them, Hawthorne felt the gravity of what lay ahead, settling firmly on his shoulders.

Hawthorne rose from his chair with ease, crossing to the antique sideboard where a crystal decanter of amber whiskey gleamed in the firelight. The decanter, a gift from an old friend in Scotland, held a rare single malt aged for over thirty years.

He removed the stopper. With a faint pop, the earthy, and peaty aroma filled the air. The Vice President took four heavy-cut crystal glasses from the tray and placed them on the sideboard with a deliberate care that matched his mood. Pouring the whiskey, he allowed just enough in each glass to coat the bottom generously, the liquid swirling like molten gold under the light.

He handed them to each of the men without questioning if they would like a drink or not, let alone if they enjoyed strong liquor.

There was no clinking of glasses with joy. Instead, there was the sort of silent camaraderie of people whose fate was entirely entwined.

Hawthorne momentarily met the eyes of each man in turn, then brought the glass to his lips, savoring the warmth of the alcohol as it burned softly down his throat. It was a grounding sensation for the difficult conversation that was about to begin.

For a moment he stared at the flames in the fireplace.

Then the Vice President's gaze drifted from the flickering fire to the three associates seated before him. Marcus Voss, sharp and composed as always, sipped his whiskey with the quiet confidence of a man who understood power intimately.

Dr. Alan Kepler, radiated a calm authority that came from decades of navigating the undercurrents of international intelligence.

And, finally, Dylan Frost. The youngster, lounging with the casual irreverence that mocked the seriousness of the moment, yet whose mind worked like a precision instrument.

Hawthorne's stomach churned with an uneasy mix of anger and fear, emotions he rarely allowed himself to feel, let alone acknowledge. He had come too far, built too much, to be brought down now. The sheer horror of it! Knowing that the decisions of these men, sitting on opposing lounges in front of his fire, could determine the fate of everything he had worked for – gnawed at him like a slow acid burn.

His thoughts wandered backward, unbidden but relentless, to the coal mines of western Pennsylvania. He could still feel the crushing weight of the earth above him, the damp chill of the tunnels, and the ache in his arms from wielding a pickaxe for hours on end. He had been just sixteen when his father died, leaving him the man of the house. There had been no choice – school had to wait while he worked the mines to keep food on the table for his mother and younger siblings. The darkness of those days was still with him, a gloomy shadow he couldn't quite shake, no matter how far he had risen.

He had been strong then – physically strong, hardened by the relentless grind of survival.

The football talent scout had seen that strength, plucking him from the mines and handing him a scholarship to the University of Notre Dame. He had embraced the opportunity with the same ferocity he had once used to claw coal from the earth. On the football field, he had been unstoppable, a force of nature. And when the cheering crowds faded, he turned that same drive toward the law, building a career that took him from courtrooms to the corridors of power.

Returning to his home state, Hawthorne built a reputation as a staunch advocate for labor rights and fair energy policies, first serving as Pennsylvania's Attorney General, where he tackled corporate corruption and championed worker protections.

This success propelled him to the governor's office, where he revitalized the state's economy by balancing traditional energy industries with emerging renewable technologies. After two terms as governor, Hawthorne was elected as a U.S. Senator, where his bipartisan approach and focus on working-class issues gained him national prominence. His compelling story and legislative achievements made him a natural choice as the running mate, balancing the presidential ticket and helping secure the White House.

Now, as Vice President of the United States, the distance between the coal mines and Number One Observatory Circle seemed immeasurable.

And yet, it wasn't.

The weight of responsibility still pressed down on him like the massive weight of the mine, though now it was the future of a nation – and his own hard-won legacy – heavily resting on his shoulders. He remembered his father, who had died before seeing any of his achievements, and his grandfather, the swollen, deformed joints of his fingers roughened, and his lungs scarred, by decades of the same thankless toil.

In an unusual show of honest introspection, he silently acknowledged to himself that he had broken many laws on his route to the highest office. He had done plenty of corrupt deals, but show him a politician who hadn't?

No, he'd made his bed, and he was only too happy to lay in it. His route to the top was interlaced with deals with greedy CEOs, wealthy donors, and unethical billionaires who had only too happily lined his pockets in exchange for lucrative government contracts. He was guilty as all hell. Those who had challenged him, he had gotten rid of, either through lies, intimidation, blackmail, bribery, and where required, violence.

If he were honest, he would gladly break a great deal more laws before he achieved his greatest ambition: The Presidency of the United States of America.

But it was worth it for what he'd achieved.

America was a safer, better, and more prosperous place because of the rules he'd broken, and the decisions he'd made. He didn't see himself as a villain. Far from it. He was a fucking saint – a man who made the kind of brutal, gut-wrenching decisions that would break most decent people. He carried the weight of those choices, bearing the guilt in silence, all to shield everyday Americans from the harsh truths that kept them safe.

Did he have vices?

He thought about the women. About the aggression that simmered inside him, rising unbidden like the cravings of an addict. Of course he did! But show him a politician – hell, show him a single human being – who claimed they didn't wrestle with their own darkness, and he'd show you a liar.

No, he could live with his faults.

He and Niccolò Machiavelli could agree on one thing...

The ends justified the means.

Everything Hawthorne had built would crumble if the wrong secrets escaped, if the wrong people acted on their sudden pangs of conscience.

His eyes settled on Voss, Kepler, and Frost again. These three – an architect of advanced weapons, a spymaster, and a scruffy digital genius – were all that stood between him and disaster. It was disturbing, he thought, that so much could hinge on so few. But then again, his entire life had hinged on small moments, improbable chances, and sheer willpower. These three could stop the chaos before it began. He simply must make sure they understood just how high the stakes truly were.

Hawthorne raised his glass of whiskey, the amber liquid glowing in the firelight. He spoke quietly, but his voice carried the power of a man who had dug himself out of one life and into another.

He studied the others in the room, then the set of his mouth formed a pugnacious line. "All right, who's going to bring me up to speed with this disaster?"

"That will be me," Dr. Kepler said, his voice cold and hard.

"Good." Hawthorne's eyes narrowed. "And when you're finished, you can tell me what the fuck we're to do about it?"

Chapter Three

Paxton recognized the high-pitched whirring sound of their surveillance drone.

It buzzed overhead, its faint mechanical hum blending with the howling wind that whipped through the snow. Paxton could feel its presence before he saw it, the unmistakable noise of its rotors slicing through the cold air. He looked up, squinting against the bright sunlight reflecting off the white expanse, and spotted the drone hovering above him.

His eyes quickly shifted to the curved touchscreen wrapped around his wrist. It was sleek, designed like an old Viking band. His fingers hovered over the surface for a moment before tapping the eagle-eye symbol. The band came alive, its interface glowing with sharp, vivid detail. A moment later, the drone's viewpoint appeared on the screen. The image flickered across the landscape, before locking onto the scene below, revealing Raven's lifeless body in stark detail.

The drone's sensors kicked in, analyzing the blood splatter – calculating the trajectory and angle of the shot, before quickly determining the bullet's origin. Paxton watched the digital overlay as it marked the exact starting point of the fatal round, pinpointing its trajectory with mathematical precision.

The whir of the drone increased in pitch as it adjusted its course, rotating so that its camera could follow the direct line of sight the shooter had taken.

Paxton stared at his digital Viking band.

It kept playing the live video footage from the drone.

The image began to rotate right to left, in a search pattern behind them. It was scanning the rocky outcrop toward the upper reaches of the Ural Mountains a couple hundred feet above where he was positioned, in a place where granite boulders rose above the pine trees and snow to form an impenetrable cliff face.

It used LIDAR.

The acronym stood for Light Detection and Ranging. Utilized extensively in archeology, it was often used to form a map of the ground below tree canopies.

Paxton watched the live drone feed intently on his curved digital screen, the display wrapping around him like a command center from the future. The LIDAR pulses mapped out the granite outcrop in sharp relief, each laser scan layering onto the image until the rugged terrain seemed almost tangible. Boulders and crevices appeared one by one, each crag and fissure captured with eerie accuracy.

The 3D map took shape, revealing a complex maze of rocks and ledges, every detail adding another piece to the puzzle. As the drone continued its meticulous scan, Paxton's eyes narrowed on several points of interest highlighted in pulsing red. These were places with just the right amount of cover and elevation to give a shooter an unobstructed view.

He focused on a narrow ledge halfway up the outcrop, tucked behind a screen of low scrub and shaded from above. It was exactly the kind of hidden vantage point a skilled sniper would choose. The drone shifted lower, directing the LIDAR toward this specific spot, refining the map as it gathered each new layer of data.

Still nothing.

It circled around, expanding its search grid.

Paxton depressed his mic. "Speak to me Falcon. Have you got eyes on the shooter?"

"I'm working on it!" Falcon said.

A moment later, the drone stopped moving. It fixed on what appeared to be a massive eagle's nest, built some ninety-plus feet into the air, and wedged into the side of the cliff.

"Got them!" Falcon said.

Paxton's eyes narrowed on the massive eagle's nest.

It was perched high on the cliff face. The structure clung to the granite wall, an intricate weave of large sticks and thick branches wedged tightly into the cracks and crevices. The nest was massive, likely weighing two or three tons – a structure that seemed both impossibly fragile and enduringly solid, as though it had been part of the cliff for centuries.

In all probability, it had taken the eagles over a hundred years to build. A generational nest, extended by each new family, who added to its size and strength with their own gifts of sticks and branches.

"What am I looking at?" Paxton asked over the radio.

Falcon said, "Just watch the eagle's nest."

Paxton stared at the image.

The drone's camera zoomed in, focusing on the underbrush beneath the eagle's nest. It was so small, it was almost imperceptible, and Paxton knew he would have missed it if Falcon hadn't pointed it out.

There were two small pieces of steel bolted into the rockface and crisscrossed to form a support beam and platform upon which the eagle's nest had been built.

Paxton grinned. "Well, well. It's man-made!"

"What's more," Falcon said, adjusting the focus of the drone's camera lens to fixate on the middle section of the eagle's nest. "Look at this!"

Paxton stared at it.

For a few split seconds, he wasn't sure he could see anything. Nothing that stood out as unnatural. From what he could see, there was still every possibility that those steel beams formed the support of a climbing rig or an old pulley system, now used by an ingenious eagle who claimed the space as its own.

Then he saw it.

A single barrel.

No, two barrels.

They were well camouflaged to look like natural branches that formed the walls of the nest. The eagle's nest created the perfect location for two or possibly even three snipers to watch over the precious Tactical Nuclear Weapons of their small terrorist factory.

The snipers must have used a caving ladder to reach it, and then pulled it up after each climb, leaving no easy access and ensuring their fortress remained out of reach.

Despite the nest's fragile appearance, Paxton could imagine it would be lined with thick armored steel behind its façade of natural sticks and branches. This would make it secure to defend and difficult to attack.

Paxton depressed the mic. "Bulldog, do you have any idea how to reach those snipers up there?"

"If it's all the same to you, Rembrandt, I would prefer to bring them down to us."

Paxton said, "Good suggestion. Make it happen."

"Copy that. Just give me a minute and I'll knock those birds right out of their nest."

Paxton stared at Alicia's crumpled body.

It was an absolute tragedy. An expert assassin, taken out by a sniper's shot, just before ordering them to abort the mission.

Luck was a brutal mistress.

If he was still a Navy SEAL, he would have made sure she wasn't left behind. Her body would be returned stateside for a proper burial. But they weren't still in the Navy. Right where she rested, Alicia had already been buried. There was no way they were going to take her where they were going.

It was impossible, no matter how much he would have liked to.

Paxton pressed the mic again. "All Ghosts, on Bulldog's mark, we storm the foundry and complete our mission." He paused, his throat strangely tight, and then added, "This one's for Raven."

Chapter Four

Bulldog moved with the fast, efficient speed of an experienced professional.

Keeping low and hidden in the snow, his fingers worked quickly as he unzipped the canvas backpack case and pulled out the familiar weight of the RPG-7. The launcher gleamed dully in the low light, a functional and deadly piece of hardware that he'd maintained with almost religious care. He slid the padded casing aside, revealing the detachable components neatly stowed within.

First, Bulldog attached the wooden shoulder stock to the launcher's tube, locking it into place with a practiced twist. The connection clicked with a satisfying sound, firm and secure. He then unfolded the iron sights, his thumb brushing against the rear notch as he calibrated it to the appropriate range. Somewhere between instinct and muscle memory, honed through years of practice, he hit the perfect mark.

Reaching back into the case, he extracted the warhead, its bulbous tip unmistakable. Bulldog twisted the grenade's stabilizing fins to ensure they were locked in the closed position before sliding the rocket into the launcher's muzzle with a smooth motion. He rotated it gently until the pins engaged, the faint metallic snick confirming it was seated properly.

It was the Soviet era classic rocket-propelled grenade armament, not the modernized version built by AirTronic USA. It, along with everything they had brought with them into the country, could have been purchased in Russia.

The Russian government were going to know in an instant who attacked the terrorist cell and could almost certainly guess the US agency behind the attack. But there was no way in hell the CIA was ever going to admit that, much less ever provide them with evidence to use as propaganda.

The RPG-7, a relic of the Soviet era, had the rugged, utilitarian look of something designed to survive any warzone. Its green-tinted launcher was scarred and scratched from years of use, the tapered rocket protruding menacingly from the muzzle.

It wasn't state-of-the-art, but the weapon was tried and true.

At six feet tall, Bulldog's thick neck, broad shoulders, and barrel-like torso made him look shorter than he was, giving him an appearance that matched his nickname.

He knelt and braced the RPG-7 on his shoulder, aiming at the base of the nest. From this angle, the so-called eagle's nest looked like what it really was – a manmade stronghold, reinforced and camouflaged to blend seamlessly into the cliff face. Through the sight, Bulldog could make out the structural base of the nest, a tangle of branches cleverly lashed together with steel wiring.

Bulldog exhaled slowly, the familiar weight of the RPG-7 pressing against his shoulder as he sighted down the tube. His target loomed in the distance, a steel-reinforced bunker nestled into the hillside. His thumb nudged the safety lever, and his finger found the trigger.

The moment he squeezed it the launcher barked with a sharp report.

The booster charge fired first, propelling the grenade forward in a blur of motion. A plume of smoke briefly trailed behind the weapon as the projectile cleared the launcher, its fins springing open mid-flight. Bulldog felt the push of pressure as it whooshed away.

Less than a second later, the sustainer motor kicked in, its ignition a faint flare in the sky as it carried the warhead toward its destination. The sudden acceleration was remarkable, the incendiary device tearing through the air at nearly 900 feet per second. The fins imparted a slow, deliberate spin, stabilizing its flight as it hurtled toward the bunker unerringly on target.

Bulldog lowered the RPG-7, watching as the warhead struck home with a brilliant flash.

The explosion was instant and violent.

Branches and debris erupted outward in a fiery blast, and the entire structure gave way, crumbling from its foundation. Bulldog watched as three figures tumbled from the nest, their sniper rifles spinning uselessly through the air before they disappeared into the rocks below. The explosion sent shards of concrete and steel spiking outward, a shockwave rolling through the valley.

Pride and pleasure warming his chest, Bulldog packed the RPG-7 into its case and attached it to the much larger backpack. He pulled the pack over his shoulders. Then he grabbed his PP-19-01 Vityaz submachine gun, clipped his boots onto skis, and began skiing downhill toward the steel foundry...

Chapter Five

The little girl screamed.

Paxton secured his boots into their bindings, the familiar click of metal locking into place bringing a sense of focus.

He glanced down, mentally mapping his route.

The snow-covered mountain was steep, littered with jagged rocks and patches of ice. Navigating it would be treacherous, but the quickest path to the foundry cut straight down. He took a series of deep breaths, planted his poles, and pushed off, leaning forward to gain momentum as he carved his first turn.

The wind whipped past him, sharp and cold against his face as he picked up speed. His skis cut smoothly through the snow, and he adjusted his stance, shifting his weight to keep control on the steep incline. The world blurred at the edges, his focus narrowing on the path ahead. He ducked low, his body moving instinctively with each shift and curve of the slope, absorbing the jolts and bumps as he maneuvered around obstacles.

Paxton was an expert skier.

The plan was for him to take the fastest route off the mountain and he would be followed by his team who would offer suppressing fire if needed. Then, their roles would reverse, and he would cover them as they finished their descent.

Paxton leaned forward, his skis slicing through the icy snow with surgical precision as he led his team down the slope. Below, the steel foundry sprawled like a grim industrial fortress, its smokestacks pumping black smoke into the overcast sky. The moment they crested the ridge, he saw movement – workers scrambling to arm themselves.

The crack of gunfire shattered the ice-cold air, and a burst of bullets kicked up snow thirty feet away from Paxton's skis.

"Contact!" Paxton barked over the comms, shifting his stance to pick up speed. He swung to the right, aiming toward a series of trees to provide partial cover during his descent while his team fanned out behind him.

Echo moved to his right, laying down suppressive fire, while Bulldog and Hammer angled toward a ridge to the left for an overwatch position.

More shots erupted from the several workers who spilled out of the steel foundry like an angry army of ants after its nest had been kicked over. They brought with them a cacophony of Kalashnikov Assault Rifles. A line of men crouched behind a stack of steel girders, firing wildly. Paxton noticed a few workers – those closest to the molten steel – continued going about their work, seemingly oblivious to the firefight erupting outside.

Madness. Yet such insanity seemed almost normal in his line of work.

Paxton noticed the worker's shots were all falling wide.

At a guess, he figured these weren't professional fighters. They were steel workers who had access to Kalashnikovs to double up as guards, or even to use as deterrents against bear attacks.

Paxton wasn't particularly concerned.

It would take a lucky shot to hit him from this distance as he moved with speed. It was possible, but so was getting struck by lightning. Neither of which he had ever wasted any thought about.

Instead, he concentrated on rapidly covering ground and carving his way through the dense forest of pine trees.

Up ahead, Paxton noticed the train beginning to move.

The old, hulking beast hissed as it started to lurch forward, its wheels screeching against the ice-slick rails. In the cab, a man leaned out of the window, barking orders in Russian. He fired a PPSh-41 submachine gun toward Paxton's team, its drum magazine rattling with every burst.

The engineer shouted at his daughter to get inside and stay down.

Halfway down the hill, the terrain grew even steeper. Paxton spotted a stretch of sheer ice and tightened his grip on his poles, leaning back just enough to ease his descent without losing momentum. His heart pounded as he skimmed over the ice, his skis barely holding their grip, until he finally hit snow again and steadied himself.

The foundry loomed larger below, its steel-gray walls and high chimneys now visible through the thinning mist.

Paxton veered to the left, navigating a final outcrop of rocks before cutting straight down toward the flat expanse at the base of the mountain. He could feel the burn in his legs, but he pushed through, his focus locked on the buildings ahead.

The engineer's cabin began to retreat into the distance, and the echoing sound of submachine gun bursts began to die off, leaving the scattered and crisp reports of the Kalashnikovs intermittently being fired into the mountain slope. One by one, Paxton heard the short, controlled bursts of return fire neutralizing the attackers. Then the sounds went dead as he skied toward the main entrance to the steel foundry.

With one final burst of speed, Paxton reached the bottom, skidding to a stop. Snow sprayed up around him as he unhooked his boots from his skis, breathing heavily.

Paxton found himself smiling.

He enjoyed skiing.

Always had.

Many years ago, before he'd become a Ghost, he had competed at the 2010 Vancouver Winter Olympics in Alpine Skiing, and then again at Sochi 2014.

In 2010 he'd taken a fall and had gone home without anything. But in 2014, at Sochi, he had learned his lessons and came home with a gold medal for his efforts.

Paxton crouched low in the snow, his breath misting in the frigid air as he reached down to unclip the Scarpa Maestrale RS boots from their bindings.

The matte black boots, scuffed and dusted with ice, were lightweight yet rugged, designed for missions exactly like this – where the line between skiing and combat blurred. Vibram soles gripped the icy ground beneath him, ready for the uneven terrain of the foundry ahead.

With a twist of the lever at his heel, he switched them into walk mode, the articulated cuff giving him freedom of movement as he rose to his full height. The boots, reinforced with high-performance polymer, provided both the stiffness needed for skiing and the flexibility to sprint if the situation demanded

Paxton dropped his heavy backpack and grabbed the Benelli M4 Super 90 from its holster on the side of the pack. Its weight reassuring in his hands as he pressed forward toward the foundry's massive entrance. The shotgun's black finish blended seamlessly with the shadows, while the red-dot sight mounted on the Picatinny rail glowed faintly, ready to mark targets in the dim interior. His gloved hand slid along the polymer stock, pulling it tight against his shoulder, and his finger hovered near the trigger guard, ready to engage.

Paxton glanced at where the rest of the remaining steel workers with Kalashnikovs had gone silent. It was his turn to provide cover for the rest of his team.

But not a shot was fired.

They were already dead. Raven would be pleased.

Then, one by one, Bulldog, Falcon, Hammer, and Echo each skied to a stop beside him.

Paxton grinned.

He lifted the Benelli M4 Super 90 shotgun up, ready to shoot anyone left alive.

It was time to head on inside, and to discover what terrorist weapons existed within the foundry, and if this mission had been worth Raven's life.

Chapter Six

P axton stepped into the massive industrial complex.

The steelworks were alive with activity, a symphony of metal clanging and machinery humming with production, as though the firefight that had just erupted outside had never existed. Enormous ladles filled with molten steel were suspended in mid-air, glowing a fierce orange as they were carefully maneuvered by overhead cranes. Sparks flew like fireworks as the molten metal was poured into molds, illuminating the dark, cavernous interior with an intense, fiery glow.

The air was thick with heat and the acrid smell of burning metal, mingling with the constant roar of furnaces and the rhythmic clatter of machinery. Paxton observed several workers below, clad in protective gear, moving amidst controlled chaos. The scale of the operation was staggering, with towering structures and intricate networks of pipes and conveyors stretching into the shadows.

Despite the overwhelming noise and heat, Paxton's mind was focused.

The place seemed mostly deserted.

Paxton exchanged a glance with Bulldog, who, with the loss of Raven, had now stepped up in the team as his 2IC. He signaled with his hands for them to split into two teams and make their way through the foundry.

Everyone was guilty by default.

Take no prisoners.

Lay the explosives and destroy the terrorist cell.

Then get to the extraction point.

It was that simple...

Paxton advanced with Echo and Bulldog with Falcon – leaving Hammer to follow up with his Geiger counter. His job was to locate any miniature nukes.

The machinery clanked and whirred around them, a constant cacophony that masked their movements. Still, his team moved with stealth, slipping through the shadows of the Ural Steel Foundry. The massive crucibles towered above them.

It felt like they had stepped into the bowels of the underworld.

They advanced cautiously, their silenced weapons at the ready. The few workers present were clad in aluminum or reflective metal suits, resembling creatures from another planet. One by one, the workers glanced up, their eyes widening in surprise, but they didn't have time to react. Shots cut through the air, and the workers fell, their bodies crumpling to the ground without a sound.

Paxton led his team through the labyrinthine foundry, past the roaring furnaces and the rivers of molten steel. They reached the main office, a structure built to overlook the entire foundry. The vantage point provided a clear view of the industrial behemoth below.

Paxton signaled to Echo and together they moved in.

The door to the office was breached swiftly and silently. Inside, the office was completely empty. Its workers were most likely dead outside in the snow. Mowed down by superior forces. They were amateurs who didn't stand a chance against professional killers – CIA Ghosts.

Paxton scanned the office, his eyes sharp and focused.

He frowned, running his eyes across the foundry. "Rembrandt to Ghosts – Report."

"The eastern side of the foundry has been cleared," came Bulldog's reply.

"The place is looking good from the air. Sentinel drone video feed shows no movement approaching the foundry or inside it. Right now, I've only got five moving bodies within the foundry – all Ghosts." Falcon's voice came over the radio. "I think we're on our own."

Paxton looked at Echo. "You got anything?"

"No." Echo shook her head. "The west is clear."

"Okay, Ghosts," Paxton said. "The foundry's clear. It won't remain that way for long. Time to go to work, doing what we came here to do."

Paxton said, "Hammer, how are you going with those radiation readings?"

"I'm working on it," Hammer said.

"Good." Paxton said, "Bulldog. You and Echo better start setting up the fireworks... we're going to have incoming soon."

"I'm on it," Bulldog said, already removing his large backpack and began pulling out various tools of destruction. He was utterly absorbed, like a man selecting instruments for a symphony of chaos. First came the blocks of C-4, neatly wrapped in their olive-drab casings, their malleable shapes catching the dim industrial light.

He laid them out methodically, a craftsman preparing his trade. Next, he unspooled a length of detonating cord, the thin, flexible line hissing softly as it slid through his calloused hands. Finally, Bulldog reached deeper into the pack, retrieving a pair of thermite charges, their sleek, metal casings designed to burn hot enough to melt through steel.

Paxton returned his gaze to Hammer, who moved methodically across the vast foundry floor, the rhythmic click-click-click of the Geiger counter breaking the oppressive silence. Hammer was built like his namesake, a solid wall of muscle striking hard and fast as if every step and turn were preordained. He held the Geiger counter with a steady hand, its analog needle quivering just enough to suggest it was working properly, but not enough to indicate danger.

Paxton's grip tightened on his shotgun as his eyes darted across the maze of molten steel vats, conveyor belts, and piles of scrap metal. The air was thick with the tang of scorched iron and sulfur, and the heat pressed against his skin through his tactical suit.

He couldn't shake the feeling that they were being watched.

"You getting anything, Hammer?" Paxton asked, his voice low but firm, transmitted through their encrypted comms.

Hammer shook his head without looking back. "Negative," he replied. His voice was gravelly but calm, with the no-nonsense tone that Paxton had come to rely on. Hammer adjusted the device and scanned a steel beam stacked with others, letting the counter hover near the surface. The clicking remained steady, monotonous.

"No residual radiation. No spikes," Hammer confirmed after another sweep.

Paxton exhaled through his nose, a mix of relief and frustration bubbling in his chest. The CIA intel had been firm – too firm – to be entirely wrong. This facility was supposed to be ground zero for a black-market nuclear operation.

Yet so far, they'd found nothing but heat and noise.

Which meant someone was lying to them.

"Could they have shielded it?" Paxton asked, moving to Hammer's side. The Geiger counter chirped faintly, registering the ambient background radiation present in any industrial setting but nothing more.

"It's possible, but doubtful. Not here. Lead shielding that thick would stand out like a sore thumb." Hammer adjusted the sensitivity on the counter and gestured toward a pile of scrap metal awaiting recycling. "I'll sweep that next."

Paxton nodded but felt his gut tighten. Hammer was thorough, but again, this operation wasn't adding up. If the radiation was absent, it meant one of two things: the nukes weren't here – or they'd been moved.

He scanned the upper levels of the plant with his rifle's scope, tracing the catwalks and shadows, looking for anything out of place. Above, the metal scaffolding groaned faintly as if complaining under its own weight.

Paxton's instincts were screaming at him to move faster, to find the truth hidden in the depths of the foundry before it found them first.

"Keep at it," Paxton said quietly. He glanced at Ghost, their tech specialist, who was setting up a compact thermal imaging drone on a nearby workbench. "If it's not here, we're missing something."

Hammer gave him a sharp nod and moved toward the scrap pile, the Geiger counter clicking steadily. But Paxton couldn't shake the growing certainty that the real threat was somewhere just out of reach – waiting for them to make the wrong move.

There was no sign of nuclear radiation.

If they had used this place as a cover for a trading post for Tactical Nuclear Weapons – the sort of small ones theoretically capable of being used on the battlefield, such as rockets, grenades, suitcases or bombs, then there would have been trace elements of radiation that would be sending their Geiger counters berserk...

And yet, the needles were whisper quiet. Someone had lied to them.

And Raven had died for nothing.

And that meant their entire mission had been a sham. It was time to get away and forget the entire operation. Paxton was about to order the mission aborted, and for the Ghosts to make their way to the extraction point...

Then he heard it.

A faint, almost imperceptible sound. Someone was crawling inside a metal cupboard that formed part of the desk.

He and Bulldog exchanged a quick glance.

Their eyes darting from each other back to the cupboard. It looked like the back of a desk, and barely big enough to hide anyone.

But was it possible the place led to a secret compartment?

Paxton aimed the shotgun at the door.

He motioned for Bulldog to open it.

Bulldog nodded and swung it open in one quick movement.

Paxton stepped forward with the Benelli M4.

A piercing scream erupted from inside, raw and frightened, echoing against the steel and concrete.

Chapter Seven

The young woman looked terrified.

She was crammed into the small space, her knees hugged tightly to her chest, wide blue eyes shimmering with panic beneath a fringe of disheveled blonde hair. She was wearing a plain black skirt and a crisp white blouse, now wrinkled and damp with sweat. Her face, framed by loose strands of hair, was pale and tear-streaked, betraying the fear that had driven her to such a desperate hiding spot.

Paxton moved without hesitation, the shotgun in his hands a blunt reminder of the danger in the air. Her scream rose again as his shadow loomed closer, but with one quick motion, he grabbed her arm and pulled her out of the cupboard like a doll.

"I'm not going to hurt you," Paxton said in fluent Russian. "I just need your help. I need you to answer some questions. Do you understand?"

Tears streamed down her eyes. "No, please..."

Paxton said, "You're not in any danger."

He quickly showed her an image on a small notepad, which he withdrew from his thigh pocket. It depicted a stark black trefoil with three evenly spaced blades radiating from a central black circle, set against a vivid yellow background, signaling danger with bold simplicity.

It was the internationally accepted symbol for just one thing...

Nuclear Radiation.

Her frightened eyes darted toward the symbol, but she kept her lips pressed firmly shut.

Paxton said, "Have you seen anything like this?"

"No, no... nothing!"

"Not anywhere around here?" Paxton gestured toward the train cars parked inside the foundry. "Do any of those carriages ever carry anything with that symbol?"

"No," she said determinedly.

"Are you certain?"

She shook her head. "I know what the nuclear radiation symbol is! We're a steel foundry. We melt iron ore and make steel. Sometimes we melt down disused steel parts, recycling them into low grade steel rods. We're not a military site. We don't make weapons. And we don't have anything to do with nuclear waste."

"Okay," Paxton said, releasing the pressure on her arm. "I'm going to let go now. There's no one else around. You don't need to scream or anything. I give you my word, nobody here is going to hurt you..."

Paxton released her.

She straightened the pleats of her thick, long skirt.

The woman seemed to make a point of straightening it, as though such a routine task was able to help her redeem her composure. It seemed odd, but Paxton had seen plenty of people who had survived near death experience generally turn to routine tasks in the moments afterward. He wasn't concerned. If it helped her collect herself, so be it. Better for her to regain some composure if she was to be of any use to him in terms of Intel.

The look of abject terror in her face had begun to fade.

She started to appear human again.

If he was capable of such feelings, he would have felt sympathy for her. She was just going about her regular job, and a bunch of assholes from the other side of the planet just killed all her colleagues.

As far as he understood, that made him the bad guy in this situation.

He frowned.

Sometimes he was glad he couldn't feel emotions.

He spotted a packet of Belomorkanal on the desk beside the typewriter, the common Russian brand of cigarettes marketed to young women.

Paxton said, "Do you want a smoke?"

Her eyes furtively darted across the bodies of her dead colleagues outside the office, her face unreadable. "What?" she asked.

"I saw the pack of cigarettes. Do you want one?"

"Yes," she replied, relief showed on her face at the thought of doing something so mundane, despite the insanity and death that appeared to now surround her.

She brushed her hand across her pleated skirt and stepped toward the pack of smokes.

Two shots fired from behind him.

Both shots struck the side of her head, leaving clean entry wounds, and massive exit wounds – along with a brutal spray of human flesh where her mind had been a split second earlier.

Her body slumped to the floor.

And she was dead before it reached the ground.

"She was just a secretary trying to do her job." Unable to remain indifferent to his team member's actions, Paxton turned to Bulldog who had taken the execution style shots. He was annoyed as he met Bulldog's hard, ice-cold eyes. "I just gave her my word no one was going to hurt her."

"She was going to kill you!" Bulldog explained. He'd killed his fair share of people and wasn't going to cry over some secretary who potentially worked for a terrorist organization. "You can thank me later."

Paxton shook his head and drew a slow breath. He saw no evidence that she had an intent to harm. But he had been known to make mistakes.

Very few of them, but he had made some.

Rarely.

Bulldog – AKA Cole – was his oldest friend. His best friend. They went all the way back to the beginning of SEAL training. All the same, he'd just killed a woman in cold blood. A woman he'd just personally promised not to harm! He wasn't certain if he was more irritated over being made into a liar or over the woman's death.

Paxton didn't get angry.

Instead, he stared at Cole with disbelief in his eyes, and asked, "Show me."

"Take a look for yourself."

Paxton stared at her. She wasn't carrying anything. She was unarmed. He looked at the old metal typewriter. The steel foundry was so antiquated they still used a typist. "See, she's just a typist."

Bulldog shrugged. "Roll her over, Paxton."

He rolled her over.

Nothing.

Paxton frowned. "I don't see anything?"

"Look at her skirt," Bulldog said.

Paxton checked out her long skirt.

Stitched into the pleated skirt was the outline of a weapon's holster. Her hand had already reached it – a Makarov PM pistol – another second and she would have had the chance to squeeze off a round or two, killing him.

Paxton picked up and studied the weapon.

The Makarov PM was a classic Soviet-designed sidearm.

The compact, semi-automatic handgun was widely issued to KGB agents during the Cold War and remained in use by modern Russian security forces and intelligence operatives like the Federal Security Service – FSB – the successor to the KGB.

He glanced at Bulldog, gave an appreciative nod, and said, "Thanks, Cole."

"You're welcome. Anytime."

Paxton frowned at the FSB sidearm in his hand.

He said, "She was no secretary here. She's a bit young to be part of the KGB, but with a weapon like this, she was almost certainly part of the FSB. It all but confirms she was here as the last line of defense protecting something important."

Bulldog nodded. "The question is, what?"

Paxton shook his head. "No, if she was here as the last line of defense, the real question is why was she hiding in a cupboard?"

Bulldog shrugged. "Even the FSB can get scared during a firefight."

"No, I don't buy that."

"Then what?"

Paxton checked out the semi-open cupboard under the desk again.

Something about it looked off.

It didn't appear deep enough for someone to hide inside, let alone crawl. The desk was backed up against a wall. There was only two to three feet between the cupboard and the brick wall. Something didn't match up with the image he had seen when he opened the door and dragged the secretary out of her hiding place.

A wry grin formed on his lips. "I think what I have to ask is, where was she going?"

Bulldog seemed surprised by the question. As if he thought the answer was clearly obvious. The woman hoped to hide in the cupboard.

Paxton pulled open the cupboard door again.

His parted lips curved upward in satisfaction. "Bulldog, I do believe we just found ourselves a secret tunnel."

Chapter Eight

Number One Observatory Circle, Washington, D.C.

Vice President Hawthorne didn't like what he heard.

He glared at Dr. Kepler. "Alan, how the hell does an Eastern European criminal arms dealer discover a conscience?"

"Apparently this one found God," Dr. Kepler said good naturedly.

"I believe in God, and I'm still happy to make a deal with a man like Boris Volkov!" The VP shook his head. "What does religion suddenly have to do with any of this?"

"My Intel says his newfound love – or possibly fear – of God was secondary to a recent diagnosis of cancer."

"I'm not surprised." The VP took another sip of whiskey. "After so many years trading so called dirty bombs, and Tactical Nuclear Weapons, it's a wonder he hasn't died of cancer earlier."

Dr. Kepler said, "That's just it."

Hawthorne frowned. "What's just it?"

"After a lifetime of sin and dirty trades, our friend Boris is dying. He feels it's God's way of punishing him for the sins of the past decade."

Hawthorne said, "Those sins made him a rich man."

"While he was alive," Dr. Kepler replied.

Voss, said, "It enriched the three of us, too."

"Yes," Hawthorne agreed. "But you don't see any of us suddenly developing a social conscience and deciding we're better off trying to tell the world exactly what we have done!"

"No, and it's a good thing, too." A shadow of fear crossed over Voss's normally impassive demeanor. "If the world knew the truth, there would be outrage. By the time the various justice departments managed to decide who was going to personally prosecute us, or more likely tear us apart in some Black Ops CIA prison, we'd end up preferring to die of Boris' cancer."

Hawthorne doubted that type of hyperbole, but he wasn't going to waste his time arguing the point. Instead, he turned his attention on Dr. Kepler. "How did you discover that our man wanted to defect?"

"The same way we tend to learn most things in the CIA." Dr. Kepler gave a wry and somewhat mischievous grin. "We got lucky."

"Oh?" Hawthorne asked.

"Dylan." Dr. Kepler gestured toward the computer whiz kid. "Do you want to take this one?"

"Yes, sir." Dylan Frost replied in a mildly mocking tone, but it was clear that he was pleased with himself. "The CIA hosts a secure website where people can submit tips."

"Wait, are you telling me Boris tried to make contact directly with the CIA?"

"He sure did."

Hawthorne's heart took an extra few beats than it should have. "Should I be packing my bags for some third world country to start a new life?"

"No, sir. I believe I've suppressed it."

The dim lighting of Vice President Daniel Hawthorne's private office seemed to shrink the already confined space. Bookshelves lined with legal tomes and relics of his mining town past loomed over the desk. Across from him, Dylan Frost perched awkwardly on the edge of a chair, his long hair falling into his face as he tapped away on a sleek laptop. The faint hum of the device filled the silence.

Hawthorne leaned back, his fingers tented, watching Frost with narrowed eyes. "So, explain this to me again. Slowly, this time, exactly what happened."

Dylan smirked, pushing his hair behind one ear. "Okay, so here's the deal. Boris got cold feet. Tried to play whistleblower. He sent a message through the CIA's open submission portal. You know, the one they advertise to the public for tips and Intel?"

"Of course." Hawthorne nodded. "What did Boris say?"

Frost shrugged. "Pretty basic stuff. He offered to hand over names, connections, all that jazz. Claimed he'd give up his entire network, including you, in exchange for safe passage and a new identity. He practically begged for extraction."

Hawthorne's expression darkened. "And the CIA got this?"

"Not anymore." Dylan's fingers flew over the keyboard, pulling up a mirrored version of the submission form. "I've had a worm embedded in their database for months, monitoring open submissions. The moment Boris hit 'send,' I received an alert. I was able to intercept the message before anyone at Langley could see it."

Hawthorne arched an eyebrow. "And what did you do with it?"

Dylan leaned back, clearly enjoying himself. "I wiped the submission clean from their database. As far as the CIA's concerned, it never existed. Then, I re-routed the message to a dummy account named 'CIA Director Special Projects.' Sounds official, right? To Boris, it looked like his plea for help went straight to the top."

Hawthorne's lips curled into a tight smile. "And Kepler?"

"I looped him in right after. We decided to give Boris exactly what he wanted – or at least, what he thought he wanted. We set his contacts up at the steel foundry in the Urals. Told him he'd be meeting a team of elite operatives for extraction. Asked him to bring evidence. Every bit of intelligence he has on those he's been working with from the CIA. This in exchange for full immunity and medical treatment."

Hawthorne turned to Dr. Kepler. "Alan, you sent a team of Ghosts?"

"Yes, sir. My absolute best team."

"What did you tell them?"

"The steel foundry is a terrorist cell – which is, in fact the truth – and that the entire place is to be destroyed. The rules of engagement are that all personnel at the foundry are terrorists, and they're to take no prisoners. By the time they're finished, Boris, everyone there, along with all incriminating data linking all four of us to Boris and the rest of the deals, will be nothing more than molten steel."

"Excellent. Well done." Hawthorne drew a breath. It was going to be all right. "When does the operation begin?"

Dr. Kepler glanced at his cell phone. "One of our NRO SIGINT satellite constellations identified a large explosion in the Ural Mountains just a few minutes ago."

Hawthorne knew that the National Reconnaissance Office had a deal with SpaceX and Northrop Grumman to develop and deploy a network of spy satellites in low-Earth orbit. The CIA, NSA, along with the Pentagon all had access to that data.

"Will the NSA or the Pentagon take notice of the explosion?" Hawthorne asked.

"Not likely. Not yet anyway. It's the kind of detonation that indicates a small vehicle or miniature bunker was destroyed. Nothing large enough to warrant anyone's concern at this end of it."

"Good. So what does this mean?"

"It confirms the Ghosts have launched their attack." Dr. Kepler took another sip of his whiskey. "This will all be over in the next thirty minutes, sir."

Hawthorne didn't buy his confidence. Instead, he growled, "What are the chances of this coming back to bite me?"

Dr. Kepler said, "Zero."

"There is no such thing as zero." Hawthorne was a detailed planner, and he expected exact, yes or no, results. He didn't care for this sort of ad hoc discussion. It was the kind of junk he expected from some sycophant lobbyist in Congress.

Dr. Kepler revised his opinion. "The risk is very low."

"Good. I want it lower still."

"How can you get it any lower?" Dr. Kepler asked. "I've already sent my best team in with enough C4 and thermite to melt the steel foundry to a giant molten pile of dross."

"The team you sent to do it." He paused, "What about them? Are they trustworthy?"

"They're all Ghosts..." Dr. Kepler said, "This is what they do."

"Even so. After the job is done, I suggest you make that status as Ghosts a little more physical than metaphorical."

Dr. Kepler arched an eyebrow. "You want me to clean the slate?"

"Pick whatever euphemism works for you," Hawthorne said. "But at the end of the day, I need you to send in another team and kill them all."

"Look. I think you're overreacting. Just give me some time. The team working this mission are the best Ghosts in existence, not easy to replace. They do this kind of thing all the time. Trust me, they'll get the job done."

"All right. They're your guys. But to prevent leaks, and so help me God, you had better bury them all."

Dr. Kepler said, "The wet team won't be happy about killing some of their own."

Hawthorne shrugged. "So don't tell them."

"You think I can send them in without them working it out?"

"Who's in charge of the team you sent to destroy the steel foundry?"

"A man code-named Rembrandt."

"And he's good?"

"The best operative we've ever had." Dr. Kepler said, "Hell, you won't find a better one in the CIA, MI6, DGSE, Mossad, BND, SVD, any of the Intelligence Agencies around the globe. He is the very best."

Hawthorne nodded. "Good. So tell them Rembrandt has gone rogue, and he and his team need to be taken out."

"Look, it's so wasteful." Kepler sighed. "I'm not keen on losing Rembrandt. If mistakes are made, and I really must assassinate my best seek and destroy team, I'll order it myself. But let's see how this plays out."

"They're your Ghosts. I'm willing to sit on it for another hour or two until we know the outcome of the attack."

"Good." Dr. Kepler said, "I have a second team onboard the extraction vessel. If things go wrong, I'll send them in to end Rembrandt and his team while they're asleep."

"Excellent." Hawthorne said, "What if one of your Ghosts find Boris alive?"

"You're worried that he'll speak to them? Ask to defect, before my team have the chance to eliminate him?"

"It's a dangerous possibility."

"These are professionals. They've been told they're going into a terrorist cell known to be trading in small nuclear weapons and dirty bombs. Their rules of engagement indicate they are to kill everyone on sight, not negotiate or interrogate anyone."

Hawthorne didn't like loose ends when the stakes were so high. "And if the unlikely should happen?"

Dr. Kepler said, "I have my own man on the team. Someone who will do whatever I say. Someone who owes me a favor. If that happens, he'll kill Boris before he has a chance to disclose any information about us."

"Are you sure?" Hawthorne shook his head. "I mean, these aren't the kind of secrets that get a person thrown in jail. This is treason. Over here, the intelligence that man has will get us shot or put away for life in a CIA black site. A place where nobody will ever hear from us again."

"It's all right, I have a man on the team. One of the better Ghosts. A young man. He's broken the rules and I offered him a way out. He took it, but he knows he owes me big time."

"What did you tell him?"

"What he needs to know. That if the truth gets out, I'm fucked and I'll bring down every single Ghost with me."

"He knows what to do?" Hawthorne persisted.

"Absolutely." Dr. Kepler spoke more confidently than Hawthorne felt. "He promised to kill anyone who even looks like they're talking to one of the Ghosts."

"And what if Boris has already talked to one of them?"

Dr. Kepler set his jaw and said, "Then, my man knows his next course of action is simple – he must kill the Ghost, destroy all evidence, and bury the truth forever."

Chapter Nine

Steel Foundry, Ural Mountains – Russia

Paxton stared at the open cupboard under the desk.

It led to a small passageway, only just big enough to crawl through, which passed the brick wall behind the table, before turning to the right in a sharp dogleg, and disappearing into the darkness.

"Hammer and Echo secure this place," Paxon said. "Keep an ear out for any movement alarms on the eye in the sky sentinel on your watches. That explosion won't go unnoticed. The sentry drone will alarm as soon as company is coming. Notify me the second you know. We're not going to take on an entire army – which I'm almost certain is what's coming for us. I fully intend to be off this mountain before anyone arrives."

"Understood," Hammer and Echo replied in unison.

Paxton looked at the rest of the team. "Bulldog and Falcon – You're with me."

Hammer removed his heavy backpack and gestured toward almost an entire pack full of explosives. "What do you want me to do with all of this, Rembrandt? Just so you know I'm not planning on hauling any of it back."

Paxton nodded. "Yeah, we're going to take enough to blow up whatever we find down here, but in the meantime, you should rig this place for fireworks."

Hammer removed a block of C4. "How big?"

"The bigger the better!" Paxton looked around. "Make a show of it. Nothing in your demolitions kit is going to destroy an entire steel foundry, but we might need a distraction when we're leaving."

"Agreed." Hammer looked at the secret tunnel. "What about the nuclear site – if you find one?"

"I don't know. Let's see what we have once we get there. But, if there's a secret bunker through here, it will be well protected. I have to find out if your explosives will penetrate."

Paxton exhaled sharply. "What we really need, is something that can go through this tunnel to achieve the same goal?"

Hammer looked at the gigantic crucible. It held several tons of molten steel that glowed like lava. "See what you can find down there. I might just have an idea how we can neutralize the problem."

Paxton nodded. "I like your thinking."

He then opened the cupboard and began crawling through the hidden tunnel.

Paxton pushed his way through the back of the steel cupboard, the narrow space barely allowing him to move. The air was stale and cold, a stark contrast to the blistering heat of the foundry above. His flashlight cast a dim glow, illuminating the metal walls around him. He reached the end of the passage and struggled to lift a steel doorway.

It gave way with a soft groan, sliding backward.

He glanced downward, revealing the entrance.

The hatch creaked as Paxton swung it fully open, its rusted hinges protesting the intrusion after decades of neglect. He knelt at the edge, his gloved hand gripping the cold metal rim, and peered down into the yawning darkness below. A faint, stale draft of air whispered up to meet him, carrying the metallic tang of decaying steel and the unmistakable chemical sting of old lubricants and coolant.

Inside he saw a secret ladder.

His flashlight beam cut through the gloom, illuminating the unmistakable architecture of a Soviet-era nuclear silo. The shaft extended deep into the earth, its cylindrical walls lined with ribbed, corrugated steel panels, many streaked with the red-brown patina of rust. Paxton's gaze caught on the gigantic hydraulic pistons along the sides, dormant now but once designed to raise a missile into firing position. Above, a fragmented catwalk hung precariously, its metal grated floor twisted like it had been wrenched apart in an earthquake.

Further down, the silo widened into a cavernous chamber where the missile itself would have once been housed. The cradle was still there – a massive, skeletal framework with bolted clamps, now empty. A faded Soviet insignia loomed on the far wall, the red star and hammer-and-sickle barely visible beneath years of grime. Nearby, a line of outdated gauges and switches adorned a rusting control console, their glass covers shattered or clouded over with dirt.

It was a monument to Cold War paranoia and destruction, and even in its decrepit state, the silo radiated an oppressive menace. Paxton's stomach churned as his flashlight passed over a tangle of cables and disconnected wiring spilling across the floor like veins of a dead beast.

His big body tensed.

There was a damned nuclear silo beneath the steel foundry – almost certainly dating back to the Cold War.

The CIA had a list of every nuclear silo ever built – anywhere in the world – but especially in Russia. That meant they knew for damned sure that the foundry was built on top of one.

Yet Intel had specifically left that information out.

It couldn't have been an accident. CIA Ghost Intel didn't make mistakes. Someone had left this info out intentionally...

Which meant, someone had lied to him...

The question remained – who?

Paxton swallowed hard.

And if such important information had been left out, what other secrets was Peregrine intentionally keeping from him?

Chapter Ten

P axton led the way down into the concrete passage.

He swung his legs over the edge of the hatch, the cold metal of the ladder biting through his gloves as he gripped it tightly. The darkness below was oppressive, absorbing the weak beam of his flashlight as he tested the first few rungs. The ladder groaned, its bolts straining against decades of corrosion. He glanced back at Bulldog and Falcon, their faces lit only by the faint red glow of their night vision goggles.

"Watch your step," Paxton muttered, his voice low. "If this thing gives, it's a long way down."

Bulldog nodded, slinging his rifle across his chest. "Always a nice day out with you, Rembrandt."

Paxton started the descent, one hand and one boot at a time, his senses attuned to every creak and shudder of the aging ladder. The stale, chemical-laced air grew thicker the deeper they went, and the echoes of their movements reverberated eerily in the hollow shaft. Above him, Bulldog and Falcon followed, their silence a demonstration to the intense Ghosts' training they had endured.

As they neared the bottom, Paxton's flashlight caught the edge of the cradle that had once housed a missile. Up close, it was a grotesque skeleton of rusted beams and broken bolts, its purpose unmistakable. The air carried a faint, acrid scent of decay mixed with the faint whiff of ozone from live electrical tools. Someone had been working here recently.

Maybe he or she still was.

Paxton swung off the ladder and landed silently on the concrete floor, crouching low as he surveyed the room. Bulldog landed beside him with a muted thud, while Falcon moved off to the left, her carbine sweeping for threats.

The space was cavernous, lit by the flickering light of old, jury-rigged halogen lamps. The remnants of the control console sat nearby, its switches and gauges shattered or smeared with grime. Paxton's eyes were drawn to the far end of the chamber, where a makeshift workbench had been set up.

With his Benelli shotgun leading the way, he stepped cautiously into the cavernous missile silo, the cold, damp air carrying the faint taste of rust and decay. His boots echoed against the reinforced concrete floor as his eyes adjusted to the dim, fluorescent lighting that flickered intermittently, casting eerie shadows across the room.

Ahead of him, lined up straight and tall like grim soldiers of destruction, were several small rockets like the display of a terrorist's weapon's dealership.

The launchers, squat and utilitarian, rested on sturdy tripods. Each one pointed slightly upward, as if poised to fire at an unseen enemy. The devices themselves were small, no larger than a water heater, painted in faded olive drab with stenciled black serial numbers. The warheads at their tips gleamed under the weak light, the polished metal reflecting a distorted image of the silo's decaying walls.

Paxton walked closer, his gloved hand brushing the cold metal of one launcher. He studied the mechanism, noting the simplicity of its design. The warhead, a W54 nuclear payload, sat snugly within its mount, its edges smooth and unassuming. It was almost absurd to think that this compact device, weighing barely fifty pounds, could unleash a fireball capable of obliterating a small town.

He ran his eyes along the row of launchers, noting how they were arranged with military precision, each spaced evenly apart.

A chill ran down his spine.

Paxton had known about the Davy Crockett's reputation as one of the smallest nuclear weapons ever built by the U.S. military. Yet seeing them here, up close, was something else entirely. They were grotesquely out of place. Relics of an age when annihilation hung by a thread and every shadow was cast by the fear of global extinction.

For a moment, he stood still, listening to the silence of the silo, broken only by the faint hum of old electrical systems still running after decades.

"What is this little arsenal?" Falcon asked. "Some sort of Soviet era, oversized tripod mounted RPG-7s?"

"No," Paxton stared at the small rockets. "Those are nuclear weapons."

Falcon's mouth dropped open. "No shit?"

"Yes, but the Soviets didn't build them."

"If not the Soviets, then whose are they?"

Paxton fixed his flashlight on a small American flag on the inside of the weapon's hull. "These are ours."

"What the hell are our antiquated nuclear weapons doing in an old Russian missile silo?" Falcon gasped.

Paxton frowned. "They were called Davy Crockett tactical nukes, but for them to be hidden away in a foreign nation, way down here? Well, it would have to mean that someone back stateside has done one hell of a deal with the devil."

Chapter Eleven

I t took less than five minutes to secure the disused missile silo.

Paxton returned to the array of rockets. There were eight in total. Something about that seemed to ring an alarm bell in the back of his mind.

He was about to voice his thoughts, when Bulldog said, "Hey Paxton, you're the linguist here. Isn't there something about the number eight in Japanese culture that's significant?"

"Chinese," Paxton corrected him. "The number eight is considered extremely lucky because its pronunciation is similar to the word for 'wealth' or 'prosper' in Mandarin. This phonetic similarity has led to a deep cultural association between the number eight and riches, success, and good fortune."

"So what do you think?" Bulldog asked.

"I think the buyers might be Chinese..."

"Or?"

"Or it's a coincidence." Paxton shrugged. "The terrorists got their hands on as many of these rockets as they possibly could, and that number just happened to be eight."

Bulldog said, "Lucky them."

"That luck doesn't appear to be working out well for them so far," Paxton said. "I'm guessing most of the people involved lost their lives topside."

"That's my guess too," Falcon agreed.

Paxton stared at the eight Davy Crockett nukes. He glanced at Bulldog. "You spent time in the Joint Nuclear Operations Task Force. Do you know much about these?"

Bulldog nodded. "Yeah, I did four years in the JNOTF."

The JNOTF was a highly classified joint-service unit tasked with training for and responding to potential nuclear threats. This task force worked closely with agencies such as the Department of Energy (DOE), the Defense Threat Reduction Agency (DTRA), the Army's Nuclear and Counterproliferation Force (NCF), and elite units like the Air Force's 20th Air Force – which oversaw U.S. intercontinental ballistic missiles.

"Did you ever see one of these?" Paxton asked.

"Yeah, we studied them at the college as part of our more rounded understanding of nuclear weapons and specifically miniaturized nukes."

"What can you tell me about them?"

Bulldog fixed his flashlight on the row of miniature nukes. "The Projectile, Atomic, Supercaliber 279mm XM388 for the Davy Crockett contains a W54 Mod 2 nuclear warhead."

"I was thinking in English, Bulldog?"

"It's a compact pure fission device weighing 50.9 pounds and, when packaged in the M388 round, weighs 76 pounds. The weapon had an official yield of 20 tons of TNT and included 26 pounds of high explosives."

Paxton ran his eyes across the rocket. It wasn't much bigger than an oversized RPG-7. "How did they work?"

"The projectile featured controls such as a two-position height-of-burst switch that could be set to either 2 feet or 40 feet airburst, a safety switch with 'safe' and 'arm' positions, and a time setting dial allowing for a delay between 1 and 50 seconds before the fuse armed. If the time delay exceeded the time-of-flight, the weapon would hit the ground without detonating. The time dial also had a 'safe' setting, functioning as a second safety switch."

"Excellent. Just what humanity needed to invent, a way to lob nukes at one another from close range." Paxton moved his flashlight until its beam shone on an open section of one of the nukes. It looked like someone had been tinkering with the weapon already.

"What is that?"

"The components that deal with its launching mechanism." Bulldog looked into the barrel. "The complete round measures 31 inches in length and has a diameter of 11 inches at its widest point. A subcaliber piston at the back of the shell is inserted into the launcher's barrel for firing. The M388 atomic projectile was mounted on the barrel-inserted spigot via bayonet slots. Upon propellant discharge, the spigot acted as the launching piston for the M388 atomic projectile, necessary due to the fission round's inability to tolerate heavy acceleration stress. During flight, four fins deployed at the end to stabilize trajectory and flight."

Paxton stood silently, the dim light of the missile silo casting long shadows across the rows of disused Davy Crockett launchers. His attention shifted to Bulldog, who crouched nearby, inspecting a cluster of crates and disassembled devices scattered across a workbench. Bulldog's rugged face, etched with years of field experience, was unreadable as he methodically examined the contents.

"Take a look at this," Bulldog muttered, gesturing to a chaotic mix of components. Paxton moved closer, shotgun still in hand, his eyes narrowing as he followed Bulldog's pointed finger. Among the clutter were chunks of high explosives, spools of wiring, electronic timers, and fragments of disassembled shells. But what drew Paxton's attention was the unmistakable presence of lead-lined containers – likely used to store radioactive material.

Bulldog straightened, brushing dust off his hands. "Someone's been busy," he said, his voice low and gravelly. He nodded toward the Davy Crockett warheads. "Looks like they're planning on stripping out the fissile material from these nukes."

Paxton's brow furrowed as he glanced from the dismantled equipment to the row of warheads. "For what?"

"Dirty bombs," Bulldog replied grimly, crossing his arms over his chest. "They're not trying to make another nuke – they're mixing the radioactive material with conventional explosives. It won't cause a nuclear blast, but when it goes off, it'll spread radioactive particles everywhere." He paused, letting the gravity of the statement sink in.

"Why?" Paxton asked.

"Purely for terror."

"Really?" Paxton asked, trying to determine how making a nuke ineffective might cause more terror. He knew this was a weak point of his. He'd suppressed his emotions from childhood – many people say they have, but in his case, a neurologist had spent hundreds of hours trying to reprogram him to forget about his emotions. The process had worked, and he'd long since learned to ignore all his feelings. The downside of which meant it was hard for him to imagine what made something particularly frightening for someone else.

"Humor me, Bulldog. Why?"

"Think about it, Rembrandt! A dirty bomb doesn't just cause the immediate damage from the explosion, but entire areas are rendered uninhabitable. This is what terrorists seek: Panic, contamination, mass casualties. Those who survive suffer acute radiation sickness and tend to die painful, cancerous deaths. All of which will end up on every news channel across the globe."

Paxton's jaw tightened as the implications sank in. "The terrorist playbook," he said, his voice clipped.

Bulldog nodded, his eyes sweeping the room like a predator scanning for its prey. "And judging by this setup, whoever's behind this is either ready to move or close to it."

Paxton returned to the problem at hand. "Work out if we can remove the atomics so we can safely take them with us, or if we'll have to destroy these here. I'm going to have another quick look around."

Bulldog nodded. "Understood."

Paxton said, "Falcon, see if you can find anything here to transport those eight weapons if we do end up going the route of moving them."

"I'm on it," Falcon said, approaching the lead-lined containers they had seen earlier.

Paxton moved cautiously through the missile silo, his boots crunching on the layers of dust and debris that had settled over decades of disuse. The air was thick with the scent of rust and mildew, and every creak of the aging metal infrastructure seemed amplified in the cavernous space. His flashlight beam swept across the walls, revealing faded stenciled warnings and peeling paint, but something about the far corner caught his eye.

There was a seam in the concrete – barely visible, but unnatural in the otherwise smooth surface of the silo's walls. Paxton stepped closer, running his gloved hand along the crack. His fingers brushed against a faint depression, and after a moment of searching, he found a concealed latch.

Paxton tightened his grip on the Benelli shotgun, its matte black barrel steady in his right hand as he approached the hidden seam in the concrete wall. The weapon felt solid and reassuring, a perfect counterbalance to the tension humming in the air.

He kept it angled low but ready, his finger hovering just outside the trigger guard.

Every instinct told him to proceed with caution.

With his left hand, he reached for the faint depression he'd spotted earlier. The cold metal latch resisted at first, rusted with age, but with a grunt of effort, Paxton forced it to turn. The hidden door groaned open, the sound echoing eerily in the silence of the silo. He stepped back slightly, angling the shotgun for quick reaction as the flashlight beam from his headlamp flooded the newly revealed space.

The stale air from the compartment hit him, thick with the smell of sweat and confinement. Illuminated by the pale light of Paxton's flashlight, his eyes locked on the figure inside. A man was hunched inside the cramped space.

His finger instinctively shifted toward the trigger, as he prepared for anything.

The man inside sprang upright, hands shot up in the universal gesture of surrender as he exclaimed in a thick Russian accent, "Don't shoot!"

Paxton froze for a fraction of a second, the Benelli steady in his hand, every muscle coiled like a spring, ready to act. "Out. Now," he commanded, his voice like steel.

The man shuffled forward, his wide, fearful eyes darting between the gaping barrel of the shotgun and Paxton's impassive face. The man straightened, his gaunt face coming into view, framed by a thick beard and sharp, sunken eyes.

The new target stammered, "Please don't shoot. I'll tell you everything. This is what they're looking for!"

Paxton's gaze narrowed. "Step out. Slowly," he ordered, his tone cold and steady.

"Yes. I will. I'm the informant!"

"Informant?" Paxton said, his shotgun held in his right hand as comfortably as a normal person might hold a Glock and pointed its barrel at the man.

"My name is Boris Volkov." The man held his gaze, as though trying to judge if his name meant anything to him. He seemed to realize Paxton hadn't heard the name. Instead of persisting, he said, "Listen. I have done many bad things in my life. I need you to understand, I have not done these on my own. I have been in business with your people for many years. I have promised Peregrine to provide details of everything in exchange for amnesty."

Paxton frowned.

Peregrine knew about this.

Yet, in the mission briefing, the man had never mentioned the name Boris Volkov – nor was there any mention of defection by a Russian arms dealer.

"Amnesty?" Paxton asked. "From what?"

"The people here who have been working with your government – the ones who have betrayed your own people for personal gain."

"That's pretty much every politician."

"No." Boris lifted his hand, revealing a small flash drive. "I have the secrets here. Everything's recorded. I've done my part, now please, get me out of here. They will kill me if they ever find out I betrayed them…"

A shot fired.

The 9mm parabellum had struck the man's chest, right beside his sternum. Paxton had seen enough chest wounds to know which ones are fatal and which ones aren't. Judging by the almost jet-like ejection of blood coming from the man's chest, it was clear the round had nicked a vital organ – most likely the aortic arch, or upper abdominal aorta. Either way, he would bleed out quickly.

Boris Volkov's remaining time alive would be counted in seconds, not minutes.

Paxton glanced at Falcon.

The surveillance kid continued to hold his Glock aimed at the dying man. A strange, almost dark, expression crossed the kid's face. It was almost like he was challenging Paxton's authority.

Then, a moment later, the threat had passed, and Falcon lowered his weapon.

Paxton put his hand in the man's chest, trying to keep him alive for a few precious seconds.

The dying man lowered his hand, and Paxton surreptitiously took the flash drive out of it.

Boris met his cold, hard gaze. He panted in whispering words, "The... truth is the... greatest revenge. Don't... trust anyone. Peregrine works for them. There is... a mole... in your team."

Chapter Twelve

P axton looked at Falcon.

The kid looked proud of what he'd done.

And what had he done? He'd shot a man Paxton was interrogating. The information he was gaining could have been highly valuable.

There was no immediate threat.

Paxton had been in complete control of the situation. He had a Benelli M4 shotgun pointed at the man's face at a range of two feet.

The guy looked sick.

Like someone dying of cancer.

If he traded in uranium-filled so-called dirty bombs that was hardly surprising.

So why had Falcon felt the need to suddenly shoot him dead mid discussion? Who was Falcon really trying to protect? What secrets was he trying to keep hidden? And most importantly, who was Falcon really taking his orders from?

Paxton asked calmly, "What did you do that for?"

Falcon seemed nonplussed. "The mission stated no survivors."

"Sure, but he was about to give us information."

Falcon shrugged. "I was just following orders."

Paxton's piercing green eyes stared at Falcon and he nodded. He was following someone's orders all right, but they weren't his.

Chapter Thirteen

The kid.

Falcon's orders weren't coming from him. So who were they coming from? And more importantly, what was he going to do about it? Fighting between members of a Ghost team was dangerous during a mission. Challenges of authority could turn deadly.

All the same, he couldn't let this pass...

He opened his mouth to challenge Falcon, but heard the garbled radio being relayed from the entrance to the missile silo, where they had climbed down.

It was Hammer. "Rembrandt! You'd better get up here, we've got company!"

"How many?"

"A lot!"

"Can you do any better than that with the math?"

"Much more than we can deal with. At least a hundred."

"A hundred!" Paxton cursed. "Where did they come from?"

"There's another train. It looked like another ore carrier, but as soon as it reached the crest of the Ural Mountain and began its descent, the soldiers started to alight the train on skis."

"How long do we have?"

"Ten to fifteen minutes. Twenty if we get lucky."

Paxton depressed his mic. "Okay, let's hope we get lucky. In the meantime, you'd better make sure your fireworks topside is ready to go and set to do maximum collateral damage!"

"I'm on it!" Hammer replied. "What are you doing?"

Paxton grinned. "I'm just going to get rid of some of our rubbish before we exfil."

Chapter Fourteen

P axton looked at Bulldog. "We can't leave this amount of nuclear material in the hands of a terrorist organization or we'll have dirty bombs going off all around the globe for decades to come!"

"Agreed." Bulldog nodded. They had both seen first-hand what happened when terrorist groups got a hold of powerful US ordnance.

Falcon said, "There's no way we're moving it."

"You're right," Paxton concurred. "But we might be able to destroy it somehow."

"How?" Falcon asked. "Our C4 isn't going to do anything to WD4 rockets."

Paxton shot Bulldog a fierce grin. "You're the only one out of us who has ever even seen the Davy Crockett nukes. Got any ideas?"

Bulldog grinned back. "What if we use one of those Davy Crockett's to light up this entire silo? I mean, the explosion will be recorded at global nuclear listening stations, but that's far less our problem than if this fissile material is allowed to be sold to terrorists."

"Definitely." Paxton frowned. "How are you planning on doing so without blowing yourself up, or making yourself sterile in the process?"

"I'll use one of the C4 timers to depress the Davy Crockett nuke's trigger. Set it for thirty minutes, and we can be long gone before it explodes."

"Great. Get to it." Paxton looked at Falcon. He still didn't trust the kid, but there was nothing he could do about it right now. He said, "Falcon, get topside and see what you can do to help Echo and Hammer with the fireworks."

"Yes, sir," Falcon replied, and began climbing the ladder.

Paxton put aside his fears for Falcon's loyalty and got to work helping Bulldog quickly assemble a fuse for the C4 trigger.

There wasn't much to it, and together they were finished within a couple of minutes.

Bulldog plugged in the last of the system's mechanism and sent an anxious look at Paxton. "There's something else you need to know."

"What?"

"There were eight containers with Davy Crockett nukes."

"Right." Paxton recalled doing the count himself.

"Only seven of them still have the nuclear fissile element inside."

A dark shadow of fear crossed Paxton's features. "What are you saying?"

"I think one of the nuclear components is missing..."

Paxton's lips formed a hard line. "And that means that potentially there is a nuclear dirty bomb out there...somewhere."

It was the sort of things nightmares were made of.

Hammer's voice, loud with alarm, called over the radio. "Rembrandt! It's time to go!"

Chapter Fifteen

P axton emerged from the hidden passage, his boots scuffing against the cracked concrete floor of the steel foundry secretary's office. The room was straight out of the 60's, with faded linoleum tiles curling at the edges and a rusting desk piled with yellowed papers. A single grimy window overlooked the jagged mountain landscape beyond, and through it, he spotted a train winding its way along a precarious track carved high into the cliffs. Its metallic sheen glinted faintly in the pale sunlight, a serpent making toward the unknown.

He stepped closer to the window, squinting. Below the train, on the snow-covered slopes, a darker, shifting mass caught his attention. As his focus sharpened, his stomach tightened. Skiers – many dozens of them – were carving down the mountainside with a precision that spoke of training, not recreation.

Their trajectory was deliberate, heading straight for the foundry.

"We've got incoming!" Echo's voice crackled over the comms, clipped and urgent.

The faint, rhythmic crack of sniper fire followed.

Paxton turned and pushed through the office's creaking door, stepping into the chaotic space beyond. Echo and Falcon were perched on an elevated walkway, sniper rifles braced as they fired in quick, controlled bursts. Their suppressors hissed, each shot sending one of the approaching skiers tumbling lifelessly into the snow.

"Any idea of the numbers?" Paxton asked, trying to judge the total of their skiing adversaries.

"Too many to count," Falcon called out without looking away from his scope. "They're moving fast."

Paxton's eyes swept the room, taking stock.

The foundry was alive with the hum of preparation. Hammer stood near the furnace, his face streaked with soot and sweat, a grim smile tugging at the corners of his mouth.

Behind him, the explosives were already wired, their detonators neatly arrayed on a metal workbench.

"All set," Hammer said, hefting a small remote detonator in his massive hand. His voice was steady, but there was an edge of excitement to it. "One push and this place becomes a memory."

"Good," Paxton said, moving to his side. He kept his gaze on the skiers in the distance, now closer, their dark shapes weaving like ants on a relentless march. "When do you want to blow this thing?"

Hammer said, "The more people we let enter the foundry the better the collateral damage."

"Okay, let's head to the southern side of this position, and get ready for departure!"

"Copy that!" Echoed all members of the Ghost team.

Then, to Hammer, Paxton said, "When you think there's the right amount of people inside the foundry, go ahead and light the firecrackers!"

Hammer's grin widened. "Music to my ears."

Paxton pulled his shotgun from its sling.

The faint crack of sniper fire and the hiss of ski edges on snow were growing louder. The enemy was close now, close enough that he could make out their dark uniforms and the glint of weapons slung across their backs.

"Here they come," he said, raising his weapon. "Let's give them a warm welcome."

And then, the chaos began.

Chapter Sixteen

T he Ghosts retreated to the southern end of the foundry.

Paxton crouched behind a rusting steel beam, his finger resting lightly on the trigger of his shotgun as the attackers poured into the building. Through the thin veil of dust and shadows, he counted them, his pulse steady despite the growing tension. One after another, they streamed in – AK-47s unslung from their shoulders and now held in their hands, tactical vests bristling with gear, their movements quick and purposeful. They spread out like a plague, taking positions around the machinery, the catwalks, and the rows of storage crates.

"Hold," Paxton murmured into his comm, his voice a low, almost inaudible growl. "Wait for Hammer's count."

Beside him, Hammer knelt, one hand gripping the detonator tucked against his chest. The man's face was calm, but his eyes gleamed with a fierce intensity. He was counting softly, his lips barely moving, the seconds ticking down like the beats of a war drum.

The foundry felt alive now, buzzing with the clatter of boots, shouted commands, and the metallic scrape of weapons being locked and loaded. Above, Falcon and Echo remained motionless in their sniper nests, their scopes trained on the soldiers below but waiting for the signal.

When Hammer hit fifty, he stopped counting. His thumb hovered over the detonator for a split second.

Then, he pressed it.

The explosion was instantaneous.

A deafening boom ripped through the foundry as the C4 and Detcord placed at the base of the massive container holding liquid metal detonated. The steel structure, weakened and fractured, groaned like a dying beast before tipping over with a sickening inevitability.

Paxton jumped backward as the world seemed to erupt.

Thousands of gallons of molten steel surged out of the crucible in a blinding, incandescent wave of hell. It hit the foundry floor with a roar, a fiery tsunami consuming everything in its path.

The first attackers were instantly vaporized.

Their screams cut short as the molten steel devoured them.

Others tried to flee, but the metal was too fast, washing over them and leaving nothing but blackened, misshapen remains. Those who managed to avoid the initial flow weren't spared – steel beams collapsed under the heat, showering them with burning slag. A few scrambled for the catwalks, only for the red-hot steel to melt the supports and send them crashing down in a cacophony of metal and flesh.

Paxton realized they were too close.

He shouted, "Run!"

They raced behind a railway car parked on the tracks to the southern end of the foundry.

A superheated gust of air blasted past him, his thick ski gear burning in the searing heat. He threw himself on the snow, rolling over to cool himself – the snow turning to steam as it touched his burning hot ski gear.

He exchanged a glance with Hammer, who said, "I did mention you might want to retreat a bit further."

"Thanks," Paxton said. Then, with a suppressed laugh, he added, "Next time, maybe be a little more forceful with me when I clearly don't copy. Especially when it comes to explosives."

"I will!" Hammer agreed.

Paxton depressed his mic. "Rembrandt to Ghosts. Everyone still alive?"

One by one, each of them sounded off over the radio. Miraculously, none of the team were injured. They were all unharmed. Paxton ordered each of them to make their descent and start skiing toward the extraction point.

Paxton glanced over at Hammer, who crouched low behind a hastily constructed snow bunker, his frame blending into the frigid landscape. The bunker, a rough but sturdy structure built from compacted snow and reinforced with steel plating scavenged from the foundry, bristled with menace.

It provided just enough cover to shield him from incoming fire while allowing him to pivot and unleash destruction.

In front of him, mounted on a tripod embedded into the icy ground, was his M134 Minigun. The weapon gleamed in the pale winter sunlight, its six barrels slightly frosted from the cold but still deadly. An ammunition feed snaked to a massive drum beside him, which looked almost comically large but felt perfectly in place next to the mountain of a man operating it. Hammer had rigged the Minigun to a modified power pack on his back, the cables slithering over his snow-covered armor like living veins.

"Let's go," Paxton said.

Hammer said, "One minute, I want to make sure our guests stay around for the final show!"

Paxton shook his head. "You get going. The rest of the Ghosts are already making their descent. I'll hold them off."

"This is my duty."

"Not anymore." He nodded. Paxton was in charge. It was his responsibility to make sure his team got home alive. Besides, he was the best skier among them. "You did good work. I'll make sure our targets are here for the final fireworks, then I'll be right behind you!"

"Okay." Hammer gestured toward the Minigun. "Try and keep them in the foundry. As soon as the last men standing arrive, you'll leave the Minigun and race us to the extraction point?"

"Agreed."

Paxton watched Hammer quickly clip onto the skis and set off down the mountain.

He then positioned himself behind the machine gun.

The Minigun spun lazily as he tested the motor, the low mechanical whir a chilling prelude to the chaos it could unleash. His hands, gloved but still impossibly large, rested on the custom grips, his finger brushing the trigger with a predator's patience. His breath clouded in the icy air, the only sign of life from his otherwise stock-still figure.

Paxton's eyes scanned the frozen expanse ahead, sharp and unyielding. A predator guarding its kill. He was a sentinel, immovable and unrelenting, his snow bunker a fortress of ice and death. The sound of boots crunching in the snow reached his ears, faint but unmistakable.

Without hesitation, the Minigun roared to life.

The barrels spun into a blur, spitting out a blinding stream of tracers that tore through the snowstorm like fireflies on a rampage. The thunderous roar of the Minigun echoed across the valley, drowning out the desperate shouts of attackers attempting to breach the perimeter.

Snow exploded into the air where bullets struck, forming a blizzard of shrapnel and ice.

Paxton didn't flinch as return-fire sparked harmlessly against the edges of his bunker. He grinned – a feral, wolfish grin – as he held the line, a one-man army turning the battlefield into a frozen wasteland of smoke, steam, and devastation.

His eyes landed on the steel river of fire which was about to hit the cooling lake, where ice-cold water was about to meet liquid, molten steel at 2,800 degrees Fahrenheit. Paxton kept firing, preventing the attackers from escaping through the southern end of the foundry.

Just a few more seconds...

The river of molten steel poured relentlessly forward.

It reached the cooling lake at the far end of the foundry. The sudden contact with water created an explosive burst of steam.

The lake became an inferno.

Steam shot upward with the force of a volcanic eruption, engulfing the attackers nearest the shore. Paxton watched as they were thrown back, their bodies contorted grotesquely as superheated vapor boiled them alive.

They opened their mouths to scream...but superheated gas filled their lungs killing them instantly. Fast and likely painless.

Their end left the entire area in silence.

In a rush to escape, Paxton turned away from the chaos.

More of the armed skiers – those who had circled around the foundry and therefore avoided the mass death – began circling around the inferno. Paxton fired the last burst of machine gun rounds until the Minigun barrel began to run empty.

A split second later, he pulled his heavy backpack over his shoulders, clipped on his skis and began his descent straight towards the bottom of the valley.

Chapter Seventeen

Paxton skied down the slope at speed.

The snow sprayed in thick arcs behind Paxton's skis as he carved a hard turn, the chill air biting at his face despite heated adrenaline coursing through his veins. Behind him, the rapid bark of AK-47 fire shattered the stillness of the Siberian wilderness. Bullets whipped past, some hissing into the snow, others smacking against the thick trunks of towering pines.

He cut through the powder with precision.

Behind him, a swarm of dark shapes grew larger, their pursuers gaining ground, their rifles spitting wild, undisciplined bursts of fire.

"Are you still coming, old man?" Hammer – the oldest by far in the team – asked over the radio.

"I'm right behind you," Paxton snapped back, gritting his teeth as he focused on the terrain ahead.

The forest opened up briefly, revealing a small river cutting across their path. Paxton's eyes darted to the fallen log spanning the icy water. It was wide enough for a crossing but coated in a slick sheen of snow and ice.

He didn't slow.

Bending low, he built speed, his skis hissing over the powder.

In front of him, a dead tree appeared out of nowhere.

Paxton hit the top of the log hard, launching himself off its edge. For a brief, weightless moment, he hung in the air, his shadow gliding across the snow-dusted riverbank below. Then his skis hit the opposite side, the impact jarring but controlled as he absorbed it with his knees. He was off again, carving a tight turn to clear the next cluster of trees.

He was good, but not clairvoyant. That last effort was more luck than skill.

The loud crunch sound of a body hitting an unmoving object followed, as one of his pursuers wasn't as lucky. It was followed by the sound of something tumbling into the river, but enough attackers made it across to keep the pressure on.

A sharp report of rifle fire followed.

Paxton ducked instinctively as a bullet tore through the air above him. He swung left, seeking the cover of a rocky outcrop, then broke right again, his skis narrowly avoiding a boulder jutting from the snow.

The forest thinned as the slope steepened. Paxton's heart was pounding hard and fast as he knew what was coming.

This was it.

He hit the edge of the cliff hard, his momentum carrying him far into the open void.

The world seemed to fall away.

The Ob River lay hundreds of feet below, its frozen surface shimmering like silver under the pale sun. He felt the rush of air whipping past his face as he raced toward the long drop and the empty space below.

Two skiers screamed as they followed him to their deaths.

Paxton waved goodbye to the falling attackers.

His fingers gripped the cord and yanked.

The paraglider's canopy erupted above him with a sharp snap, catching the air and pulling him upright. The sudden deceleration tugged at his body, but the tension eased as the glider steadied. Below, the Ob River stretched out like a frozen highway, a path leading southward toward the Gulf of Ob and the Sea of Kara.

Up ahead, Bulldog, Falcon, Hammer, and Echo's gliders flew in a trail formation, their white canopies dotting the gray sky.

Paxton exhaled a shaky breath, gripping the handles of his craft. He flipped a switch and his paraglider's little electric motor began to rotate with a comforting whir. The small propeller mounted at his back began spinning, propelling him forward through the frigid air.

Chapter Eighteen

I t felt freeing to be on the paraglider.

Always had to Paxton.

Not just the flight itself, but the knowledge that it led to their extraction point. Usually, at this point, the worst of their mission and the highest point of danger, was over.

There was no way their attackers were following them.

Not yet, and not where they were headed.

Paxton adjusted the controls of his glider, feeling the electric motor hum steadily behind him as it propelled him forward. The icy Siberian wind whipped past, biting at his face despite the protection of his balaclava. Below, the river stretched out like a silver ribbon, snaking through the vast, snow-covered valley. The mountains flanking the river rose sharply, their jagged peaks cutting into the pale sky.

He glanced to his left, where Hammer's paraglider was keeping a steady pace, his canopy billowing against the backdrop of snow and stone. To his right, Echo flew slightly higher, her smaller frame almost dwarfed by her glider's wide span.

The team moved in near-perfect formation, each adjusting subtly to the shifting air currents and the occasional turbulence caused by the valley walls.

The powered paragliders offered a surreal kind of freedom, their quiet motors almost inaudible over the rush of wind. Paxton felt the rhythmic tug of the harness straps on his shoulders as he guided his glider, using slight shifts of his body and small pulls on the controls to maneuver. It was equal parts skill and intuition, a delicate balance that felt second nature after years of experience.

The valley stretched out before them, a vast expanse of untouched wilderness. Pine forests blanketed the lower slopes, their dark green needles dusted with snow. Occasionally, Paxton spotted signs of life – tracks in the snow, a herd of elk moving through the trees, even the distant smoke of a lone chimney rising from a hidden village. Yet mostly, it was desolate, the sound of the wind was broken only by the occasional creak of ice on the river below.

The team pressed on as they carved through the frigid air. Paxton's sharp eyes scanned the horizon, his focus unrelenting despite the monotony of the landscape. The Ghosts had survived countless missions together, but this one felt different.

The stakes were higher, the terrain more unforgiving, the enemy more relentless...and there had been nuclear bombs.

As they rounded a bend in the valley, the river widened below them, its icy surface shimmering like glass. Paxton tightened his grip on the controls, angling his paraglider slightly to the right to avoid a rock formation jutting out of the valley wall.

The land stretched on, its icy beauty at once awe-inspiring and treacherous. Paxton kept his gaze forward, his mind calculating the next steps even as the cold gnawed at his limbs.

The valley stretched wide below them, the frozen Ob River glinting like a fractured mirror under the pale winter sun. Paxton's breath caught as he scanned the mountain peaks on either side, their faces carved by centuries of wind and ice. A particular point jutted defiantly from the mountainside, a stark protrusion of dark granite shaped like a spear tip thrust toward the sky. It stood out against the white expanse, its base a tangle of snow-laden pines, its tip exposed and raw.

As they glided silently above the valley, movement on the point caught Paxton's eye. It was a lone skier, clad in dark winter gear, racing along the narrow ridge, their form hunched with determination.

The figure halted abruptly at the edge of the precipice, ripping a rifle from their back.

"Contact, right!" Paxton yelled over the comm.

The sharp, staccato burst of an AK-47 broke the silence, echoing like a drumbeat across the valley. Paxton felt his chest tighten as the bullets zipped past them, harmless but jarring. Then, a hollow thwack reached his ears, followed by a gut-wrenching sight – one of Falcon's cords snapped on one side, the canopy above him crumpled, folding like a broken wing, before collapsing in a sudden, violent twist.

Paxton's stomach dropped as he saw Falcon jerked violently in mid-air.

"No!" Paxton shouted, his voice raw. "Falcon, hold on!"

Falcon's glider spiraled down, his body twisting as he fought for control. He grabbed at the remaining lines with both hands, desperately trying to steer what was left of his rig. For a brief moment, it appeared like he might regain some semblance of stability. The rocky slope of the mountain loomed closer, but Falcon angled himself expertly, navigating toward a relatively clear patch of snow.

"He's got it," Hammer said over the comm, his tone tight but hopeful.

Paxton wasn't so sure.

His eyes tracked Falcon's descent, watching as the damaged glider caught a gust of wind and wavered dangerously. The mountain's terrain rose sharply below him, dotted with sharp outcroppings of sandstone and snow-covered boulders.

Falcon's course looked precarious, but for a heartbeat, it seemed like he might make it.

Then Paxton's worst fear unfolded.

Falcon's trajectory brought him too close to a massive sandstone arch jutting out from the slope. He saw it coming, shouted into the comm, but there was no way to warn Falcon in time. The glider clipped the edge of the arch with a sickening crack. Falcon's body slammed into the rock.

Paxton winced as the impact sent a spray of red across the pale sandstone. His team member's head hit first, the force crushing his skull and snapping his neck in an instant. His lifeless body crumpled, tumbling down the slope in a twisted heap of limbs and shredded fabric.

"Falcon!" Echo's voice broke over the comm, a mix of disbelief and anguish.

Paxton's jaw tightened, his breath catching in his chest. He forced himself to look away, focusing on his own glider and the path ahead, but the image was seared into his mind. There was no recovering from an impact like that.

He was gone.

Falcon was dead.

And if he wasn't, he wouldn't be alive for much longer. That wasn't selfishness on the Ghosts' part. It was a simple fact.

"Keep moving," Paxton ordered, his voice rough. "There's nothing we can do for him."

Paxton hated the thought of losing another member of his team.

Even so, a ruthlessly pragmatic part of him felt reassured that at least now he didn't have to work out if he really did have a mole inside his team...

And it possibly saved him the grim necessity of terminating the man himself.

Chapter Nineteen

T he explosion hit like the fist of God.

It was enough to lift Paxton out of his reverie. He felt it first – not as a sound, but as a sensation deep in his chest, a low, bone-shaking rumble that seemed to rise from the earth itself. His paraglider shuddered violently, the lines trembling in his hands as though the very air had become unstable. A split second later, the sound reached them, an earsplitting roar that swallowed the valley whole, louder than anything Paxton had ever heard.

It wasn't a simple "boom."

The sound formed an infinite cascade of overlapping detonations, a primal, rolling fury that reverberated across the mountains.

The air itself felt alive.

A sudden, concussive wave slammed into them, punching hard against their bodies and canopies. Paxton's paraglider bucked like a wild animal, his harness digging painfully into his ribs as he fought to stabilize. Below him, the snow-covered valley rippled unnaturally, a brief, surreal moment of movement like a giant shrugging off a heavy burden.

Then came the light.

Even three miles away, the blinding white flash stabbed through his peripheral vision, so intense that it left jagged afterimages burned into his eyes. A second sun, impossibly bright and ferocious, bloomed in the direction of the foundry, silhouetting the jagged mountains around it.

Heat followed.

Not an all-consuming fire, but a wave of warmth that seemed wrong in the frozen landscape, as though nature itself had been upended. Paxton could feel it even at this distance, faint but unmistakable, crawling over his exposed skin.

The Ghosts struggled to keep their canopies level as the shockwave surged past them, disrupting the airflow and sending violent eddies through the valley.

Below, the landscape seemed to convulse.

A dark mushroom cloud began to unfurl into the sky, its base swelling with fire and smoke, its upper reaches flattening into a grim, gray anvil. Snow cascaded from the peaks as the mountains trembled, avalanches spilling down like rivers of ice and rock.

Nuclear bomb, he thought.

Paxton forced himself to focus, hands gripping the toggles with white-knuckled intensity as he scanned the others. They were battered but alive, their gliders still aloft despite the turbulence. He exhaled slowly, his breath visible in the freezing air.

"What the hell happened?" Paxton asked Bulldog. "I thought the top of that missile hatch was meant to be able to contain a nuclear explosion."

"It should have," Bulldog replied.

Paxton frowned. This was going to make matters worse for everyone. "Then what's the story with the sudden formation of a second sun on the horizon?"

"No, I'm hearing you," Bulldog replied. "The top of the silo was breached. No other way for that sort of explosion to become visible above ground."

"Was the Davy Crockett rocket bigger than we thought?" Paxton asked. "I mean, had it been enhanced somehow to make its chain reaction more powerful?"

"I don't think so," Bulldog replied. "If I had to guess, I'd say that the top of the missile silo had been removed since the end of the Cold War. Maybe by whoever brought those Davy Crockett nukes down there to make it easier to bring them inside? Either way, it's done now."

"Yeah." Paxton frowned. "Now we'll have to contend with the Air Force who will have to send someone out to investigate."

Chapter Twenty

The four Ghosts flew in silence.

After a little while, Bulldog radioed Paxton via a secure – private – channel.

"The Russian Air Force will have aircraft in the air by now," Bulldog said. "It won't be long until they're flying overhead."

Paxton drew a breath. "I've been thinking that too."

"Any ideas?"

"Not really."

"Have you radioed the extraction team?"

Paxton said, "They're on their way."

"They're aware they need to set everything up for us if we end up coming in hot?" Bulldog persisted.

"They're aware," Paxton confirmed. "I just hope they reach the extraction point in time."

"Look, there's something we need to talk about," Bulldog's voice continued over the private radio channel. "I meant to talk to you about it after the mission, but there's a chance we don't make it. Or possibly only one of us makes it, and so I need to say this now."

Paxton looked toward Bulldog, AKA Cole Knight. AKA his best friend and longest friend in all the world. They went through SEAL training together. It was because of Cole that Paxton managed to make it through the swim test, despite his unusually high bone density and muscle composition making buoyancy seemingly impossible for him.

It was extraordinary to hear him talk of death. Quite out of character. Cole was far more emotional than Paxton had ever been – or would ever be – but he was still way down there toward the inanimate rock side of the emotional equation.

Paxton said, "What's going on Cole?"

Cole cleared his throat. "I need to tell you something…"

"So tell me." Paxton asked, "What is it?"

"Do you remember Rowena Vandyke?"

There was something about the way Cole had said the name that made it almost sound reverent. Paxton remembered her. More importantly, he remembered how much Cole had remembered her.

"She's the blonde girl you were going to marry?" Paxton said, "The one with the nice smile, vivacious, with a mischievous personality?"

Cole said, "That would be the one."

"What about her?" Paxton asked, always quick to the point.

"I should have married her."

"Okay."

"I'm serious. People say they should have placed their numbers on the winning lottery tickets, or hit that shot and won the game, bought the house or the share just before it boomed… this isn't like any of that. This was completely different. This could have been everything anyone ever dreamed of."

Paxton smiled. "Not everyone has that dream."

"Trust me," Cole said. "If anyone ever had what I had, this would have been their dream too."

"We're all just one wrong turn away from a completely different story." Paxton wore a bemused smile on his face. He didn't get Cole in this human emotion, any more than he got most people in any of the sort of weird things they did. "Take Carter for example. If he'd pulled his paraglider slightly to the left or even the right, his cord wouldn't have been cut, and he would still be alive."

"I know, but it's not quite the same…"

Paxton shrugged. "I bet Carter wouldn't be pining about some girl who he could have married."

"This is different."

"How?"

"Paxton!" Cole snapped. "Stop being an emotionless asshole for a minute and listen to me."

Paxton suppressed a grin. "I thought I was listening to you?"

"Look. This isn't what I needed to explain."

"Okay, so tell me what you need me to understand," Paxton suggested. His unbalanced emotional and moral compass was struggling hard, despite his best efforts at empathy. He simply had no idea what his friend wanted or needed. Perhaps he just had to remain quiet and listen.

Cole said, "Did I ever tell you why I didn't marry Rowena?"

"I'm not sure," Paxton said, noncommittally. He had a near-photographic memory and could even recall sitting down with him after he'd made the decision to join the Ghosts instead of getting married, but somehow, when they had talked about it, Paxton had made the conscious decision to sort of delete the information as irrelevant. A decision had been made by his friend, and there was no point wasting useful data space in that computer inside his skull.

Paxton imagined Cole's pained expression. If he had any feelings at all, he would have felt guilty about not seeing the value in the original conversation.

For Cole's part, it was a good thing that he didn't have the same near-photographic memory. Instead, he assumed he'd never spoken specifically about it with Paxton.

"I should probably tell you what happened."

Paxton studied the scenery below him. "Should you, really?"

Cole ignored that and persisted – almost as though he knew exactly how Paxton would respond. Yet he was determined to reach the point of his story anyway. "I didn't ask her to marry me."

Paxton said nothing. *Yeah, we've been through this, he thought...*

"I should have," Cole continued. "Asked her to marry me that is. I wanted to. Oh man, I was mad about this girl. She was like nobody else I had ever met. No other experience in my life even comes close to comparing with the time I spent with her. It was that wild, uninhibited, madness named love... do you know what I mean?"

"Not really..." Paxton admitted.

"I'm sorry man. I hope one day you get to experience it." Cole's tone was solemn. "I hope one day you do. I'm sorry, there's no possible way you could understand what I'm going through..."

Paxton smiled. "Love is the best thing in the whole world to have and the worst to lose."

"Shit!" Cole swore. "Why Paxton... you do get it!"

He opened his mouth to mention that he got it from a Ken Follet book, but then closed it again. Cole seemed so happy from their shared sense of understanding, he didn't have the heart to break it.

Paxton said, "Tell me why you didn't marry this amazingly, wonderful woman."

"I don't know. That's the honest truth."

Paxton looked at him, hoping there was more of an explanation than simple regret to provoke such strong sentiments from his friend.

Perhaps it was just the sudden death of Alicia and Carter that he felt the need to share. Humans were strange that way.

He was about to try and say something to acknowledge Cole, when his friend continued speaking.

Cole said, "I didn't ask her to marry me, although I wanted to. Instead, she asked me to marry her."

"But you turned her down?"

"Bingo."

Every time Paxton thought he was following someone's emotions and starting to understand them, they would do something like this, which made no logical sense. With genuine curiosity, he asked, "Why?"

"I was very tempted. Another week earlier, and the deal would have been done. But instead, Peregrine had approached me personally and asked me to join the Ghosts."

"So you decided to ditch the girl of your dreams to become a Ghost?"

"Yeah, it sounds pretty stupid when you say it like that."

"A little," Paxton admitted. "Care to share your explanation?"

"It wasn't right," Cole said. "The justification doesn't make sense."

"They rarely do."

"Look. It was like this. Everyone gets married. Ninety percent gets divorced... or was it fifty percent? I don't know. And a hundred percent of people I've met who are married are unhappy. So why chase a fantasy? I've never been a gambler. It's all about the odds. No, I was being given the opportunity of a lifetime to make a real difference. Be the superhero that rights the wrongs in the shadows."

"Okay. What did you do?"

"Instead of accepting her proposal, I broke up with Rowena the next day and agreed to be a born-again Ghost."

Paxton heard the cry of an eagle in the distance. "Cole, I don't mean to be a heartless asshole, but why has all this come out now?"

Cole lifted a placating hand. "I'm getting to that."

"Oh. Go on then."

"I was happy with my decision for a long time. The job was amazing. The pay was astronomical. A decade's income for every year in the job. And the work was rewarding. The only problem was, as time went on, I had a niggling feeling. One of the worst. A seed of doubt grew. Had it all been the biggest mistake of my life? Should I have married the girl of my dreams and screw statistics? Maybe I would have been the lucky one to have it all?"

Paxton doubted that, but it was his story, and so he was happy for him to tell it. Yet he felt that Cole seemed to be holding something back. Paxton knew him well enough to know when he had a secret he was dying to tell.

He asked, "What did you do?"

Cole swallowed hard. "I broke the rules... and it's changed everything!"

Chapter Twenty-One

Paxton flew on, utterly baffled. The man had just survived taking on a terrorist organization in the middle of Siberia, overcoming dozens of attackers, but now was worried about certain societal rules with a girlfriend he hadn't seen in years.

"What happened?" Paxton asked.

"Like many men before me, I became obsessed with her. Not just Rowena. The idea of a life that I missed out on. A happiness that I would never get to achieve. Eventually, against the rules, I tracked her down and spied on her."

"Did you hurt her?" Paxton asked.

"No! Of course not!"

"Okay, so our Ghost conventions haven't been badly broken." Paxton shrugged. "No harm not foul."

Cole's tone took a hard stance. "I'm still getting to it."

"All right."

"So I tracked Rowena down. As a Ghost, I do this for a living. Finding her, stalking her. It was easy."

"Okay."

"At first it was just to see her from a distance," Cole said. "But soon, it became my place of respite. Somewhere I'd go after having seen some really bad things. Stuff that most humans – normal humans – no offense Paxton, should ever see."

Paxton lifted a hand in the sky toward him, a placating gesture. "None taken, I am what I am."

"Then, one day, I turned a corner and Rowena opened the door. Two girls came out with her. They were about four years old. Twins."

"New man?"

"No. Mine." Cole sighed. "You see, it turns out Rowena was pregnant when we split."

"You're the father."

"Yes."

"And you didn't know that at the time?"

"No, of course not. I never would have joined the Ghosts, if I did!"

"They're definitely yours?" Paxton asked, his tone measured.

"I'm a twin, although my sister died not long after birth. Some kind of heart complication."

"I'm sorry."

"I'm telling you as twins are genetically in my family." Cole let out a shaky breath, his lips twitching into a half-smile. "One of the girls – she couldn't have been more than four – she was trying to tie her shoe. And as she's crouched there, struggling with the laces, she sticks her tongue out, just a little, right between her teeth. You know how I do that when I'm focusing?"

"Yes." He had seen Cole do that while he was concentrating at the range, planning for a mission, and probably even now, when he was trying to find a way to broach this conversation with him.

"She's your daughter," Paxton said.

"Yes! It hit me like a ton of bricks," Cole continued, his voice quieter now. "I used to do the exact same thing. My mom teased me about it for years – said I looked like I was tasting the air whenever I got too absorbed in anything. I hadn't thought about it in forever, but seeing her do it." He paused. "I knew right then."

"Have you done a DNA test?" Paxton asked. "I mean, it wouldn't be hard. You wait until they leave for school or daycare – or wherever four-year-olds go for the day. Then you get a hair sample from their brush, and we run the DNA."

"No." Cole shook head. "I don't have to. It's not just the tongue thing, Paxton. It's in the way she moved, the way she tilted her head when she was thinking. It wasn't just familiar – it was me. No DNA test could convince me more than that moment did."

"Okay."

"That's when I knew," Cole said. "Rowena. The girl of my dreams got pregnant the last time we'd slept together. Back when we both thought we were going to get married and spend the rest of our lives with one another. That was three days before I accepted the job as a Ghost."

Paxton said, "You want out?"

"Yes."

"Okay."

"They won't let me." Cole's voice was melancholy. "Ghosts don't retire – they simply stay dead."

"I have some savings in a little bolt hole in Neft Daşları... you could go there."

"Neft Daşları!" Cole said, with a frown. "I don't think immigrating to Azerbaijan is really what Rowena was looking for."

"I wasn't suggesting you take Rowena and the girls and move to Azerbaijan." Paxton laughed. "I meant, go there, collect my retirement plan. It's in Bitcoin. I placed it there as a contingency plan back in 2012, so it should be worth something by now. And then pick somewhere nice, somewhere all four of you would love. A tropical island, a snow-covered wonderland in one of the Scandinavian countries. Hell, go to Australia if you like."

"Wait, how much Bitcoin did you store there in 2012?"

"Not much. About the equivalent of US $50,000. At the time I figured if I got into trouble, I could always use it to happily retire into some sort of remote eastern European country."

"Paxton, do you have any idea what Bitcoins are worth in today's market?"

"I don't really keep up to date with money things. It was just an easy, untraceable means of transferring money."

"Bitcoin was worth about $12.50 in 2012. 50k purchased then, in today's prices, would be worth an absolute fortune."

Paxton smiled. "Good. I'm happy for you. That will make it easier to retire and take your girls somewhere nice."

"You should retire too," Cole said. "I'm serious. With those sorts of dollars, we could both live like kings!"

Paxton shrugged. "Money's never really held an important place in my life. I guess I've always had enough to provide for me. I like being a Ghost. It's a good use of my time on earth. It makes me feel – right. Maybe even good. It's as though I'm using the gifts I've been given for the right purpose. No, you take that Bitcoin I've got stashed. You have something nice to do with it. There's nothing I could use the money for that would make my life any better."

"Paxton! You've always had enough money?"

"Guess I've been lucky that way."

"Paxton, you're an orphan. You grew up in an group home."

"So?"

"Most orphans never grow up with any money."

"And look how well I turned out!"

"I'm serious. You got an education because your intelligence is through the roof and so you got a scholarship. Then, your football coach at the school saw your potential and decided to make sure you got fed enough to eat. Then you finished school, fell into the Navy, followed by joining the Ghosts..."

"See, you've proved my point. I've never needed money in my life." Paxton made a bemused smile. "Take it Cole. You won't need to start again in life. You've served your country well. You've done enough. It's enough that you'll never have to worry about this money thing again. Take Rowena and move somewhere completely different. Get a professional ID and a back story. Start again where they will never know who you were."

"Really, you think so?" Cole's voice sounded alive and animated.

"Absolutely. You have a chance to live the way you want. I'd take that."

"Okay, I think I will. Thank you." From afar in the paraglider nearest his, Paxton saw Cole looking his way. "You're okay, Paxton. You really are. You're the best man I've ever met."

Paxton doubted that very much.

All the same, he said, "You get one life Cole. If you have a chance at true happiness, you should take it."

Chapter Twenty-Two

After the sun set, the ice-cold air surrounding them turned brutal. Night wrapped the valley in a heavy shroud of darkness, broken only by the faint glow of starlight reflecting off the snow-dusted peaks. Freezing, Paxton constantly moved his toes and fingers as he and the remaining Ghosts continued to move like phantoms. Their motorized paragliders hugged the edges of the mountain range, weaving in and out of the tree line to avoid detection.

Below them, the forest loomed in shadowy silence, broken occasionally by the pale gleam of the Ob River winding toward its terminus.

The Gulf of Ob opened ahead of them, vast and icy, a sheet of black water stretching toward the horizon. The air was even colder here, the wind sharper, tugging at the canopies of their gliders as they banked low over the water.

Paxton scanned the terrain ahead and the sky behind, his senses taut with anticipation. He depressed the mic, speaking to the remaining Ghosts. "Almost there, everyone..."

Hammer and Echo acknowledged with soft clicks over the channel, conserving their voices as they focused on navigating the darkness. The hum of their motors blended with the rush of wind, a low thrum that was hypnotic against the silence of the wilderness.

A distant sound interrupted the silence.

It was faint at first, then came the unmistakable thwump-thwump-thwump of rotor blades cutting through the air. Paxton tensed, his grip tightening on the paraglider's controls. The sound grew louder, reverberating through the valley like the approach of a hunter.

Echo said, "They found us!"

"Stay the course," Paxton calmly replied. "We're nearly there."

Hammer said, "But we're sitting ducks out here!"

"Just a little longer," Paxton said. Craning his neck, his eyes narrowed as he caught sight of the chopper, silhouetted against the faint glow of the horizon.

It was a Russian Mi-28 Havoc gunship.

The helicopter's menacing profile bristled with weaponry; its sleek, angular frame designed for hunting in hostile terrain. On its nose, was a powerful search light, which swept across the valley out into the open Gulf of Ob.

"They're closing in fast," Hammer said. "What's the play?"

"Keep heading toward the Gulf," Paxton ordered. "Stay out of their spotlight."

The Ghosts pushed forward, their gliders cutting low over the waves as they broke free of the valley and soared out above the Gulf of Ob. The water below was a cold, undulating black, its surface broken only by scattered patches of ice. Paxton cast a glance over his shoulder and felt his gut twist. The gunship had followed them out, its rotors flashing as it streaked toward the Ghosts with predatory intent.

The Russian gunship dipped lower, its nose-mounted cannon swiveling to lock onto the paragliders. A sharp crack rang out as the 30mm Shipunov 2A42 autocannon opened fire, its tracer rounds tearing through the night. Paxton veered hard to the right, his paraglider shuddering as rounds whizzed past, punching through the water below with violent splashes.

No one was hit. Seems they all got lucky...

Or more likely, the pilot was having fun.

The helicopter fired an S-8 rocket, the glowing projectile streaking toward them like a comet. Paxton's heart hammered as he banked sharply, narrowly avoiding the explosion that erupted in the water below, sending a plume of spray and mist into the air.

The weapon was designed to hit large, mechanical machines, and its homing equipment was unable to lock onto the paragliders.

As the chaos erupted around him, something beneath the surface caught Paxton's eye. A massive shadow moved deep beneath the Gulf's icy waters, its size was dwarfing anything he'd ever seen.

It was only a glimpse – a flicker of movement illuminated briefly by the gunship's searchlights – but it was enough to send a chill racing down his spine. The shadow rolled lazily, a faint flash of what might have been a tail or a fin cutting through the gloom before vanishing again.

The powerful gunship shifted position, its autocannon swiveling again.

Paxton knew none of them would be able to dodge the next volley. He looked down at his paraglider harness strap, his mind racing. His options were limited, and staying in the air wasn't one of them.

"Time to go, everyone," he shouted over the radio.

Then he yanked his knife from its sheath.

With a quick, decisive motion, he sliced through the strap.

Gravity took hold instantly.

He plummeted thirty feet toward the freezing waters of the Gulf of Ob. The wind roared in his ears as he fell, his body twisting as he fell into the darkness far below...

Chapter Twenty-Three

P axton pin-dived into the water.

He dropped feet first, body straight and toes pointed.

The icy water hit him like a sledgehammer, knocking the breath from his lungs and sending a shock of pain through his body. He plunged deep, the frigid darkness swallowing him whole. For a moment, everything was silent save for the rush of water and the pounding of his heart.

Paxton's body sliced through the frigid water like a spear, the cold biting into his skin through his unsuitable ski gear. As the surface churned above him, he turned gracefully in the water, orienting himself headfirst toward the depths.

His arms cut forward, and his legs propelled him with strong, deliberate kicks.

The pressure built around him, squeezing his chest, and his lungs burned for air. He swallowed hard to equalize the pressure in his ears, forcing himself to focus.

Without goggles, his vision was little more than an obtuse blur.

At around forty feet, the massive shadow of the submarine emerged from the watery gloom. The behemoth loomed, dark and silent, moving with the slow, ominous grace of a prowling killer whale.

Paxton reached out, his gloved hand brushing against its smooth, cold hull. He let the silent giant carry him, sliding his hands across the steel until he found the open lockout trunk, a rectangular recess near the top of the submarine.

On the Virginia Class Nuclear Attack Submarines, the lockout trunk was built to accommodate up to twenty Navy SEALs. It offered ample space for just four Ghosts.

Inside the trunk, a small panel of controls glowed faintly, illuminated by the submarine's internal power. Dive regulators hung neatly along each side, attached to the sub's onboard air supply system.

Paxton immediately grabbed one, placing it into his mouth and inhaling air deeply. The air was metallic and dry but welcome. He exhaled, watching the stream of bubbles rise lazily toward the surface.

One by one, the rest of the team appeared, their forms appearing out of the murky water. Paxton handed each of them a regulator as they arrived in the trunk. They nodded, and each returned the universal diver's "okay" signal with a circle of thumb and forefinger.

When the last of his team was secured, Paxton pressed the large close button, to secure the external hatch.

Its hydraulics whirred and the steel door shut to form its watertight seal.

To his left was the control panel, simple and functional. Two large buttons dominated the interface: one green and one red. Above them, clear labels etched into the metal read: Flood and Drain.

Paxton pressed the green button, and immediately the system droned to life. Jets of air hissed into the chamber, forcing the water out through hidden vents. The level dropped rapidly, and within minutes, the lockout trunk was dry and filled with breathable air.

The team pulled off their regulators, panting slightly but ready. Below, a muffled sound echoed through the hull, followed by the grinding noise of the submarine's inner hatch wheel being turned. A moment later, the hatch swung upward, revealing a dimly lit compartment below.

A figure in a navy jumpsuit gestured them inside.

Paxton pulled himself through the lockout trunk's hatch and stepped into the submarine's dimly lit interior. The air was thick. It tasted of metal, machine oil, and the faint musk of too many men confined to too little space.

The boat's Executive Officer was waiting for him, a tall, lean man in his late forties with sharp features and keen eyes. His uniform was immaculate despite the close quarters, and he wore the air of authority like a second skin.

"Welcome aboard the *USS Indiana* nuclear attack submarine," the XO said briskly, his voice low but firm. "Which one of you would be Rembrandt?"

Paxton said, "That would be me."

"Welcome aboard, sir." The officer shook his hand tightly.

Paxton took the man's hand in his own massive paw, giving it a firm shake back. "Thank you. We appreciate the lift."

"You're welcome." The officer cleared his throat. "I am to remind you and your team that you will be debriefed stateside, and you are not to interact or speak to any of the crew on board."

"That's fine." Paxton nodded. "We know the drill."

Paxton felt the ground shift under his feet. He had to grab hold of a railing to prevent himself from sliding down the suddenly sloping submarine.

He exchanged a quick glance with the XO.

With a wry smile, the XO said, "Given the sort of reception you've had on the surface, we thought it a good idea to descend, and disappear from prying eyes."

Chapter Twenty-Four

On Board the *USS Indiana* (SSN-789)

"Captain Grayson gives his apologies for not meeting you. As you can imagine, he's needed on the bridge right now."

Paxton nodded. "I believe it."

"To keep you isolated from the rest of the crew, I'm sorry we can't provide showers, but I'll take you and your team to your quarters where you'll find a hot meal."

"Thank you."

Abruptly, Paxton and his team all gripped the cold metal railings with both hands as the *USS Indiana* pitched downward into an emergency dive.

The sudden sharp angle had caught them off guard.

Paxton was forced to plant his feet firmly against the grated floor to keep from sliding. Around him, sailors moved with the ease of those who had spent years on board, bracing themselves against bulkheads and latching on to whatever handholds they could find. The narrow passageway slanted steeply now, transforming into a treacherous slope.

The sort of thing Paxton imagined kids would have loved to slide down.

It didn't take too much imagination to see the sort of injuries someone his size would incur if he fell and slid down the steep slope that ran most of the entire length of the submarine.

The overhead lights flickered briefly as the submarine adjusted to its new depth, and a low groan resonated through the hull. Paxton felt the press of gravity shift against his shoulders, making it harder to stay upright. His boot slipped slightly, and he cursed under his breath, tightening his grip on the rail.

Paxton scanned the faces of the crew as they navigated the slanted passageway.

They were focused and disciplined, with each motion deliberate. To them, this was routine. To him, it was a test of balance and nerve. He envied their calm as they used years of training to adjust their movements to the tilt of the deck. He reached for another handhold, muscles straining as he pulled himself forward, one step at a time.

Also, he doubted the sub's crew had been awake for thirty-eight hours.

Behind him, Hammer let out a grunt of effort, catching himself on a pipe running along the wall, as he nearly fell.

"You good?" Paxton asked without turning his head.

"Yeah," came the reply, clipped but confident. "Just trying not to eat metal."

The submarine continued its sharp descent, the hum of the engines now a steady vibration beneath Paxton's boots. He kept his eyes forward, moving with the flow of the crew as they pressed on through the sloping corridors. Every step was a battle against the pull of gravity, but he could feel the *USS Indiana* leveling out slowly, the angle less severe with each passing second.

By the time he came to the next bulkhead door, the deck had begun to even out. Paxton exhaled, releasing his white knuckled death grip on the railing and flexing his fingers, which ached from the strain. He glanced back at his team, who were catching up with similar expressions of relief.

Paxton followed the XO closely, ducking slightly under the low ceiling. The narrow passageways felt like a maze, lined with exposed piping, wiring, and bulkheads painted in utilitarian gray. Red emergency lights glowed faintly at regular intervals, adding to the submarine's otherworldly atmosphere.

They passed crew members moving with quiet purpose, their faces drawn with the mix of fatigue and focus that came from extended underwater deployments. Every step Paxton took echoed softly against the steel floors, adding to the sensation of being deep inside a metal cocoon. The hum of the submarine's nuclear reactor was a constant, low vibration that seemed to seep into his bones.

The XO stopped at the entrance to the forward torpedo room and gestured toward a series of floating bunks that had been temporarily installed within one of the empty torpedo bays.

Two armed Marines stood guard just outside the room. Their weapons holstered, but their eyes alert. They straightened slightly as the XO entered, but otherwise remained still.

"Sorry about the sleeping arrangements," the XO said, apologetically. "This is the best we could do on such short notice."

"After where we've been, it looks perfect." Paxton smiled. "Thank you. And please thank Captain Grayson for his hospitality and the use of his boat."

"I will. If you need anything, please let one of your guards know and we will see if we can accommodate you."

Paxton nodded. "Will do."

Paxton ducked through the narrow hatch into the torpedo room and stopped short as the unmistakable aroma of spiced meat, warm tortillas, and melted cheese hit him like a freight train. For a moment, he just stood there, inhaling deeply. The savory scent was stirring a primal hunger he hadn't realized was clawing at him until now.

"Smells like Taco Tuesday," the XO said with a faint smirk, his arms crossed casually as he leaned against a rack of spare torpedo casings. He nodded toward the makeshift buffet spread out on a collapsible table in the corner. "It's tradition aboard the *Indiana*. Hope you and your team enjoy Mexican."

Paxton's eyes swept over the spread: trays of seasoned ground beef, shredded chicken, refried beans, and bright bowls of diced tomatoes, chopped onions, shredded lettuce, and sharp cheddar cheese. A steaming pot of Spanish rice sat beside a stack of warm tortillas and a small mountain of tortilla chips. Bottles of hot sauce in varying levels of heat lined the edge of the table like soldiers awaiting deployment.

His stomach growled loudly, prompting a chuckle from one of the Ghosts behind him.

The XO said, "Guess that answers the question of whether or not you're hungry."

"Famished," Paxton admitted.

"I'll leave you to it." The XO stepped outside to leave. "In case I don't see you until we disembark, enjoy your travels and your well-deserved rest."

"Thank you," Paxton replied.

Then, without further preamble, he grabbed a plate and wasted no time piling it high with food. He layered warm tortillas with beef, chicken, and all the toppings in quick succession, then added a generous scoop of rice and beans on the side. For good measure, he snagged a handful of chips and an extra tortilla to mop up the inevitable mess.

As he sat down on a nearby bench and dug in, the first bite hit him like a revelation. The sharp spice of the beef, the cool crunch of lettuce, and the warm, salty bite of melted cheese mingled in perfect harmony. He ate ravenously, his focus narrowing to the plate in front of him, the world momentarily shrinking to just the food, the warmth, and the relief of filling his empty stomach.

Between bites, he noticed a neatly folded set of clothes on the edge of the bench. A dark-gray T-shirt, a pair of sturdy cargo pants, socks, and underclothes were stacked with military precision. Beside them sat a watertight bag, transparent but reinforced – and clearly designed for critical items.

Paxton wiped his hands on a napkin and set his plate aside reluctantly. With careful efficiency, he retrieved his fake Russian passport that he'd been using and the small flash drive Boris had handed him before the chaos. Both items were tucked carefully into the watertight bag, along with a million rubles in notes, which he sealed and tested for any signs of leakage. The mission was over, but he never liked to give up his survival items in a foreign country until he was stateside. Satisfied, he zipped the bag into one of the large side pockets on the cargo pants and tugged the zipper shut.

Then on second thought, when he was certain no one was watching, he pulled out the flash drive. Then he secured it in a separate water-tight container and hung it around his neck.

The dry clothes felt like luxury as he changed quickly, slipping out of his damp gear and into the clean, comfortable replacements. The soft cotton of the shirt and the snug, functional fit of the pants were a welcome upgrade from the soaked, grimy outfit he'd been wearing.

His hunger rekindled as soon as he finished changing.

Paxton returned to his plate, polishing off every bite before leaning back with a contented sigh. For the first time in hours, he felt human again – dressed in warm dry clothes, fed, and momentarily at peace. But as his fingers brushed his chest and the flash drive, a sharp reminder of the mission reminded him that this temporary moment of peace wouldn't last long.

Paxton ducked his head as he stepped through the low doorway into the forward torpedo room, his eyes adjusting to the dim red lighting. The air was cool, filled with the faint tang of metal and oil, a scent he associated with submarines. The room was a long, narrow space dominated by rows of gleaming torpedoes stacked on racks along the port side. A few had been shifted to create space, their steel casings pushed carefully against the bulkhead like sleeping sentinels.

In the newly cleared area, temporary sleeping arrangements had been set up for him and his team. Sturdy cots with thin, gray mattresses were arranged in two neat rows, each separated by just enough space to move through. Overhead, mesh netting secured gear bags, and Paxton could see his own bag already stowed, the worn canvas marked with his call sign, "Rembrandt." Clip-on lights were attached to the cot frames, their muted glow barely cutting through the gloom.

The sound of the submarine's systems thrummed steadily, a background noise that vibrated through the deck plates under his boots. At the far end of the room, just below a large pipe running horizontally across the ceiling, was the hatch leading to the adjacent compartment.

As expected, two Marines stood on either side of it, weapons slung across their chests, their postures rigid. Their eyes flicked toward him briefly but betrayed no curiosity.

Paxton moved further into the room, running a hand along one of the torpedoes as he passed. The surface was cold and smooth, the deadly precision of the weapon palpable even in its inert state. He glanced back at his team, who were filing in behind him, their expressions ranging from weariness to quiet determination.

He stepped toward his cot and sank onto it, the frame creaking slightly under his weight. As he leaned back, his gaze drifted to the hatch and the guards stationed there. Their presence was a reminder that while the Navy was hosting them, this wasn't their domain.

Not that it mattered.

Paxton had his mission, and nothing – not cramped quarters, not watchful Marines, not even the hum of nuclear power coursing through the submarine – would distract him from it.

Thinking of the heightened security at the hatch to their quarters, he cleaned his Glock. Paxton didn't trust easily, and this was the only weapon that had made it back to the submarine with him.

Hammer said, "Does security outside the door to our quarters seem particularly high?"

"Meh." Paxton shrugged. "Not really. It's a necessary safety lock-out switch between the crew of the submarine and Special Forces in general. No one is supposed to know we are here or see who we are."

As they were Ghosts, this was even more paramount. Other than the XO, and if needing something from the guards, they were not allowed to speak to anyone. Every member of Paxton's team was meant to be dead. They couldn't be seen socializing with the crew of the *USS Indiana.*

"No, I mean, even higher than usual?" Hammer countered.

Paxton glanced at the serious looking Marines at the door. "Yeah, it is higher. This was a particularly important mission. I don't think anyone's taking chances for the secrets to get out."

He may as well rest.

That suited him fine. He was tired as all hell.

His gun tucked under his pillow, Paxton curled up on the cot, trying to squeeze his six-foot-six frame into a six-foot bunk. He closed his eyes, and seconds later, drifted off to sleep...

As though he didn't have a care in the world.

Chapter Twenty-Five

Evergreen Orphanage, Woodland, D.C. – 36 Years Ago

    The name evoked a sense of peace and nature.

Although four-year-old Paxton West, who was new to the building, couldn't understand why it was named "Evergreen" or "Woodland," given the absolute lack of trees visible from the entire grounds of the orphanage.

Evergreen felt both enormous and cramped to Paxton, a sprawling, weathered brick building with too many windows to count and too few places to hide. Inside, the orphanage was divided into six large dormitory rooms, each housing twenty children grouped by age.

His dormitory housed the youngest children.

Ages four to six.

The room Paxton shared with the youngest kids was filled with narrow metal-frame beds arranged in tidy rows, each topped with mismatched blankets and pillows that smelled faintly of detergent and something older and indefinable. The walls were painted a faded yellow, meant to feel cheerful, though the chipped corners betrayed years of wear. At night, the room droned with the quiet whispers of other children and the soft snores of those too tired to stay awake.

It was a place of constant noise and shared space, where privacy was as rare as a new toy. In truth, it was a lousy place to call home.

But there was a roof, some hand-me-down clothing, and enough food to eat – if only just. Paxton knew he had received a poor lot in life, but it was enough.

Or that was to say, it could have been enough...

...if it wasn't for Tyler Knox.

Tyler was seven years old and already a head taller and nearly twice as heavy as most of the other kids in the 4-6-year-old room. He belonged in the older age bracket rooms. The one for seven-to ten-year-olds. But there wasn't any space there. Not now and not in the foreseeable future.

That meant Tyler Knox was Paxton's problem.

Like most bullies, Tyler liked to pick on kids that were smaller than him. And in his room at Evergreen Orphanage that was everybody, which made Tyler, King Rat.

Tyler's bulk made him an imposing figure, and he used it to his full advantage. His round face was perpetually smudged with the remnants of whatever snack he'd scavenged, his dark eyes glinting with a mix of cunning and defiance. His clothes were stretched tight over his frame, the buttons of his hand-me-down shirt straining, and his worn jeans barely clinging to his waist. Despite his size, he moved with surprising speed, especially when it came to snatching a valuable extra roll or piece of fruit from an unsuspecting kid's plate in the dining room.

Nobody dared call him out. What would be the point?

Tyler denied everything he did with a sneer, and the staff never stepped in to stop him, too distracted or indifferent to notice. His appetite was as big as his presence, and he had no qualms about taking whatever he wanted, whether it was food, a toy, or the confidence of a smaller child. His loud, grating laugh echoed through the dormitory whenever he got his way, which was most of the time, leaving the others to grumble and whisper behind his back but to never directly challenge him. As Tyler was stuck in the younger kids' room, he was determined to make it his kingdom, one stolen snack at a time.

Paxton had only been there a week and already he had become Tyler's biggest target. He had come from a separate orphanage designed to cater to newborn babies through to three-year-old kids.

The four-year olds moved on to Evergreen.

Already, Paxton knew he was going to have to deal with the Tyler problem.

The sooner the better.

Paxton was tall for his age. Really tall. In fact, at four years old, he was just slightly towering above the height of Tyler Knox. But where Tyler had the full roundness of someone who no longer went without food daily, along with the physical growth of a seven-year-old child, Paxton had the immature, and gangly limbs of a typical four-year-old. As the two biggest kids in the room, you would have thought they could have been friends.

Paxton would have been happy to make it work.

Instead, Tyler appeared to take offense at the fact that a four year should be bigger than him and worked hard to prove his superior might at every opportunity. This meant regularly beating Paxton when the staff weren't looking.

And that's what made bedtime so dangerous.

It was probably ten o'clock at night, judging by the height of the moon outside the large windows that overlooked the sea of neighboring housing. Paxton cursed himself for not going to the toilet when he had the chance.

The children weren't supposed to leave their beds after lights out. Even if they needed to use the bathroom.

The graveyard shift was staffed with a skeleton crew at Evergreen, and as such, children were required to stay in their beds all night. It didn't matter if they were sick, unwell, in pain, or in this case, needed to go to the toilet.

Paxton tried to hold it.

He tried, but he feared he would wet the bed.

Perhaps that was for the best. He would get teased, and the staff would yell at him, but at least he wouldn't be breaking the rules, and suffering the consequences.

So Paxton waited.

An hour went by, maybe more, and he knew holding it just wasn't possible.

So, against his better judgment, he quietly climbed out of his bed and went down the hall, to the bathroom. There were no lights on, but it was a moonlit evening, and he had no trouble making his way to the toilet in the dark.

The orphanage's communal bathroom was a cold, uninviting space. Its cracked tile floors and walls echoing every sound. Along one wall, there was a row of old-fashioned toilets, their heavy porcelain tanks lined up like soldiers on parade. Each tank had a matching porcelain lid, though they were chipped and discolored from decades of use. There were no cubicles or partitions. Privacy was a luxury the orphanage apparently couldn't afford, which left the row of toilets completely exposed to anyone passing through.

One of the tanks in particular stood out. Its lid was partially broken, a jagged crack running diagonally across the surface, revealing a glimpse of the inner workings beneath. The fracture exposed rust-streaked chains and water-stained levers, a grim reflection of the bathroom's neglected state. The lid, though damaged, was still solid and deceptively heavy – its weight a constant reminder of the orphanage's reliance on old, durable fixtures that no one ever bothered to replace.

Paxton made his way to the closest toilet.

The floor was wet and smelled of strong bleach.

He quickly did his business, drawing a sigh of contented relief as he emptied his bladder and took a step back from the urinal.

A moment later, the worst thing happened.

He ran into Tyler.

The bully – like all bullies – enjoyed being in a position of power. They liked to stack the odds in their favor. Right now, Paxton could see in Tyler's malicious eyes that he figured all those odds were well stacked. Paxton might have been the same height as Tyler, but the bully was seventy pounds to his comparatively measly fifty.

To make matters worse, they were alone.

Paxton thought about screaming, but wasn't sure his voice would be carried as far as the staff's sleeping quarters at the other end of the building and two flights of stairs below. And if didn't, then what? Then Tyler would have known he was scared.

Nothing empowers a bully like seeing fear in their victim.

No, he wouldn't scream.

Tyler grabbed him. "You're not supposed to be out of bed after dark."

"Oh, hi Tyler," Paxton said in a whisper, pushing down the fear that flooded his veins. "I'm heading back there now."

"No, you're not."

Paxton swallowed hard. "Come on Tyler. It's late. Can we do this tomorrow?"

"So you can squeal to the staff?" Tyler shook his head. "No, I don't think so. We're going to do this now."

Paxton opened his mouth to ask what 'doing this' may possibly entail, but before he got the chance to speak, Tyler punched him in the solar plexus. The muscles of his small diaphragm spasmed, and for several seconds he couldn't breathe.

Tears welled in Paxton's eyes. He would have screamed now if he had the ability. Maybe then someone would come for him. Or maybe they wouldn't have. But either way, anything other than his current course of action had to have been better.

Tyler laughed and took another punch.

This time, Paxton's reflexes kicked in. He moved fast, quickly ducking out of reach Tyler's punch, causing him to overreach and nearly topple over.

Paxton tried to back away, but Tyler stepped between him and the door. He then stepped toward the row of toilets, hoping that his agility might allow him to maneuver himself around the toilets faster than Tyler.

Tyler saw what he was trying to do and moved to block him again.

Paxton was trapped.

He could be seriously injured or even die. But he didn't want to die! With terrifying realization, he knew that he no longer had anything to lose. Gritting his teeth, he prepared to take the beating of his life.

Tyler's muscles relaxed, as though he knew he'd already won. They both knew it.

He took another swing at Paxton.

This one narrowly missed connecting with his face, and Paxton began to worry one mistake might cost him his life. He had to do something about it.

On the next punch, Tyler put all his effort into hitting him.

Instead of ducking, or retreating as he had, Paxton stepped into the punch, using all his energy to push Tyler. Tyler's punch landed on his shoulder, but it didn't have much momentum and inflicted only minor injury.

Paxton kept marching forward and gave one harsh shove.

Tyler, taken by surprise by Paxton's response, tried to take a step backward. But his feet slipped on the recently bleached floor, and he toppled onto his back, with a sickening crunch.

Paxton gulped.

He'd just seriously hurt the bully.

Tyler didn't let anyone get away with anything that challenged his authority. Knocking him over and injuring him was unforgivable. Worse, Tyler's wrath would be lethal.

His heart began pounding hard and fast. Real fear rose up in Paxton's throat like bile.

The stakes had just risen, and Paxton viewed the situation logically.

It was now him or Tyler.

One of them had to go.

Paxton had to end this so Tyler could never hurt him ever again. His eyes landed on the broken porcelain toilet lid. Without a second thought, he picked the weapon up, needing both hands to lift it. Then he brought it down hard onto Tyler's head.

Contact between the boy's head and the porcelain lid made a horrifying crunching sound. Tyler's skull became wedged between the porcelain toilet lid and the tiled floor. But somehow, that wasn't enough. Flashbacks of all Tyler had done from hitting him, scaring him, stealing his food, and ultimately threatening his life, rolled through Paxton's mind. Even at the tender age of four, he knew he had to end this with finality.

So he brought the lid up again and slammed it down on the bully's head.

Again, and again, he hit the boy, panting with effort. Frightened and furious, he found himself making animal sounds. Paxton gasped and grunted, ending the danger. He was like some feral creature pushed right to the edge, and then over it.

He was finishing his enemy, until he felt a big hand pulling him up and off Tyler.

It was one of the nightshift workers, a man in his fifties.

The man stared at the broken body of the boy, who had gone completely still. Then he stared at Paxton, who had blood spatter on his face and clothes.

Then he swore long and hard.

"Son," he said to Paxton. "I think you might have killed him."

Chapter Twenty-Six

Number One Observatory Circle, Washington, D.C.

Vice President Daniel Hawthorne hung up the phone.

Dr. Alan Kepler took in the shocked look on his face. "What's happened?"

"There's been an explosion in the Ural Mountains in Russia!"

Kepler arched an eyebrow. "A nuclear explosion?"

"Yeah," the VP confirmed.

Dr. Kepler saw the implications immediately. "This is worse than we thought."

Hawthorne said, "So much worse."

Dr. Kepler said, "This shows that Boris suspected a trap from the beginning!"

"He would be a fool not to at least take precautions," Voss suggested.

Hawthorne said, "I don't even know how he moved the Davy Crockett nukes into Russia."

"No, that part I don't doubt he was capable of." Dr. Kepler smiled knowingly, and Hawthorne decided there were some things he was definitely better off not knowing. In his darkest nightmares, it was a man like Dr. Kepler who did the knowing. "Boris was telling us something with those nukes. Sending us a message."

"What was the message?" Frost asked.

Dr. Kepler's voice went cold. "If you try to betray me, I will show the whole world what you have done."

Hawthorne felt a shadow of fear cross over him. "He's a bold man."

Voss, who had made a very lucrative career on promoting war, observed, "He's a very dead man by now."

"Indeed," Dr. Kepler said. "The question is, did our secrets die with him?"

The phone rang again. VP Hawthorne took it, spoke for about a minute, and then hung up.

He surveyed each of the three men sitting in his office, and said, "The President is being taken to the White House Emergency Operations Center as a precaution until we know more. Under the recommendations of the Secretary of Defense, the President has set us to DEFCON 3."

DEFCON, short for Defense Readiness Condition, referred to the United States military's alert levels. This was a five-tier system used to measure the nation's preparedness for conflict, particularly in response to potential nuclear threats. The scale ranged from DEFCON 5, which signified normal peacetime readiness, to DEFCON 1, the worst of the scale, as it indicated an imminent onset of nuclear war.

Each step marked an escalation in military readiness. DEFCON 3 enabled the rapid deployment of air forces, and DEFCON 2 placed all military forces on the brink of action. The system, overseen by the National Command Authority, served as a vital tool during moments of crisis. It ensured the military's readiness to respond to threats at a moment's notice.

The VP then added, "The Secret Service will be arriving shortly to transport me to board the Boeing E-4B Nightwatch, as part of the COG protocols."

The Continuity of Government protocols (COG) were designed to preserve leadership and the uninterrupted function of government during emergencies. The E-4B Nightwatch was a military aircraft operated by the United States Air Force that serves as a mobile command post for the National Command Authority. It was nicknamed the "Doomsday plane" because it was designed to survive a nuclear attack and serve as the US military's command and control center in the event of an all-out nuclear war.

Kepler, Voss, and Dylan remained silent.

Each one was processing their next step. Hawthorne didn't have any doubt they would all happily sign his death warrant if it meant they would gain a "get out of their current predicament FREE" card.

Fortunately for him, the four of them were all in this together. They formed one of the smartest syndicates on earth. If they could survive another year, he would ascend to the highest office.

Then they would all know it was worth it.

That was, if they made it through this oversight that was building into one hell of a disaster. Hawthorne looked at Dr. Kepler. "You're a part of that plan too, Alan. You may as well ride with me and there you can tell me what sort of hellhole you've gotten me into, and how you propose we get out of it.

"Yes sir."

Hawthorne studied Voss and Frost with a smirk. "Sorry gentlemen. Your services, although very helpful to me, are currently underappreciated by the powers that be. As such, you're not part of this Continuations of Government. I suggest you use this time wisely to work out our next moves."

They both stood up without saying a word.

Everyone in the room knew they weren't really on the precipice of nuclear war. They also understood if Boris Volkov succeeded in revealing their secrets, they would all hope for a nuclear war to actually break out.

Two Secret Service Agents entered the room. "Marine Two is ready to take you to Joint Base Andrews, Mr. Vice President. It's time to go."

"Yes, of course." Hawthorne turned to Voss and Frost. "Dismissed, gentlemen."

Within minutes, Hawthorn and Dr. Kepler were on board the Sikorsky VH-60N White Hawk. It was run by Marine Helicopter Squadron One (HMX-1) out of Marine Corps Air Facility Quantico, Virginia.

Within seconds of boarding, Hawthorne and Kepler had taken their seats and buckled up. Then Marine Two was in the air.

Hawthorne glanced toward Hugo Lee, the Special Agent In Charge. "Does the Pentagon have any information for us yet on the nuclear explosion?"

"Not yet, sir. The President has spoken to the Russian President, and he's assured us they're not about to launch a nuclear attack."

"That's probably the sort of thing the Russian President would say just before he launched an attack." Hawthorne frowned, wishing he could know for certain that his secrets died along with Boris. "Anything else?"

"No, only that the Russian President assures us it appears to be an accident at a steel foundry in the Ural Mountains. Nothing more."

"And no indication where the nuclear bomb originated?"

"None."

But VP Hawthorne knew exactly where the bomb had originated. What's more, he knew where those eight Davy Crockett nukes had been stolen. After all, he was the one who helped make them disappear.

The question remained, was his involvement going to stay hidden?

After an eight-minute flight, Marine Two landed at Joint Base Andrews, where the fully fueled Boeing E-4 Nightwatch Advanced Airborne Command Post was ready to depart. Hawthorne was quickly moved to the Doomsday plane, and within minutes, the aircraft was in the air.

A series of military officials and intelligence officers brought the VP up to speed with what was known about the nuclear explosions – which was nothing other than it originated in the Ural Mountains, Siberia, inside a known Soviet Era missile silo, upon which a modern steel foundry now operated.

There were several explanations for the explosion.

All of them potentially innocent.

And none of them correct.

The Boeing flight lasted two hours before the explosion was deemed not to have been caused by a rogue state, and that no known Americans had been injured in the attack. The NSA de-escalated their defense state to DEFCON 4. They would maintain increased intelligence and security measures, but there was no indication the USA was under attack.

It was nearly 9 p.m. before Hawthorne returned to the VP residence at Naval Observatory One. VP Hawthorne poured another whiskey for himself and Kepler. He figured they both deserved it after the day they had had.

Dr. Kepler's secure phone pinged. He looked at the details. A wry smile on his lips. "There's been a development."

"What now?"

"My spy on the inside with the Ghosts sent a message."

"Go on," Hawthorne said, impatiently.

"The fissile materials were missing in one of the Davy Crockett's."

The VP swore. "He's sending us another message."

"Yes, he's telling us he's able to show the world what he's got, and that he's prepared to use it."

"But what good is that to him?" Hawthorne asked. "I mean, he's already dead!"

"Haven't you ever met someone in the throes of redemption?"

Hawthorne shook his head. "No. Politics is full of plenty of interesting people, with an enormous variety of traits. I haven't found that striving for redemption is strong among them."

"Allow me to increase your experience," Dr. Kepler said. "Someone in the grips of salvation genuinely believes in the future. It doesn't matter that Boris, like Martin Luther King, was never going to live long enough to see the promised land. It was good enough that he believed his actions were making the world a better place."

"Good God! Save us from the atonement of terrorists!" Hawthorne paused. "Wait... if Boris is dead, who did he pass our secrets to? Who does he imagine will fulfill his damned dream?"

Dr. Kepler drew in a melancholy breath. "If I had to guess, I'd say he's tried convincing Rembrandt. Explaining to him that revealing our treachery is in the best interests of our fine nation."

"You know him better than anyone else. Would he do something so crazy for such a foolish notion?"

"To save the USA from internal betrayal after trust?" Dr. Kepler shook his head, as though he couldn't quite understand how someone like Hawthorne, who had spent his life learning to manipulate powerful people from Congress to Senators, through to lobbyists and wealthy donors, could miss such basic human traits. "Rembrandt lives to serve his nation and protect US citizens. If he truly believes that what Boris wants is in our nation's interests, he'll die trying to achieve that goal."

"You think he'll expose us?"

"I do. And what's more, I think he has the missing nuke. This would ensure his point is made in the most profound way."

VP Hawthorne sighed. "You know what that means, don't you?"

"Yes." Dr. Kepler nodded. "Rembrandt and his Ghosts must all be terminated."

Chapter Twenty-Seven

U SS *Indiana* – SSN-789

Captain William "Will" Grayson didn't like anything about his current mission.

The seasoned submariner was in his early fifties, with a demeanor as steady and unyielding as the vessel he commanded. His close-cropped salt-and-pepper hair framed a rugged face weathered by years of navigating the depths, and his intelligent gray eyes missed nothing. He carried himself with an air of authority, his voice steady and deliberate, whether issuing orders or engaging in casual conversation.

A career Navy man, he was known for his meticulous attention to detail and an uncanny ability to anticipate problems before they arose. Despite his gruff exterior, he had a deep sense of loyalty to his crew, earning their respect through fairness and unwavering competence.

Grayson had served in Nuclear Attack submarines for twenty-eight years. More than half his life. He was dedicated to the country he loved, and the men and women under his command. Very few things frightened him.

But if he was honest, he was spooked by the CIA Ghosts on board.

There was nothing about the Ghosts he liked. They performed clandestine tasks that no government in their right mind would acknowledge they had sanctioned. Captain Grayson wondered how many politicians had stopped to question if such dark tasks should be performed at all. To make matters worse, this was a particularly dangerous mission. One he knew nothing about, only that it was being authorized by the highest levels of the Pentagon.

A small nuclear explosion was recorded in the Ural Mountains, right near the point of the Ghosts exfiltration.

That couldn't be a coincidence.

No, he would be extremely happy when they were off his boat.

The steady hum of the *USS Indiana's* nuclear reactor filled the control room, a comforting backdrop to the muted exchanges of the crew. Captain Grayson stood at the conn, his hands clasped behind his back as his intense eyes scanned the dimly lit room. The quiet efficiency of his team was calming proof to their training and his leadership.

"Conn, Radio," came the voice from the communications station. Chief Petty Officer Reynolds turned in his seat, his face illuminated by the faint glow of his monitor. "Priority bell ringer received. Orders request we come to periscope depth to establish satellite communication. Message classified priority one."

Grayson's gaze snapped to the chief. A priority bell ringer wasn't issued lightly. It was a high frequency radio transmission that could be picked up by the sonar and radio operators, indicating they were to surface to receive a secure satellite communication.

"Details?" he asked, his tone measured.

"Message content encrypted, sir," Reynolds replied. "All we have is the request to surface for satellite transmission."

Grayson nodded, the weight of the decision clear. Surfacing, even to periscope depth, carried risks, but priority one messages weren't something he could ignore.

Even in the dangerous seas near Siberia.

"Officer of the Deck," Grayson called, his voice cutting through the low murmur of the control room. "Prepare to bring us to periscope depth."

"Aye, sir," replied Lieutenant Commander Harris, who immediately began issuing orders. "Helm, make your depth sixty feet, five degrees up bubble. Speed to three knots."

"Make my depth sixty feet, five degrees up bubble, speed three knots, aye," the helmsman repeated, adjusting the submarine's trim and speed.

"Sonar, sweep the area. Report all contacts," Harris continued, turning toward the sonar station.

"Sonar, aye," the operator replied, his hands moving over the controls as he began an active scan. Moments later, he looked up. "Sonar reports no contacts within five nautical miles."

"Very well," Harris said before glancing at Grayson for confirmation.

Grayson gave a curt nod. His voice steady, "Proceed."

The *USS Indiana* tilted slightly as it ascended. The hum of the engines shifted subtly, and Grayson felt the familiar change in pressure as the submarine approached periscope depth.

"Conn, Radio," Reynolds called again as they reached sixty feet. "We're in position. SATCOM antenna deployed and link established. Secure channel ready."

"Patch it through to my console," Grayson ordered. He stepped toward the communications station, the rest of the room falling silent as the gravity of the situation set in.

The screen on the secure terminal flickered to life, displaying the image of an older man with sharp features, neatly combed gray hair, and a focused gaze that matched his code name: Peregrine. Dr. Alan Kepler, the CIA specialist in charge of the Ghost mission, wasted no time.

"Captain Grayson," Peregrine said, his voice calm but carrying an edge of urgency. "I need to speak privately to you and Umbra – the leader of the second Ghost team."

Captain Grayson frowned.

Umbra meant the darkest part of a shadow, where the light source was completely blocked. The man looked and acted like a psychopath. He might have been one of theirs, but he was still a psychopath as far as he could tell.

Even so, he was here merely for transport.

Determining what sort of weapon to use in these clandestine battles was definitely above his paygrade.

Grayson nodded. He gestured to his 2IC, and said, "Please fetch Umbra – the leader of the second Ghost team. Let him know he's got a secure message from his controller."

Umbra arrived, and together he and Grayson moved the audiovisual feed into a secure, communications room designed to receive classified information. Peregrine went through the various mission codes confirming his authority.

Captain Grayson confirmed their authenticity.

Umbra agreed.

Peregrine said, "The Ghost team your vessel has just picked up are commanded by Paxton West – code named Rembrandt. We have confirmation that he has been working with a Russian illegal arms dealer named Boris Volkov. Together, they have stolen small nuclear weapons. One of those, were blown up to cover their tracks from its storage silo in the Ural Mountains."

Captain Grayson said, "We are aware of the explosion."

Umbra asked, "You believe Rembrandt has gone rogue?"

"Yes, and he's taken the rest of his team with him."

"What are my orders?" Umbra asked.

Peregrine said, "You need to kill Rembrandt and his entire team."

Umbra said, "Copy that."

Peregrine said, "And one more thing..."

"Go ahead." Umbra's eyes narrowed.

"Rembrandt is the best fucking Ghost that's ever existed." Peregrine's lips formed a grim line. "Don't take chances. You and your men are to enter their quarters, and shoot them as they sleep. Do I make myself clear?"

Umbra nodded. "Yes sir."

"And Umbra..." Peregrine added. "If you screw this up, you won't be answering to me. You will be answering to whatever God you believe in."

Chapter Twenty-Eight

P axton woke with a jolt, suddenly alert.

Some sort of primitive survival mechanism at the base of his brainstem had alerted him that something wasn't right. His mind and body instantly kicked into gear.

The memories of the past forty-eight hours ran through his mind like a movie in fast-forward. Everything had gone wrong, but his team had made it back to the *USS Indiana* – a US nuclear attack sub – all except Raven and Falcon. Raven with a sniper bullet to the head and Falcon crashing into a rock arch in the valley above the Ob River in a remote part of Siberia.

Alicia and Carter.

The two youngest members of the team.

One he trusted infinitely, and the other he'd always distrusted.

Both dead.

His heart raced, adrenaline surging, preparing for a fight or flight. But he was on board a nuclear attack submarine. Once he was back in Washington there would be hell to pay. Powerful people would try and silence him.

But right now.

He was safe.

That's when he noticed the Marines stationed outside his door were no longer there. This was completely against protocol. He nudged Bulldog, Hammer, and Echo awake.

In a whisper Paxton said, "We're in serious trouble."

Chapter Twenty-Nine

U mbra grinned maliciously.

It felt like a gift.

A wave of elation coursed through his veins, the familiar rush of adrenaline that marked the chaos of battle and start of the hunt. Umbra turned away from the submarine's secure communications hub.

He felt a solid hand grasp his shoulder.

His gaze darted to the vise-like grip of the captain. The man's gray eyes landed on his, his face set with controlled rage.

"Yes?" Umbra said, a bemused smirk on his parted lips.

Captain Grayson said, "I don't care what Peregrine's orders are. While you and your demonic Ghosts are on my boat, you are under my command."

"With all due respect, Captain, my Ghosts operate outside the Navy's jurisdiction. We answer to a higher chain of command, and our mission parameters don't require your approval. While we're on your boat, I'll respect your authority over the vessel. But when it comes to our own operations, we're in charge. Stay out of our way, and we'll stay out of yours."

"The *USS Indiana* has a crew complement of 138 persons. Those are the lives I care about. As for all of you Ghosts, you can go back to hell where you all belong for all I care." Captain Grayson met his gaze. "But if you or any of the Ghosts damage my boat, I will end this farce so help me God. Do I make myself clear?"

Umbra nodded. "Crystal, sir."

"I'm serious. There are pipes and gauges and touchscreens that control the pumps strewn throughout the submersible. Just one of your stray shots and you're likely to send us all to the bottom."

"Understood."

Umbra stepped out of the secure communications room.

His pulse quickened, a steady drumbeat in his ears as anticipation coursed through him. Many years ago, he went by the name of Vaughn Sinclair. He trained as a US Army Ranger and served three tours of duty in Afghanistan. He had always liked to hunt. It was a sort of unbidden desire that churned in his blood since his father had first taken him out into the woods with a Savage Axis .243 hunting rifle.

He'd hoped that Afghanistan would fulfill some of that need.

It didn't.

Yes, he killed people.

It was war, but he was kept on a very tight collar, the leash held by his commanding officer. Then one day he was recruited as a Ghost. It was wonderful as he was given covert missions outside the law. With unbridled autonomy, he was able to perform the way he worked best, without rules and orders keeping him restricted.

After all, if you wanted someone dead, why attach a series of restraints to such orders?

But the missions were few and far between and most of them were simple assassinations. The targets were generally unaware of their impending demise, and long-distance shots were frequently used to achieve government sanctions, ignobly ending their lives without knowledge or fear. Most of them were simply alive – going about their business – and then dead. Sometimes, necessity allowed him to kill with his hands by stealth.

He enjoyed close eliminations best. But few situations required such methods, and the excitement of being a Ghost had quickly waned. But now he had been given an opportunity to hunt another Ghost...

Rembrandt.

The name was a legend whispered among operatives in the deepest shadows. A man whose skills and tactical brilliance had taken on a mythical quality. Umbra had never met him, but he knew the stories. Umbra sighed with satisfaction. For the first time in years, he felt the genuine thrill of the hunt.

Chapter Thirty

U mbra desperately wanted to savor the moment.

He moved silently with his team through the narrow passageways of the submarine, his Glock drawn, his senses honed like a raider closing in on their enemy. He felt the rhythm of the hunt, that primal surge of adrenaline coursing through his veins. The forward torpedo room was just ahead, the glow of the red emergency lights giving the space an ominous hue.

His team moved with alacrity. Six men trained for missions exactly like this.

He pushed the door open, his sharp eyes scanning the room. Four bunks were set up neatly against the far wall, each with a body-shaped outline under the gray blankets. They were exactly where the Captain had said they would be.

He nodded once, the gesture precise.

No words were needed.

The sound of gunfire cracked sharply in the confined space as two shots were placed into each bunk in near-perfect unison. Umbra's lips curved into a contented smile as he waited for the expected sound of pain, a groan, anything.

Nothing.

His satisfaction twisted into suspicion. He raised a hand, a signal for Jordan, his second-in-command, to investigate. Jordan nodded and stepped forward, his Glock held at the ready as he leaned toward the nearest bunk. With his free hand, he yanked back the blanket.

Umbra's pulse spiked at the sight of what lay beneath: not a body, but a single carbon dioxide fire extinguisher. Wrapped around its center was a thin strip of pale, waxy C4, secured by a web of fine detonation cord. Detcord – a narrow, flexible, plastic-coated explosive – snaked tightly around the extinguisher's surface, gleaming faintly in the red light. It was like a coiled viper, deadly and waiting.

"Oh shit!" Jordan hissed, his call of alarm breaking the tense silence.

"Everyone out!" Umbra barked, his voice like a whip crack.

The words had barely left his mouth when the detonation ripped through the torpedo room. The fire extinguisher exploded with a deafening roar, the compressed CO2 blasting outward in a fury of shrapnel and a thick, choking haze.

The force of the explosion hurled Jordan backward.

He didn't even have time to scream before a jagged shard of steel tore through his chest, killing him instantly. Behind him, Tompson staggered, his hands flying to his neck as blood poured between his fingers. Umbra saw the deep gash and knew immediately that Tompson wouldn't survive. The man's wide, desperate eyes locked onto his, but Umbra was already moving.

The shockwave threw Umbra off his feet, slamming him against the doorframe. His back hit the steel with brutal force, the impact driving the air from his lungs. He landed hard on the cold deck, momentarily dazed, his ears ringing and his vision swimming.

The room was chaos.

The air was filled with the hiss of released CO2, the smoky haze reducing visibility to almost nothing. The cold, biting fog stung his lungs as he gasped for breath. Around him, the sharp tang of blood and burning plastic cut through the metallic chill. He struggled to push himself up, every movement a battle against the disorientation caused by the blast.

Umbra's mind raced.

The mission was falling apart, and now his men were dead or dying. Worse, the prey they'd come for wasn't here. He clenched his jaw, rage boiling beneath the surface.

Then a second carbon dioxide fire extinguisher exploded. The gust of air throwing him backward, his head slammed against the steel wall of the hull, knocking him out cold...

In his delirious dreams, his mind wondered what just happened?

Rembrandt was at least as good as the legends told.

Probably even better.

Chapter Thirty-One

T he torpedo tube door swung open.

With a faint hiss Paxton emerged, his SCBA mask gleaming in the dim red light. It had been taken from the submarine's damage control locker. The small air tank strapped to his back ensured his breathing remained steady, unaffected by the dense haze of CO_2 filling the room. Through the swirling fog, he spotted the outline of a man gripping his throat, blood spilling through his fingers. Without hesitation, Paxton raised his Glock and fired once. The man's body went limp, collapsing heavily onto the deck.

Behind him, Hammer was already out of the tube, moving quickly toward the large hatch that separated the torpedo room from the crew's sleeping bunks. Bulldog and Echo followed, their movements rapid and precise as the team worked to stay concealed by the dense, smoky haze.

Paxton reached the door first, his boot almost touching the threshold, when something clamped around his leg.

The grip was iron-tight, twisting sharply at his ankle.

Pain shot through his knee as it buckled, sending him crashing to the deck. His Glock skittered out of his grasp, disappearing into the fog.

He rolled instinctively, grappling with an attacker he couldn't see.

The two of them wrestled in a chaotic tangle of limbs, the hard deck biting into Paxton's back. The man was strong, his movements sharp and unrelenting. Paxton felt fingers clawing for his throat, but he twisted away, their fight carrying them toward an area where the haze thinned just enough for shapes to become discernible.

Echo appeared; her Glock aimed at Paxton's attacker. Her stance was firm, her finger ready on the trigger, but before she could fire, the sharp crack of a gunshot echoed through the room. Three shots slammed into her back in rapid succession. She fell without a sound, crumpling to the deck, her weapon clattering beside her.

Paxton caught a glimpse of the new attacker as he turned the gun toward him. Desperation surged through Paxton as he rolled, dragging the man he was wrestling with on top of him just as the enemy fired again.

The bullets struck his foe's body above, the man's frame jerking violently before going still.

Paxton pushed the corpse off, his hands scrambling for Echo's fallen Glock. He felt the familiar weight in his grip, turned, and fired once. The bullet struck true, and Echo's killer fell, his weapon clattering to the deck. Silence returned to the room, broken only by the hiss of CO_2 and the hum of the submarine's systems.

Paxton hauled himself to his feet, his SCBA mask still in place. He staggered toward the door, glancing briefly at Echo's lifeless form before forcing himself to look away. Outside the torpedo room, a submariner lay unconscious next to the bunks, likely thrown there by the explosion. Paxton met Bulldog and Hammer's eyes.

"Time to get off this boat," he said, his voice steady despite the chaos.

"Agreed," Bulldog replied, with Hammer nodding grimly.

Paxton turned toward the corridor ahead. Through the haze, he saw movement—three submariners approaching quickly, their postures tense and alert. His eyes darted on a swivel, searching for an escape route. His gaze landed on a floor grate, the metal covering a narrow ladder leading to the level below. He moved swiftly, pulling it up with a sharp clatter.

"Head down," he barked.

Without hesitation, Bulldog and Hammer dropped through the opening, disappearing into the shadows below. Paxton followed, the clang of the grate closing above them echoing faintly. They descended into the depths of the submarine, vanishing into the labyrinthine corridors to make their escape.

Chapter Thirty-Two

P axton swung his legs over the edge of the hatch and slid down the ladder.

His boots clanged against the rungs as he descended into the submarine's lower deck. Hammer and Bulldog were already moving ahead, their forms cutting through the narrow corridor illuminated by strips of faint red lighting. Paxton hit the deck and broke into a sprint behind them, his SCBA mask still in place, its muffled hiss the only sound competing with the thrum of the submarine's systems.

They charged through a compartment filled with bunks, the cramped space empty but for the faint shadows of personal effects hanging near the beds. The smell of metal, sweat, and oil was thicker here, oppressive in the confined space. Paxton's mind raced as they darted through, knowing the clock was against them. Every step brought them closer to the engine room—and further from the team of Ghosts hunting them.

The door to the engine room loomed ahead, a heavy bulkhead with a wheel lock that Bulldog spun open with practiced speed. The three of them slipped inside, the sound of the submarine's nuclear reactor humming like a living heartbeat in the background.

The space was alive with pipes, gauges, and a faint, almost imperceptible vibration. Paxton's eyes flicked to a glowing caution sign near the reactor's shielding as they hurried past.

At the far end of the engine room, another ladder rose sharply upward. Hammer was first, hauling himself up with swift, sure movements. Bulldog followed close behind, his bulk moving faster than seemed possible for a man of his size.

Paxton climbed after them, his body coiled with adrenaline, every muscle tense with the expectation of an ambush.

They emerged into a higher deck, slipping past the crew mess hall. The faint aroma of reheated food still lingered in the air, a surreal reminder of the everyday life continuing elsewhere in the submarine. Crew members' voices could be heard faintly through the walls, unaware of the deadly pursuit playing out in the vessel's depths.

Ahead, the corridor stretched toward the submarine's central control room. Hammer glanced over his shoulder, his expression hard. "Which way?"

Paxton's eyes darted to a side passage, leading to the escape trunk. "There," he said, pointing. But before they could move, the sound of boots echoed down the corridor behind them. The thudding steps grew louder – three submariners approaching fast.

His gaze darted to the floor. Just ahead, a metal grate covered a ladder leading down to the bilge level. He strode forward, gripping the edge of the grate and yanking it up. The clang of metal echoed in the confined space as he gestured to Hammer and Bulldog.

Paxton pointed toward another grate.

Hammer didn't hesitate, lowering himself onto the ladder and sliding down with controlled speed. Bulldog followed, his heavy boots scraping against the rungs as he descended into the dark. Paxton glanced over his shoulder.

The approaching submariners were almost upon him.

Without a word, he slipped into the hatch and pulled the grate closed above him, his heart pounding as he plunged deeper into the submarine's labyrinth.

A few minutes later, they emerged at the entrance to the lockout trunk.

The cylindrical chamber was lined with polished steel and surrounded by controls, valves, and small blinking lights. Paxton and Bulldog moved quickly, the weight of urgency pressing down on them. The muffled hiss of their SCBA masks filled the confined space, blending with the faint hum of the submarine's systems. Behind them, Hammer pulled himself into the trunk, his movements quick but controlled as he reached for the hatch to seal it.

The sound of boots pounding down the corridor grew louder. Just as Hammer grasped the edge of the heavy steel hatch, a deafening crack echoed through the narrow space. Hammer staggered, a red bloom spreading across his side as he clutched the wound, his face contorted in pain.

Paxton swore, grabbing Hammer by the collar and pulling him deeper into the trunk.

Bulldog slammed the hatch shut, his broad hands spinning the locking wheel with a sharp, metallic screech. Another bullet ricocheted off the outer edge, but the hatch slammed closed just in time. Bulldog secured it, turning the wheel until it wouldn't budge.

"Flood it!" Paxton shouted.

Bulldog didn't hesitate.

He punched the flood button, and with a sharp hiss, water began pouring into the chamber from overhead valves. The level rose rapidly, climbing up their boots and soaking them in seconds. Paxton leaned over Hammer.

The old man of the team looked at him fondly. "You've done well, Paxton."

Paxton didn't know what to say, so he said, "Thank you."

Hammer started choking and gurgling on the blood that was filling his lungs, and drowning him from the inside. Through gasps, Hammer said, "Paxton... don't let the bastards win."

"I won't," he promised.

Hammer didn't respond. His eyes stared upward without seeing anything.

Paxton let go of him, letting his lifeless body float in the water that continued to rise inside the lockout trunk. It climbed past their knees, then their waists. The lockout trunk felt impossibly small now despite it being capable of supporting up to twenty Navy SEALs. The water surged upward. Paxton kept his eyes on the gauges, watching the pressure equalize. Outside, faint banging sounds reverberated through the hatch as the submariners tried to force their way in, but it was too late for them.

Bulldog pointed toward the fully encapsulated Zodiac, a small, inflatable boat, attached to the wall of the lockout trunk. Inside, housed a series of weapons and supplies to form a readymade attack vehicle for Navy SEALs to utilize.

Paxton nodded. "I see it."

He pulled the dive mask over his head and placed the air regulator into his mouth. A moment later the chamber filled completely, water closing over their heads. The hiss of their masks was all that remained as the last bit of air escaped, replaced by the cool silence of the flooded trunk.

Paxton and Bulldog untied the Zodiac and hit the green open button.

The hydraulic pumps pushed the massive steel door outward.

The hatch swung open to reveal the dark, endless expanse of the ocean outside. He pushed off, swimming into the cold blue depths.

Chapter Thirty-Three

U mbra woke up with a jolt.

He'd been knocked out. What the hell had gone wrong? He was supposed to kill Rembrandt as he slept, but instead, the man had known they were coming for him. He had hidden a series of CO_2 fire extinguishers under their bedsheets and waited for them to come.

The explosion had knocked him back. It had shaken him, but he was still conscious. Then a second explosion blew him back again.

That time he wasn't so lucky.

He took a quick stock of his injuries. Whatever they were, they weren't fatal. He sat up and heard a series of submariners working on the hatch to the lockout locker.

No way! How could Paxton and his team have reached the lockout locker?

Umbra grabbed his Heckler and Koch MP5 submachine gun. Sensitive submarine parts be damned. He'd sink the entire submarine if he had to just to prevent Paxton from escaping his grasp. When he reached the hatch to the lockout locker, Captain Grayson and the XO were standing there seemingly doing nothing.

Umbra said, "Open the damned door!"

Captain Grayson said, "It's flooding. You know as well as I do that there's nothing I can do from this side of that water-tight door."

Umbra said, "Then dive! Bring us to a depth of a thousand feet. Let them escape into those sorts of crushing depths!"

"There's not enough time!" Captain Grayson replied. "We wouldn't be halfway to that depth before they were out the door and merrily swimming to the surface."

Umbra said, "Okay, so bring us to the surface."

Grayson shook his head. "We're in the Kara Sea, on the coast of Siberia. This entire waterway is riddled with the Russian navy. There's no way we're going topside here."

Umbra pointed his Heckler and Koch MP5 at the captain. "I strongly suggest you change your mind before we find out just how much damage a submachine gun can cause inside your precious nuclear submarine."

Grayson glared at the threatening CIA Ghost. A shadow of fear crossed his otherwise disciplined expression. "I believe you're serious."

"You had better believe it..."

Grayson exchanged a furtive glance with the XO. "All right Mr. Jenkins. I suggest you take us to the surface."

Chapter Thirty-Four

I ce cold water stung Paxton's unprotected skin.

The lockout trunk had opened into the cold, dark expanse of the ocean, the faint glow of the submarine's internal lights from the lockout trunk casting eerie streaks against the steel hull. Paxton motioned to Bulldog, and together they pulled the tightly packed container holding the Zodiac from its storage compartment.

It was a sleek, compact package, purpose-built for Navy SEAL missions – efficient and deadly.

Underwater, their movements were steady, each man careful not to disturb the fragile silence of the deep. Bulldog held the container steady while Paxton worked the restraining straps. The final buckle released with a muted snap, and Paxton reached for the activation cord.

A sharp hiss broke the stillness as the Zodiac's internal CO_2 canister deployed. The gray material unfurled in an instant, its sleek shape snapping into form as the chambers filled with gas. The boat's buoyancy tugged it upward, and Paxton placed a firm hand on its side, ensuring a controlled ascent as it surged toward the surface.

The Zodiac broke through the water's surface with a soft splash, its inflated form bobbing gently in the waves. Paxton emerged moments later, pulling himself over the side of the craft. Bulldog followed quickly, his strong arms gripping the edge as he hauled himself aboard.

For a brief moment, they both sat in silence, catching their breath as the waves lapped against the inflatable sides.

Paxton moved swiftly, pulling the compact electric motor from its secured compartment at the stern. Bulldog steadied the boat, his broad shoulders tense as his eyes scanned the horizon. Paxton locked the motor into place, its design made for stealth.

He started the electric motor.

Taking a quick visual bearing, Paxton spotted the distant silhouette of the Yamal Peninsula, a dark shadow against the faint glow of the overcast night.

The Zodiac glided forward, cutting through the gentle swells with ease, the motor propelling them toward the distant coast. Behind them, the submarine was just a memory – a tomb where Hammer and Echo's lives had been lost.

Shivering with adrenaline, cold, or a combination of both, Bulldog shifted beside him, checking the gear in the Zodiac with careful precision. The quiet hum of the motor was the only sound, a thin veil over the tension that hung in the air. They were alive, moving forward, but the shadows of what they had left behind would follow them until the end.

Neither man said a word.

Paxton glanced over his shoulder, the icy Arctic wind cutting against his face. In the distance, barely visible against the dark water and faint horizon, a Russian navy frigate cruised steadily. Its silhouette was unmistakable, an ominous reminder of how close they were to hostile territory. He doubted the crew on that ship would spot their Zodiac in the endless expanse of water, but he felt a flicker of relief knowing they were heading in the opposite direction.

That relief vanished when the *USS Indiana* suddenly broached the surface.

The sleek, black hull of the Virginia-class nuclear submarine erupted from the water, its momentum creating massive waves that rocked the Zodiac. Paxton's heart clenched as he saw a figure climb through the conning tower hatch – a man, wild-eyed and holding a submachine gun.

Cursing, Paxton opened Zodiac's motor throttle all the way.

The man on the submarine opened fire, the rapid bursts of gunfire tearing through the air. Bullets hissed and splashed around them, some punching into the water with deadly force, others ripping into the sides of the inflatable Zodiac. The tough material held, designed to float even under fire, but the hiss of escaping CO_2 betrayed the growing damage. The boat jolted slightly under the assault, but it stayed afloat, for now.

Bulldog, already moving, grabbed one of the SEAL team's submachine guns from the gear stashed on the Zodiac. Paxton, still steering, reached for his Glock, firing a few precise shots toward the madman on the *Indiana*.

Bulldog leaned over the side of the Zodiac, returning fire with controlled bursts. The sharp staccato of the weapon echoed across the water, their rounds pinging harmlessly off the submarine's hull but forcing the gunman to duck momentarily.

The Russian frigate loomed closer, its hull cutting through the waves with imposing speed. Paxton's eyes flicked between the Russian frigate and the *Indiana*, praying silently for a miracle.

It came a second later.

The appearance of the enemy vessel seemed to spook the submarine. The *Indiana*, unable to maintain its position, began to submerge. It quickly disappeared beneath the water in a smooth dive.

"That was lucky," Paxton gasped, his adrenaline-fueled laugh strained. "I never thought I'd be so glad to see a Russian frigate!"

But Bulldog didn't answer.

Paxton turned to look and felt his stomach drop. Bulldog slumped against the side of the Zodiac, his submachine gun still in his hand. A dark stain spread across his chest, blood pooling beneath him, and mixing with the seawater sloshing at the bottom of the boat.

"Cole!" Paxton shouted, releasing the throttle and grabbing his friend. Bulldog's breathing was shallow, his face pale, but his eyes fluttered open.

"Keep... moving," Cole rasped, his voice weak but resolute.

Paxton clenched his jaw, his mind racing.

The coast of the Yamal Peninsula was still a distant shadow on the horizon. The Zodiac sputtered slightly, the motor working against the growing weight of the damaged inflatable. Paxton pressed his hand against Bulldog's wound, trying to stem the bleeding while he steered with his other hand.

"We're going to make it," Paxton said, his voice firm despite the knot of dread in his chest. "Just hang on."

The Arctic waters stretched endlessly ahead, the waves relentless, but Paxton's grip on the motor remained steady.

Paxton pulled the Zodiac up onto the icy shores of the Yamal Peninsula.

He tried to lift Cole out of the rubber boat, but his friend wouldn't have any of it. Paxton studied his last fellow team member. A dark red mixture of blood and seawater sloshed around at the bottom of the Zodiac.

He didn't look to see where his friend had been shot.

It didn't matter.

Cole had lost more blood than the human body could live without. If they were anywhere near a hospital – somewhere with blood products to infuse – he might be operable, and able to survive. But out here, on the edge of Siberia, there was no chance.

A simple, cruel fact.

Paxton said, "What do you need?"

"I need to confess my sins."

Paxton shook his head. "Then you need a priest. Whatever sins you have committed, I am certain mine are far worse."

Cole knew he didn't have long to live. He came straight out with it. "It was me."

The words hit Paxton like a sledgehammer, leaving his thoughts splintered and scattered. He frowned. "You?"

"I'm sorry."

"How?"

"Peregrine offered me my freedom and issued me a formal death certificate. He was letting me resign from the Ghosts."

"In exchange for what?"

"I had to sabotage the mission if Boris Volkov was alive and tried to communicate with any of the team. If he made contact with any Ghosts, I was to kill him and the Ghost he contacted."

Paxton said, "But Falcon was the one who shot Boris Volkov."

Cole nodded. "Yeah, making it so I didn't have to."

"What would you have done if you knew Boris had already given me the flash drive?"

Cole said, "I don't know. Peregrine would have wanted me to kill you."

"Would you have?"

"I don't know, Paxton." He swallowed hard, struggling to breathe. "I want to say that it never would have happened. Yet if it meant being with Rowena again and being able to be a father to my two girls... that's not even a question. I would have killed you and any other person who stood in my way."

"It's all right, Cole." Paxton squeezed his hand. "I forgive you completely. I don't have kids, or a woman I care for, but from what I understand, given your situation, I would have done the same thing too."

Cole was dying, but Paxton could see there was some relief in the man's eyes.

There was nothing that could be done.

Cole tried to whisper something...

Paxton had to come close to him to hear what it was.

Cole spoke again. This time his words were clear and determined. "Promise me you will find Rowena Vandyke. Make sure she and my girls are okay."

"All right." Paxton nodded. "You have my word. I'll find her and make sure they're fine. They won't have to worry about a thing."

Chapter Thirty-Five

Eisenhower Executive Office Building – Washington, D.C.

Dr. Alan Kepler stepped briskly through the grand entrance of the Eisenhower Executive Office Building, the chill of the morning air clinging to his overcoat. The building's ornate façade and imposing architecture always struck him as an odd contrast to the modern power that pulsed within its walls. It was a relic of another era, but today it served as the gateway to one of the most influential offices in the country.

He moved through the security checks rapidly, handing over his identification and enduring the brief but thorough scans. The guards barely glanced at him; his presence here was routine enough to draw no special attention, yet rare enough to maintain its weight. His credentials had been pre-cleared, and within moments, he was escorted deeper into the labyrinthine halls of the building.

The air inside carried the scent of polished wood and faint traces of coffee, a mix of history and the mundane. Kepler adjusted his tie as he was guided down a hallway lined with portraits of past vice presidents, their stoic gazes following him as if silently judging his purpose here.

Dr. Alan Kepler was feeling good. He'd dealt with the problem in Siberia, so they had passed through the danger zone. Yes, Rembrandt, the very best operative he'd ever seen, was dead. Yet it had to be done. After everything the orphan kid had been through, it seemed sad to think he had been murdered by the country he served. Still, it couldn't be helped.

America was at war and tough decisions had to be made.

Her people just didn't realize it yet.

The door to the Vice President's office opened, and a staffer gestured him inside. Kepler nodded his thanks and stepped into the room, the plush carpet muffling his footsteps. The office was both grand and functional, its furnishings chosen to strike a balance between authority and approachability. Heavy drapes framed large windows that let in pale winter light, casting long shadows across the room.

Vice President Daniel Hawthorne stood at the far end, his broad frame silhouetted against the windows. He turned as Kepler entered, his expression greeting him with barely restrained rage. "I thought you said you had dealt with it, Alan!"

"I did deal with it," Dr. Kepler said, "I had Umbra's team take Rembrandt and the rest of his Ghosts out."

VP Hawthorne then slammed a newspaper down in front of him. It was TASS, a Russian state-owned newspaper. And there, on the front page, was the *USS Indiana* nuclear attack submarine's silhouette on the surface of the Kara Sea.

It was going to be one hell of a diplomatic nightmare.

The President was going to be pissed.

Dr. Kepler said, "Do we know anything?"

"Not much. Only that the *Indiana* submerged a moment after this photo was taken by a nearby Russian frigate."

"Is there any chance it was sunk?"

"Unlikely. The Secretary of Defense and the Intelligence Officers at the NSA all assure me that if it had hit the bottom or imploded our listening stations in the North Sea would have heard it."

"But there's been no word from Captain Grayson?"

"Nothing."

Dr. Kepler nodded. "He's probably pissed at us that Umbra failed with the assassination of Paxton and his Ghosts."

"Can we be certain he did fail?" the VP asked.

"I think so." Dr. Kepler thought about that for a moment. "I can't imagine any other possible reason Captain Grayson would have brought his boat topside in the middle of the Kara Sea, a region of Siberia's waters known to be riddled with Russian naval ships."

"What do you think happened?"

"If I had to guess, I'd say Umbra failed to take me seriously when I informed him of just how intelligent and dangerous Paxton was. Thus Paxton, and perhaps some of his team escaped. They probably shot their way to the submarine's lockout trunk, and then made their way to the surface... where Grayson and his boat followed."

"You think Umbra forced his hand?"

"Definitely. I know Captain Grayson personally. There's no way he would be stupid and irresponsible enough to surface in the middle of the Kara Sea. No, mark my words. Umbra – psychotically patriotic and mission-focused to a fault – must have made Grayson surface the *USS Indiana*."

VP Hawthorne said, "Then the question remains, did Umbra achieve his objective?"

"I don't know..."

"If Paxton and some of his fellow Ghosts escaped, where would they go?"

"That's a good question. They may have taken one of the Navy SEAL's Zodiacs to reach the coast. But even then, I can't see them surviving. They are in the middle of Siberia in winter, no doubt wet and cold, with enemies on all sides, and without support. Nobody could live through that. They would have to be exceptionally lucky or incredibly resourceful to make it out alive."

"All right," VP Hawthorne said. "Some of Paxton's Ghosts may still be out there. Just how good is Paxton?"

Dr. Kepler's lips formed a grim line. "If there really is a divine creator... and HE were to make the perfect assassin, I believe that creation would look pretty much identical to Paxton."

Hawthorne arched an eyebrow. "He's that good?"

"No." Dr. Kepler shook his head. "He's a lot better."

The VP grimaced. "Then I suggest you do whatever you can from your end to make sure the man doesn't leave Siberia."

Chapter Thirty-Six

St. Elizabeths Psychiatric Hospital, Washington, D.C. – 36 Years Ago

"So they tell me the child you injured with the toilet lid is going to survive..." Dr. Alan Kepler said.

His eyes met those of young Paxton West, looking for a response. The kid's demeanor remained unchanged by the revelation. He neither seemed excited nor apologetic. Kepler might as well be telling him the weather report.

"Yes," Paxton confirmed. "He came back to Evergreen a few weeks ago."

"How did that make you feel?" Kepler asked.

Paxton looked at him curiously, maintained good eye contact, and asked, "Feel about what?"

"The fact that this boy – I understand that he was a bit of a bully – was back at the orphanage."

"He hasn't bullied me at all since he got back," Paxton said, cheerfully. "So far, anyway."

"No, I think his days of bullying is most likely long past him now."

"Maybe," Paxton replied, his expression suggesting he agreed, but wasn't going to commit to any specific notion. Not until he'd had more time to see how his once arch enemy recovered.

"What was the kid's name?"

"Tyler Knox."

"That's right." Dr. Kepler adjusted his glasses, pinching the base of his nose. "Have you noticed anything different since Tyler came back?"

"Not really."

"Nothing at all?" Dr. Kepler asked, surprised by Paxton's response.

The boy was displaying classic psychopathic behavior, but he was far from stupid. A series of psychological and psychometric tests had revealed his Intelligence Quotient placed him in the top one percent of the top percentile of people in the population.

His memory was very near photographic and his language development, even at this early age, suggested he was destined for a career in linguistics. Already, he'd picked up conversational Russian and Arabic from two other orphans. Paxton might not feel guilty for what he'd done, but there was zero chance he hadn't observed the changes in Tyler's behavior.

"I haven't noticed." Smiling, Paxton shook his head. Then, as though he knew Kepler was trying to elicit a little more out of him, he said, by way of an explanation, "Tyler and me didn't really play together much before the accident."

"Oh, really?" Dr. Kepler said, with an equally false smile.

That's interesting, Kepler thought, to see Paxton had now learned to refer to the event as an accident – most likely discovering that people could readily accept a four-year-old accidentally hurting an older child, far more than the truth: that the four-year-old had been bullied, and instead of telling an adult, had decided to end the bully's life.

Dr. Kepler drew a breath. "What about Tyler's speech? Did you notice anything different there?"

"No." Paxton spread his hands in a gesture that seemed to plead for understanding, his expression halfway between regret and explanation. "Tyler and I didn't speak before the accident, and we haven't spoken since he got back."

Dr. Kepler nodded.

Working with Paxton was an equal mixture of excitement and frustration. "Okay, let's try something different," he said.

"Okay," Paxton agreed. "Sure."

"Good. Now, can you please describe to me how Tyler appears and behaves since he has gotten back from the hospital? How does he spend his day? And what does he do with it?"

Paxton thought about that for a moment. Then, without emotion, said, "He doesn't do anything on his own."

"No?"

"No. It's like he doesn't have any thoughts of his own."

Dr. Kepler thought, *now we're getting somewhere*. "Can you explain that?"

"Sure." Paxton pressed his lips together. "He is capable of doing basic things, but someone needs to guide him, or at least start him on the process. And then, once he's finished, someone else needs to stop him again."

"Can you give me an example?"

"He spills food when he eats you see…" Paxton paused, frowning. Trying to think of the best way to explain it. Then, as though picturing the right analogy, he said, "One of the staff members will hand him a wipe and tell him to wipe his face. He almost looks normal as he wipes the food off his face, but then he doesn't stop. He would keep wiping all day if one of the staff didn't instruct him to stop."

"Anything else you have noticed?" Dr. Kepler persisted.

"Yesterday, one of the staff placed Tyler in front of a potted plant in the main hall. It was a gift from some good Samaritan at the hospital. They told Tyler to watch the plant and enjoy the nature."

"What did Tyler do?"

Paxton's expression was completely unreadable. No smile, no grimace, no horror. He simply said, "Tyler stood there all day and did as he was told. The staff had to guide him away for dinner many hours later."

Dr. Kepler said, "Tyler has what is called a traumatic brain injury. He finds it difficult to concentrate. He will never learn to read. He's lucky if he can feed himself without spilling half the food on the floor. He is no longer able to speak, and he drools incessantly. He's unlikely to ever pass the cognitive function of a toddler."

He paused, expecting Paxton to make a comment. When the silence stretched on, Dr. Kepler gave him a gentle nudge. "How does that make you feel?"

Paxton seemed to think about that.

Possibly about the relentless beatings he got. The fear the bully provoked. The times he'd stayed awake all through the night afraid of what Tyler might do to him in the morning.

Dr. Kepler watched his response with interest.

Paxton stared up at him, his piercing green eyes filled with absolute honesty. He smiled, and said, "I like him much better this way."

Chapter Thirty-Seven

Yamal Peninsula – Siberia – Present Day

The snow fell from the sky in thick wet sheets, heavier and heavier.

A storm was coming.

Siberian winters were known to produce arctic tempests that were deadly to those prepared for them, and Paxton, being currently soaking wet was far from prepared. He needed to get out of his wet clothes and into something dry if he were to survive the next few hours, let alone the night.

He quickly rifled through the small storage compartment of the Zodiac, his fingers stiff and numb from the biting cold. He almost didn't believe his luck when he pulled out a set of winter gear – a pair of insulated long pants, a heavy woolen shirt, and a thick jacket designed for Arctic conditions. The fabric was sturdy, clearly military issue, with a faded insignia stitched on the sleeve. He recognized the style – Russian Arctic uniforms. They weren't new. A faint musty smell clung to them, but right now, they were a godsend.

He quickly slipped out of his soaked clothing, his skin prickling as the icy wind whipped against his damp body. The pants were too short, the cuffs barely reaching his ankles, and the waistband strained when he clinched it tight. The shirt clung awkwardly across his shoulders, the sleeves ending just shy of his wrists, and the jacket was snug enough to restrict his movement slightly. Standard uniforms were always too small, and this set was no exception, but they would have to do. It was one of the problems with being six-foot-six and built like a human bulldozer.

In the bottom of the compartment, he found a single pair of spare socks, rolled tightly together. He yanked them apart and frowned. Too small. The fabric stretched just enough to cover the tops of his feet, but his toes were left exposed. With no time to waste, he pulled out his knife, slicing the ends off the socks to create makeshift sleeves. He slipped his feet through, the dampness of his boots pressing against the fabric. It wasn't much, but it offered a thin layer of insulation between his skin and the wet leather.

Paxton shivered violently, his body still trying to recover from the icy water, but he couldn't risk lighting a fire with the Russian Navy nearby.

A fire this close to the shore would serve like a flare to them.

Not to mention whoever was trying to kill him on board the *USS Indiana* for that matter, although he doubted they would risk coming topside again now that the Russian frigate had spotted them on the surface the first time.

He hunkered down in the shadows of the rocky shore, pulling the jacket tighter around him. His boots squelched as he shifted position, but he ignored it. Survival was a steady game of patience and adaptation. Difficult, sure. And at times he felt panicked, yet he would play it as long as he had to.

Paxton quickly raided the rest of the supplies from the Navy SEALs' Zodiac.

There wasn't much. A Heckler and Koch MP5 submachine gun. A few spare magazines and a Glock. There were a few MRE food packs, which were welcome. The military Meals Ready to Eat weren't known for their taste, but he'd spent a lot of his life eating them and had tricked his taste buds into finding them delicious.

There was a small demolition kit in a watertight container.

He unzipped it.

There wasn't much. A single block of C4. A detonator. A timer.

He looked down at Cole's lifeless body.

It would have been nice to bury him. Not that Cole ever felt that particular about it. The man wasn't religious. All the Ghosts knew it was unlikely they would ever receive a proper burial. Technically, they were already dead. Their empty caskets were already entombed in Arlington with full military honors.

Paxton stuck the detonator into the single block of C4, attached a timer, and stuck it to the bottom of the Zodiac. He then started the electric motor and set the autopilot so that it headed out into the Kara Sea.

Not much of a burial for his best friend, but it would have to do. Besides, it would serve to confuse anyone who was actively searching for him.

He watched it go, picked up the small pack loaded with supplies, and began his long journey into the icy wilderness.

Chapter Thirty-Eight

The Siberian ice storm was shaping up to be brutal.

If he didn't find shelter, the bitter cold was going to kill him.

The wind howled across the desolate expanse of the Yamal Peninsula, a relentless force that drove snow in stinging waves against Paxton's face. Each gust felt like a slap of needles, cutting through the gaps in his gear no matter how tightly he pulled the hood around his head. The Arctic jacket, though thick and designed for such brutal conditions, seemed to lose its battle against the cold. Every step was a war against exhaustion and the creeping numbness that threatened to steal his strength.

Around him, the landscape stretched in frozen monotony. Snow-covered tundra rolled out in every direction, interrupted only by clusters of gnarled, skeletal trees – scrubby larches and birches, their branches weighed down by frost. They stood like phantoms of a forgotten forest, offering no refuge, only a reminder of how alone he was. The ground beneath his boots alternated between crunching snow and patches of ice, where his footing slipped dangerously with each step.

The sky above was a swirling chaos of gray and white, the storm blotting out any hint of sun or direction. Snowflakes clung to his eyelashes, and his breath came in shallow bursts, condensing into frost on the scarf he had covering his face and mouth. Paxton glanced down at his hands, encased in thick gloves, and flexed his fingers to keep the blood flowing.

He couldn't afford to lose mobility – not out here.

He pushed forward, his gaze scanning the horizon for any sign of sanctuary. A jagged rise in the distance hinted at a rocky outcrop, perhaps a place to shield himself from the merciless wind. Even with shelter, though, he knew the truth: the cold was an unrelenting hunter, and it wanted to freeze his bones. Without a fire or a proper place to hunker down, it would claim him before morning.

The temperature felt like it had dropped with every passing minute, and without the scarf, the air would freeze in his lungs. His cheeks burned, not with warmth but with the icy bite of frostnip. He reached up to adjust his scarf, wishing it could cover more of his face, but the fabric was already stiff and wet with his breath.

As he trudged on, the storm grew fiercer, the wind howled, and the snow whipped into a blinding wall. The trees thinned, their twisted silhouettes fading into the white void behind him.

Paxton's thoughts turned grim. The Yamal Peninsula wasn't just cold – it was the grim reaper with an icy scythe, and Death was coming for him.

The only thing keeping him moving was the knowledge that stopping would mean surrendering. His steps faltered for a moment, and he shook his head fiercely, forcing himself onward.

And besides, he couldn't die.

Not yet.

Paxton didn't fear death. Nor was he overly keen to greet it either. Even so, he knew he had to survive whatever hardship came for him. No matter what it took.

Cole had asked him to find Rowena Vandyke. He would reach her, make sure she and her girls were unequivocally taken care of for life, and then he would find Peregrine and whoever else was responsible for the massacre of his team – and he would make them pay severely.

Somewhere in the distance, beyond the roaring wind, he thought he caught sight of something – a dark shadow against the endless white. A structure? A rock formation? Hope stirred faintly, but he knew better than to celebrate too soon. Shelter, if it was real, was his only chance.

Tightening his grip on his resolve, Paxton pressed forward, his body screaming for rest, his mind battling the storm's unyielding grasp.

It appeared to be a hunter's lodging. There was a chimney and a fire, and the place smelled of the rich aromas of meat being cooked.

He reached the door, his fingers grasping through the phantom building.

It was nothing more than a mirage.

Like a dehydrated man in the desert, his frozen brain was playing tricks on him. That was a bad sign. He needed to get out of the cold.

The wind whooshed through the brittle, leafless branches. Ice crystals blew into his face like thousands of tiny pinpricks. His feet and hands were numb. He floundered through deep snow. He staggered and lurched and kept moving.

Everything hurt.

But he was still going.

Adrenaline kept the pain from overwhelming him.

Sheer willpower kept him on his feet.

He decided he needed to change his plan, at least until the morning and until the storm had blown over.

Paxton stopped and blinked hard against the snow and looked for a tree well, a swath of ground with far less snow beneath the canopy of an evergreen tree. The snow collected on the tree boughs rather than under the tree, creating a natural gap.

He found one beneath a huge spruce with thick, heavy boughs. He dug away the shallower snow and pushed it all to one side to create a small wall to block the wind. Spruce boughs were a bad choice for insulation due to their prickly needles.

A fir tree would have provided softer branches.

Paxton eyed the massive spruce tree, its low-hanging boughs heavy with snow, forming a natural shelter. The storm howled around him, but beneath the tree, the wind was muted, and the ground was relatively clear of deep drifts.

This was his best shot at survival for the night.

He pulled off his gloves briefly, his fingers numb and trembling as he grabbed his folding knife from his pack. Putting his gloves on again, he stepped to the base of the tree and began slicing through the thickest boughs he could reach, the blade crunching through the frozen bark. The branches were tough, their needles coated with a thin layer of frost, but he worked methodically, letting them drop into a pile at his feet.

Once he had a sizable stack, he started digging. Using the knife and his gloved hands, he scraped away the snow beneath the tree until he reached the frozen earth. He created a shallow depression, deep enough to shelter him from the wind but not so deep as to trap the cold.

He lined the depression with the spruce boughs, layering them thickly to create insulation from the icy ground. Their resinous scent was sharp in his nose, mingling with the metallic bite of the cold. He worked quickly, his breath coming in sharp puffs of steam, knowing he didn't have much time before his body heat bled away entirely.

With the bed prepared, he gathered more branches and built a crude windbreak on the side most exposed to the storm. He stacked the boughs at an angle, overlapping them like shingles to create a barrier against the biting gusts. It wasn't perfect, but it would hold.

Finally, Paxton crawled into the makeshift shelter, pulling his jacket tighter around him. The boughs crackled faintly under his weight, their needles poking through the fabric of his clothes, but he barely noticed. The storm raged outside, the wind screaming through the trees, but here, under the spruce, it was quieter. A small cocoon of relative safety in the Arctic wilderness.

He got as comfortable as possible and let himself drift off to sleep.

Chapter Thirty-Nine

Georgetown, Washington, D.C.

Dr. Alan Kepler guided the 1989 Saab 900 Aero Turbo 16s along the cobblestone streets of Georgetown, the car's modest engine purring steadily. The classic Scandinavian design stood out amid the sleek, modern vehicles parked along the narrow roads. Its rounded body, painted a faded mint green, gleamed faintly in the dim light of the overcast afternoon. The car had been meticulously maintained, its chrome details polished to a soft shine, though a few scratches on the bumper hinted at years of loyal service.

Kepler tightened his grip on the oversized steering wheel, navigating a tight corner with the ease of someone who had driven these streets countless times. The old Saab's distinct, curved windshield gave him a panoramic view of the surrounding neighborhood: rows of historic buildings with ivy creeping up their facades, wrought iron balconies, and colorful shutters framing windows like picture frames. The building he approached might have appeared as quaint as any other.

Despite the charm, he felt a twinge of unease.

He pulled up in front of a narrow, four-story Federal-style townhouse. Its brick exterior was darkened with age, the mortar between the bricks crumbling in places, lending it an air of old-fashioned respectability. A small plaque near the door declared it to be "Kensington and Co. Law Offices," but no one who worked in the area could ever recall seeing a client walk through its doors.

Kepler glanced at the shuttered windows, each adorned with neatly trimmed flower boxes. They were just a little too perfect, as though they were tended by someone more interested in appearances than flowers.

Slowing to a stop at the side alley next to the building, Kepler reached into the glovebox and pulled out a small, nondescript black beeper. He pressed the button and waited. A moment later, a faint mechanical whir broke through the quiet, and a section of the alley's brick wall slid aside, revealing the entrance to an underground car park. A red light above the entrance flickered, scanning the area, and a security camera swiveled toward the Saab.

Kepler leaned back in his seat, letting the system confirm the car's plates and his presence.

The light turned green, and the heavy steel door groaned open, the dimly lit ramp spiraling downward like the throat of some secretive beast. Kepler released a breath he hadn't realized he was holding and shifted into gear. As he guided his vehicle inside, the door rumbled shut behind him, sealing him off from the outside world. The faint scent of oil and concrete filled the air, and the hum of distant servers vibrated faintly through the walls, a quiet reminder of the high-tech world concealed beneath Georgetown's historic veneer.

The building was owned by the CIA.

It was intentionally separated from the rest of the CIA at Langley, Virginia to serve as a cut-out between the Agency's spies and the people responsible for building their fictional lives, including an online social media presence, education and work histories, along with families. These days, Ghosts triggered more alarm bells when their online presence was non-existent.

Which was why the Kensington and Co. Law Offices existed. Internally, they were referred to as Paper Magicians. And Dylan Frost was the head of the department.

They were independent of the Office of Technical Services at Langley who specialized in fake passports, identification documents, and other forged materials. They were capable of producing all of these too, but they mainly specialized in background histories and online histories.

Dr. Alan Kepler stepped up the two flights of stairs into the main building. He was greeted by Dylan Frost who brought him into his secure office.

"How is it going?" Dylan asked.

Dr. Kepler said, "The CIA's best meteorology reports indicate Siberia's currently being lashed by the worst blizzard in years."

"Finally, some good luck."

"Indeed."

Dylan exhaled. "What can I do for you, Alan?"

Dr. Kepler said, "Before the mission, you issued Paxton and his team with Russian passports?"

"Uh-huh, yeah of course."

"Good. I need you to set an international Interpol Red Notice on Paxton's Russian passport, so it alarms as soon as he scans it." Dr. Kepler drew a breath. "Better he should rot in a Siberian prison than ever make it back here with our secrets."

Dylan swallowed hard. "I thought you said we got lucky and there's a Siberian blizzard hammering the peninsula?"

"Sure, but I don't believe in taking chances." Dr. Kepler met his gaze. "Trust me, Paxton is a survivor. And if he lives, he will take any loose rope we give him. You know what he'll do then?"

"What?"

Dr. Kepler said, "He'll use it to hang us all."

Chapter Forty

P axton woke to the sound of silence.

It was so stark, so sudden!

After the relentless howl of the storm, the silence jolted him awake as though it was a screaming noise instead of its absence. For a moment, he lay still beneath the cocoon of spruce boughs, faint light filtering through the branches. The world felt eerily still, as if Siberia itself were holding its breath.

He moved cautiously, brushing snow off and pulling his jacket tighter. The boughs above him were stiff with frost, their needles brittle to the touch. He dug his way out of the hollow he'd created, pushing aside layers of snow and branches until he emerged into the open air. The storm had passed, leaving behind an unbroken expanse of white. The air was clear, the sky a brilliant, bright blue. It was the kind of clarity that only comes in the wake of violent weather. The sun hung low, casting pale shadows across the frozen landscape.

The calm felt deceptive, as though the weather was lulling him into a false sense of security. But there was no time to linger. Paxton brushed himself off, his movements stiff and deliberate. His limbs ached from the cold, and his damp boots felt like iron weights, but he set his jaw and started walking.

The journey from the Yamal Peninsula to Salekhard Airport was a grueling 120 miles of freezing terrain. He had left his GPS built into his satphone on the Zodiac to prevent Peregrine from using it to track him. So for three days, Paxton trudged across the frozen tundra, navigating by the sun during the day and the stars at night. The snow-covered ground stretched endlessly before him, broken only by the occasional copse of skeletal trees or a ridge of wind-swept ice.

The first day was the hardest.

His muscles burned with every step, and his stomach twisted with hunger. He rationed the few MRE food packs he had taken from the Zodiac, nibbling sparingly and drinking melted snow to keep hydrated. The cold was an unrelenting companion, gnawing at his fingers and toes despite his layers of clothing. His boots, still damp from the storm, were a constant source of discomfort, and he knew frostbite was a real danger.

By the second day, his body had settled into a grim rhythm.

Each step felt mechanical, his mind focused only on putting one foot in front of the other. He passed the occasional frozen stream and paused briefly to gather his strength, but he never lingered for long. The cold was a killer, and stopping too long would only invite him in.

On the third day, he began to see signs of civilization. A wooden marker jutted out of the snow. The faint tracks of a snowmobile were partially buried. And finally, in the distance, a thin wisp of smoke rose into the sky. His heart lifted slightly, though his pace remained measured. Hope was dangerous, and he wouldn't let it slow his focus.

By the time he reached the outskirts of Salekhard, his body was on the edge of collapse. The sight of the airport's control tower rising against the horizon spurred him forward, though his legs felt like lead. He entered the airport grounds under the cover of darkness, slipping past snow-covered hangars and onto the fringes of the terminal.

For a moment, he stood still, his breath coming in shallow gasps as he stared at the glow of lights and the faint sound of planes. He'd made it, but he knew the hardest part was still ahead. With grim determination, Paxton adjusted his scarf, pulled his hood tighter, and stepped toward the terminal, blending into the shadows like the ghost he was.

Chapter Forty-One

Salekhard Airport – Siberia

Paxton crouched in the snow and studied the airport from a distance.

It was small, just a handful of squat, utilitarian buildings surrounded by a single runway that stretched into the frozen expanse. The lights from the terminal cast an orange glow against the twilight sky, and he could see a scattering of aircraft parked on the tarmac: a regional turboprop, its dull fuselage marked with a faded Russian airline logo; a smaller private jet; and a pair of rugged cargo planes, their hulking frames built to endure Siberian winters.

Paxton exhaled a long plume of frost, his breath crystallizing in the air. The sight of the planes stirred a pang of longing. He preferred to board something heading west, closer to Europe and his bolt hole.

But it was too risky.

A direct flight might leave a trail that Peregrine – or worse, Peregrine's allies in the FSB – could follow. Yakutsk was far enough east to throw them off, and from there, he could vanish into the Siberian railway network.

He left the Heckler and Koch MP5 submachine gun unloaded and buried in the snow. He hoped some kids didn't find it when the snow melted. He kept the Glock concealed in a takeout bag he'd found in a nearby waste bin. He would discard it in the airport, giving him the chance to use it if things went bad with his passport.

That made him remember his passport.

He pulled his Russian passport from an inside pocket. Paxton flipped it open, his jaw tightening as he scanned the fake name and photo. The Paper Magician who had crafted it had done impeccable work, but it wouldn't matter if the document had been flagged. He tucked it into his jacket along with a thin wad of Russian cash, adjusted his scarf, and started toward the terminal.

Inside, the airport was as spartan as he'd expected.

He made a careful reconnaissance of the terminal, still carrying the takeout bag with the Glock inside. If everything worked out okay, he would dump the Glock, cross the security checkpoint, and board the flight.

If it didn't, well...

The Glock might buy him one more chance at survival.

The tiled floors were scuffed, the fluorescent lights flickered faintly, and the air carried the faint scent of diesel and cigarettes. A handful of travelers sat on plastic chairs, bundled in heavy coats, their faces drawn and tired. The ticket counter was manned by a lone agent who barely glanced at Paxton as he handed over cash and requested a flight to Yakutsk. The transaction was rapid, and with his boarding pass in hand, Paxton moved toward security.

The checkpoint was a simple affair: a single metal detector, an old X-ray machine, and one security officer stationed at a desk. Paxton joined the short line and waited his turn, his pulse steady but his senses sharp. When he reached the counter, he handed over his passport, the laminated pages crackling faintly as the officer scanned it into the system.

For a moment, nothing happened.

Then, a red light blinked on the desk console, silent but unmistakable.

Paxton swore under his breath. Peregrine. It had to be him. The bastard must have had his Paper Magician tag the passport with an Interpol Red Notice.

The security woman looked at the flashing light, her face tightening with suspicion. "Podozhdite zdes', pozhaluysta," she said, her tone calm but firm. *"Wait here, please."* She reached for her radio and murmured a few quick words, her hand hovering over the console as if she were ready to escalate things further.

Paxton didn't wait to see what she'd do next.

His survival instinct kicked in, and he moved before she could call for backup. He shoved the desk hard, knocking it sideways, and bolted toward the nearest exit. Cries of alarm erupted behind him as startled travelers scrambled out of his path. A man in a fur hat staggered backward, his suitcase spilling open, but Paxton didn't stop.

He sprinted through the terminal, his boots pounding against the tiled floor, his breath coming in sharp bursts. Behind him, he heard shouts and the thudding of heavy footsteps. Airport security was on his heels, but he didn't look back.

Glass doors loomed ahead, the icy night beyond promising a temporary escape.

Paxton hit the doors at full speed, shouldering them open, bursting out into the freezing air. The wind bit at his face as he veered toward the side of the building, heading for the shadows where the bright lights of the terminal couldn't reach. He needed a plan, and he needed it fast. For now, all that mattered was getting out of sight before the hunt closed in.

Paxton's breath burned in his chest as he neared the entrance of the airport, his boots slipping on patches of ice hidden beneath the snow. His eyes locked on a lone figure pulling up on a snowmobile just outside the gates.

The machine, a rugged Buran 4T – a classic Russian workhorse – idled loudly, its exhaust puffing into the frigid air. The driver, bundled in thick winter gear, dismounted to help a bundled passenger climb off.

The timing was perfect.

Almost too perfect.

Paxton didn't stop to think. He surged forward, closing the distance before the driver even had a chance to register the sound of his boots crunching through the snow.

With a single fluid motion, Paxton barreled into the man, knocking him backward into the snowbank. The driver shouted in surprise, his arms flailing as he hit the ground. The passenger turned, startled, but froze as Paxton swung a leg over the snowmobile. The machine rumbled beneath him; its handlebars cold against his gloved hands.

The driver scrambled to his knees, yelling in Russian, but Paxton jammed his thumb on the throttle, sending the Buran 4T lurching forward with a spray of ice and snow. The machine roared as it shot toward the edge of the airport, its rugged frame handling the uneven terrain with ease.

Behind him, the passenger was yelling, and the driver had staggered to his feet, waving his arms in a futile attempt to flag him down. Paxton didn't look back. The airport lights shrank in the distance, swallowed by the shadows of the Siberian wilderness.

He guided the snowmobile onto a narrow path leading into the forest, the machine's track digging into the snow as it clawed forward. The icy wind whipped at his face, and branches clawed at him as he maneuvered through the dense trees.

The Buran's engine roared against the silence, a beacon of sound in the otherwise still night, but Paxton didn't slow.

Behind him, he heard a pair of police officers yell, "Stop or we'll shoot!"

Paxton weaved the snowmobile through the trees and kept going. Multiple shots from pistols echoed in the distance. Each one missed him completely. They would have been difficult shots to make for an expert marksman, and he doubted very much that the airport police were experts.

A moment later, the sound of gunfire ceased, and he rode on into the darkness of the night. He leaned forward, urging the snowmobile to go faster. Siberia stretched endlessly before him, and he needed to disappear before the wolves closed in.

Chapter Forty-Two

Pine trees whipped by his snowmobile.

The Buran roared beneath Paxton, its engine a deafening growl that echoed across the icy tundra. He raced southward toward the Ob River, the frozen expanse ahead glinting in the moonlight like polished steel. His breath came in short, sharp bursts, frost forming on his scarf as he leaned into the handlebars, urging the snowmobile faster.

Behind him, the faint whine of engines broke through the night. He glanced over his shoulder and saw two riders closing in, their headlights cutting paths through the darkness. Their snowmobiles were sleeker, newer – machines designed for speed rather than utility. Whoever they were, they weren't amateurs.

FSB agents? Local mercenaries? It didn't matter.

The first shots rang out, sharp cracks against the night.

Paxton felt the whiz of bullets slicing the air around him, and he swerved hard, the Buran fishtailing as he narrowly avoided a snowbank. The riders gained ground, their machines closing the gap with unsettling accuracy.

Ahead, the Ob River came into view, a vast, frozen artery stretching into the horizon. Paxton gritted his teeth and pushed the Buran harder. The ice looked thick, but he knew better than to trust appearances.

A crack, a weak patch, and it'd all be over.

He had no choice.

The snowmobile hit the river with a jarring thud, the track spitting ice shards as it gripped the slick surface. Paxton veered sharply, zigzagging across the ice to make himself a harder target. The riders followed, their headlights bobbing wildly as they took the chase onto the treacherous river.

Another burst of gunfire rang out, and this time, a bullet punched through the snow-mobile's windshield, shattering it in a spray of glass. Paxton ducked low; his knuckles white under his gloves.

His mind raced. He needed to lose them before they got lucky.

He angled the Buran toward a cluster of ice ridges, using the natural formations as cover. The snowmobile bucked beneath him as he weaved through the obstacles, his pursuers struggling to maintain their line.

The sound of their engines grew louder, closer, until—

A loud crack split the air. One of the chasing snowmobiles wobbled violently. The rider had hit a weak patch of ice. Paxton didn't wait to see if they recovered; he used the distraction to veer sharply, angling toward the riverbank. He glanced back to see only one headlight still on his trail, the second rider left behind, stranded or worse.

The remaining pursuer was unrelenting, but Paxton had the advantage now.

The bank loomed ahead, and he gunned the Buran up the incline, the snowmobile's treads clawing at the frozen ground. Once off the river, he plunged into the woods, the dense trees swallowing him whole.

Gliding to a stop, he cut the engine and waited.

Breath shallow, ears straining for the sound of pursuit. The forest was silent, save for the occasional groan of branches under the weight of snow. Yet it seemed his gambit had worked. The lone rider had lost him in the maze of trees.

Paxton restarted the Buran, keeping the throttle low as he made his way southward. A few seconds after he'd restarted the snowmobile, another headlight shone on him from behind.

He cursed under his breath. He wasn't the only one to try turning his lights off to hide.

A crack of gunfire cut through the silence.

Paxton hit the throttle again and raced off deeper into the forest. He was a better rider than his pursuer, but the trailing rider was on a much faster snowmobile. Paxton found himself having to cut corners and take greater and greater risks to stay ahead.

The engine whined as his vehicle sailed over a small log.

And landed hard.

Paxton's snowmobile jolted violently as it hit a hidden patch of ice beneath the snow, the handlebars jerking out of his grip. He fought to steady the machine, but the uneven terrain was unforgiving. The Buran lurched sideways, and before he could regain control, it slammed into a snowbank with a deafening crunch. The force threw him forward, and he tumbled through the snow, landing hard on his side. Pain shot through his shoulder, but he pushed himself up, ignoring the sting.

Behind him, the growl of an engine grew louder.

His pursuer was closing in. Paxton scrambled to his feet, his eyes darting frantically for a weapon. A gnarled, broken branch jutted out from a nearby tree, thick and heavy. He grabbed it, testing its weight in his hands, then turned to face the oncoming rider.

The attacker bore down on him, the snowmobile's engine roaring as it carved a path through the snow. Paxton waited, his breath fogging in the cold air, every muscle coiled. At the last possible moment, he swung the branch with all his strength, aiming for the rider's head. The wood connected with a sickening crack, and the pursuer toppled sideways. His body hit the ground hard as the man's snowmobile skidded to a stop.

Paxton didn't waste a second.

He dropped the branch and sprinted to the fallen snowmobile, his boots slipping on the icy surface. The rider groaned, trying to push himself up, but Paxton shoved him back down with a swift kick to the chest.

He swung onto the new machine, the engine rumbling beneath him, and jammed the throttle. The snowmobile roared to life, spraying snow as it shot forward. Glancing over his shoulder, Paxton saw the attacker still sprawled in the snow, clutching his side.

He turned his focus back to the forest ahead, the icy wind whipping against his face. The stolen snowmobile was faster, more agile, and for now, it was his ticket to survival. With a grim set to his jaw, Paxton disappeared into the frozen wilderness, leaving his pursuer behind in the Siberian cold.

Thirty minutes later, the lights of Labytnangi appeared on the horizon. He abandoned the snowmobile at the edge of town, brushing snow off his jacket as he approached the train station.

Inside, the warmth was almost overwhelming. He purchased a ticket with cash, careful to avoid the gaze of the sleepy clerk, and slipped onto a waiting train. The hiss of steam and the rumble of wheels against tracks were a welcome reprieve from the roar of snowmobiles and the crack of gunfire.

As the train pulled away, Paxton leaned back in his seat, letting the vibration of the car lull his frayed nerves. The Ob River and its icy battlefield receded into the distance, and with it, his pursuers. For now, at least, he was gone. Into the Siberian night, he vanished, a phantom once more.

Paxton cozied up to the side of the carriage. Then to the gentle rocking of the train's car, he dropped into a deep sleep.

Chapter Forty-Three

I t was morning by the time the train pulled into Yekaterinburg.

The city felt like a different world. Snow still blanketed the streets, but the buzz of life was palpable. Cars were honking, and pedestrians were bustling between shops. There was a dull hum of machinery in the distance. Paxton stepped off the train and merged into the flow of people, his eyes scanning for an opportunity to move further south.

At a loading dock near the edge of the city, he spotted a trucker leaning against his cab, lighting a cigarette. The man had the look of someone who didn't ask too many questions. Paxton approached with cautious confidence. A few rubles and a shared swig of vodka later, Paxton found himself in the passenger seat of a rumbling cargo truck heading toward Samara.

The driver barely spoke, grunting occasionally as he navigated glacial roads that wound through villages and open plains. Paxton didn't mind the silence. It gave him time to plan his next steps. The truck rumbled into Samara two days later, dropping him near the city's train station. From there, he bought a cheap ticket with cash to Astrakhan, the city at the northern edge of the Caspian Sea.

The train to Astrakhan was crowded, its passengers a mix of workers, traders, and weary travelers. Paxton kept to himself, feigning sleep as the conversations around him ebbed and flowed. He didn't dare let his guard down, though. The further south he traveled, the more likely it was that someone might question his presence.

Astrakhan, with a population of 500,000, was a city in southern Russia. The industrial metropolis greeted him with the smell of salt and oil in the air. The docks were a chaotic sprawl of activity—fishermen unloading their catches, workers shouting orders, and the distant horns of ships coming and going. Paxton wandered among the warehouses, his eyes scanning for something specific: a boat heading out to the Caspian. It didn't take long before he overheard a crew speaking Azeri – a form of Turkish spoken by Azerbaijani Turks.

His ear recognized it immediately.

It was spoken extensively at Neft Daşları, where he'd worked as a laborer on the oil rigs in 2012. Within seconds of hearing it, he was able to make sense of what they were saying. They were arguing over a delay in their departure. Their small fishing boat, weathered and worn, was loaded with crates of supplies.

Paxton approached the captain, a burly man with a lined face and quick, sharp eyes. Speaking in Azeri, he told him he was heading back to Neft Daşları for work, and offered cash and a promise to help unload the supplies at their destination. The captain stared at him for a long moment before jerking his head toward the boat.

He hadn't said a word.

Paxton climbed aboard without hesitation.

The fishing boat creaked and groaned as it cut through the dark waters of the Caspian Sea. The journey was long and monotonous, punctuated only by the occasional barked orders from the captain and the rhythmic slap of waves against the hull.

As the days passed, the sea shifted from hostile to eerily calm, the stillness broken only by the distant call of seabirds. On the final day, a strange sight emerged from the misty expanse – a sprawling complex of platforms and machinery rising improbably from the water...

Neft Daşları.

The offshore oil city looked like something out of a dystopian dream, or an oversized version of Waterworld, that 1990s film with Kevin Costner. The city was formed by a labyrinthine network of pipes, cranes, and barracks stretching endlessly over the waves. Roads of steel connected the platforms, their edges disappearing into the hazy distance.

The fishing boat pulled alongside one of the supply docks, where workers in grease-stained overalls waited to unload the cargo. Paxton grabbed a crate and followed the crew ashore, blending into the chaos of the docks. The salty air stung his face, but the strange hum of Neft Daşları's machinery masked his presence.

As promised, he helped unload the crates, then thanked the captain, and wandered the floating streets of Neft Daşları for the first time since 2012...

Chapter Forty-Four

Neft Daşları had been built decades ago. It seemed less like a human settlement and more like the skeleton of an ancient industrial beast, its pipes and girders twisting into the distance. Roads of rust-streaked steel connected the platforms, forming an endless maze. The air smelled of salt, but mostly of oil and metal. It was a heavy mixture that clung to everything.

Cranes creaked as they swung overhead, and the distant rumble of machinery echoed across the expanse, a constant reminder that this place was alive, even if it looked forgotten by time.

Paxton walked along one of the narrow decks, his boots clanking against the metal grates. Below him, the waves slapped against the pontoons, the dark water shimmering faintly in the light of the setting sun. Workers moved in small groups, dressed in heavy coveralls and oil-slicked boots, their voices muffled by the wind.

No one paid him any attention. In a place like this, anonymity was easy to come by.

He turned down a narrower walkway, leaving behind the main platforms and heading toward the edges of the city. The decks here were quieter, less traveled, and the rusted railings sagged under their own weight. He passed a cluster of squat buildings that looked like long-abandoned storage units before spotting his destination in the distance.

The apartment he sought, stood apart from the rest of the settlement, a small building perched on a massive floating pontoon. It seemed to defy logic, its three stories listing slightly to one side as though the sea itself was trying to reclaim it. The exterior was peeling and weather-beaten, the faded remnants of white paint clinging to warped wooden panels. One window on the second floor was boarded up, and another hung crookedly in its frame. A narrow set of stairs led up to the front door, where a single light bulb dangled, flickering faintly.

Paxton climbed the stairs cautiously, the wood creaking under his weight. When he reached the door, he hesitated for a moment, studying the scratched surface. This place felt like a relic of another life, a life he had tried to leave behind.

Taking a deep breath, he knocked firmly, his hand lingering on the door for a moment before stepping back. The door creaked open, and his breath caught.

She stood before him, framed in the dim light of the house.

His eyes narrowed. How old was she now? Mid-forties, he guessed. Time had done nothing to dull her striking good looks. Her almond-shaped eyes were a deep, captivating brown, framed by long, dark lashes that seemed to hold secrets. High cheekbones gave her face a regal symmetry, and her skin, a rich, sun-kissed tone, had only the faintest lines hinting at the passing years. Her jet-black hair was swept back into a loose braid that draped over one shoulder, a few strands escaping to soften the sharp edges of her jawline.

She wore a simple silk blouse, the fabric catching the light, and a long skirt that swayed slightly in the breeze from the open door. The simplicity of her attire only enhanced her natural elegance, her presence as arresting as the rugged beauty of her homeland.

For a moment, neither of them spoke.

Her eyes locked on his, and a slow smile spread across her lips. A smile that carried a thousand memories, unspoken yet deeply felt.

"Paxton," she whispered, her voice low and rich, carrying the faintest lilt of her Azerbaijani accent.

He pressed his lips together, a warm smile on his lips. "Hello, Leyla..."

The door swung wider, and she closed the gap between them in an instant. Her expression shifted from surprise to recognition, and without a word, she stepped forward and threw her arms around him.

She kissed him.

He kissed her back, eagerly.

Time stood still and all those years washed away. When she pulled back from him, there was a small smile tugging at the corners of her mouth. Speaking in Azeri, she said, "You have a lot of nerve coming back here after all these years, Paxton."

Chapter Forty-Five

Paxton didn't understand most people.

It had something to do with missing an important part of his brain that regulated emotions, morals, and ethics. It had taken years of effort on his part to learn what he was supposed to do in certain circumstances. After forty years of faking it, what was expected of him now generally came, more or less naturally.

He just didn't have the same sort of gut instincts as most people have.

Then, there were women who came and went from his life. Making sense of them, and what they wanted, rose that level of complexity of human existence to another level.

Of all the women who had come into his life, Leyla had been the most difficult to understand. She ran the only bar on Neft Daşları. It had been her father's, specializing in vodka. By default, she'd inherited it after he died. At the time, she'd even thought of selling it and moving on, but simply didn't know where to go.

It was at that time when Paxton had turned up.

He'd only meant to start talking to her because he needed to learn to speak Azeri at a colloquial level, and although he was a fast learner, he needed someone local to converse with. Their relationship started simply.

He was interested in her and asked a lot of questions.

She hadn't had many lovers since she'd lived at the apartment above the bar with her father, since her mother had died when she was a child. And she had even less experience in men who were more interested in talking with her than doing anything physical.

He made sure to see her every day.

At first, he was using her for her language. This was because he had a mission that would need him to be capable of speaking fluent Azeri. But somewhere, even he wasn't sure where, he'd found himself falling for her. Hard.

She was a strikingly beautiful woman.

But it wasn't that.

The world is full of beautiful women, but there was something magical about Leyla. An imp of mischief and an ability to live life with abandon, finding joy and fun, in so many things.

Love was an emotion most "normal" people struggled with. For him, literally missing the part of the brain that regulates emotions, he was at a total loss to make sense of it. They moved in together to the three-story apartment. It floated on a massive pontoon, converted into a house, which he'd bought using cash.

It was the same place where she still lived today. He'd heard stories of a sort of honeymoon period in an early romantic relationship, where one can't keep their hands off each other. An experience that wanes over time.

But for them, it had never changed. They would make love at night and then again in the mornings before they went to work.

It was a good year.

Having spoken to Cole about it in the years since, and having done some reflection, he felt like being with her had been what happiness felt like.

He didn't know it back then.

At the time, it was just an experience. But looking back, after all these years, he could see it was as close as he would probably ever get to come to truly experiencing that elusive human emotion called happiness.

Somewhere, toward the end of the year, they were chatting about traveling. Foolishly, he had spoken about the various countries he'd visited.

He should have lied.

He didn't know why, but he couldn't lie to her. Perhaps it was because of love. She simply disarmed every professional barrier he'd spent years cultivating.

Leyla, as smart as they come, looked at him after the list of travel locations, laughed, and then said, "What are you, a CIA spy?"

She was so close, Paxton didn't know what to say. So he spoke the truth. "No, not a spy. I'm a Ghost. I perform government sanctions – murders – that the US government can't acknowledge."

"Let me guess. You're here to tamper with the election?" Leyla laughed. "There's an uppity, educated candidate who wants to reduce our reliance with Russia and promote a genuine democracy. The other one is a General who rose to strength through military power, and claims a direct family connection to the Kremlin..."

She stopped laughing...and gasped.

Her brown eyes met his. "You're going to assassinate the General."

Paxton didn't say anything.

He didn't have to.

She read the truth on his face with absolute clarity, in the way a wife knows when her husband has been unfaithful.

Her world spinning, Leyla stood up. "That's why you're here. That's why you've spent all this time cultivating the Azeri languages, speaking it like a local."

"Leyla," Paxton had tried to explain.

"When were you going to do this? Were you going to tell me you were leaving? Or just walk out the door?" Her face distorted in horror. "The elections are next week!"

Paxton said, "Please wait."

A moment later, she was gone.

He thought he would never see her again.

Then, in the middle of the night, she had come home and made love with him, clinging to him vigorously as though her entire world needed it. She needed to know that the last twelve months of their lives hadn't been an entire lie.

In the morning, she cried her eyes out and asked him when he was going to leave. He told her he had to leave the next day. Then showed her that he had transferred the house into her name – leaving her the official owner, and that he wished her all the happiness in the world.

She took the news stoically and told him to go and never come back.

He took her at her word.

The next day, Paxton left to assassinate a General and sway an election. He succeeded in his goal, but the General's brother rose from his ashes like a phoenix, and won the election based on the popularity of his rising movement. The brother was far worse than the original candidate. He claimed his opponent was a criminal and executed him for political crimes. Azerbaijan swung even further into an authoritarian regime.

In doing so, Paxton had succeeded in his goal as a Ghost but failed in his mission.

Fate is what it is, and sometimes, there are unintended consequences. If he had emotions, he might have felt uneasy about the outcome. As it was, he moved back stateside and took on his next assignment.

And he never saw Leyla again... until now.

Chapter Forty-Six

Paxton stared at Leyla. His gut told him something strange and powerful was happening, but he couldn't make sense of any of it. So, as with most emotions, he simply ignored it.

He said, "I thought you would have moved on by now."

Leyla met his gaze. Her expression unreadable. Then she grinned. "And I thought you might have come back well before now."

Paxton smiled. He'd learned long ago to use that boyish smile when it was expected of him to soften the blow of a painful memory.

He frowned. "I never said I was coming back for you."

She smiled. It was a nice smile, but there was something somber behind it somehow. Perhaps a little bit of regret too. "You also never said you wouldn't."

"May I come in?" he asked.

She spread an open arm in a gesture indicating he was welcome. "Of course. It's your house."

"No, it isn't." Paxton missed the humor in her words, and then reiterated, "I transferred it to before I left."

"Paxton, get inside and tell me what you want."

"Yes, ma'am."

"Oh, so I'm a ma'am to you now?" she asked, the venom of a woman betrayed in her voice.

"I'm not sure what you are." Paxton met her gaze, smiled his best smile again, and squeezed both her hands. "But it is really good to see a friendly face."

She nodded. "It's really good to see you too." Pouring herself a drink, she asked, "Can I get you something?"

"No, thank you." Paxton glanced up at the large stairwell that climbed three flights to the top of the building. His eyes landed on the heavy door at the very top. "Do you know if my stuff is still in the room?"

"I thought about throwing it out long ago."

"Did you?"

With an impish grin, she shook her head. "No. It was important to you. Some sort of last ditch, backup plan, in case of some disaster. A personal bolt hole and get out of hell place. I've left everything in that room, exactly as you left it."

"Thank you."

She stared at him, taking him in for the first time. "Oh, Paxton... what the hell have you gotten yourself into now?"

"It's a long story. I might fill you in tomorrow morning, if that's all right?"

"Okay," she said, kind of noticing how exhausted he was for the first time. "You've traveled a long way to get here, haven't you?"

"Yes. It was the only place I could think of to turn to."

"That bad, hey?"

"Worse."

Her eyes narrowed as she knew what he was. The sort of work that he did, and the consequences of such a life. "How much trouble are you in?"

"They killed my entire team... and nearly got me too."

Her face shone with shock. "All of them?"

"Yes." Paxton said, "They were my family in every sense of the word."

Stunned, at first, she said nothing. Leyla always seemed to get him, in a way nobody else had ever truly understood him, let alone how much he knew himself. She seemed to get and accept the way he was built.

Finally, she asked, "How are you feeling?"

"I'm okay."

"Really?"

"Yes, they were all Ghosts anyway." It was easy talking to her like this. Always had been for some reason. Paxton knew he was supposed to be angry and sad, and overwhelmed by a multitude of emotions. But those parts in his brain simply didn't work. Leyla seemed to recognize this, so he didn't have to hide or pretend. He could just be honest. Be himself.

Did he wish his team to die?

No.

Could he help it?

No.

Leyla moved to the next logical question. "Do you know who was behind it?"

"Somebody from the CIA. I'm not sure who, but I intend to find out."

"What will you do?"

"What I'm trained to do." Paxton shrugged. "I'll discover who was responsible... and then I will kill them."

There was no emotion, not even a little bit of anger in his voice.

A simple, logical, response.

Leyla seemed to understand that he was finished. He had said all he intended to say. She pre-empted him, by saying, "I'm going to bed. Do you want to join me?"

He politely declined. "I'm happy to sleep on the couch."

"Don't be ridiculous." She smiled, knowing she had to be the initiator. "I could use the company."

He pictured her warm, loving body, and the thought of cuddling up to her for the night stirred something in him. "Are you sure?"

Leyla took his hand, kissed it, and said, "Yes, but first you really need a shower."

Chapter Forty-Seven

Number One Observatory Circle, Washington, D.C.

Agent Adrian Shaw was new to the VP's protective detail. His job was a security upgrade, after the nuclear explosion in Siberia had upped the ante in terms of risk to senior White House staff.

Shaw was hardworking, dedicated, and driven. Standing just over six feet tall, he had a lean, athletic build that suggested both discipline and agility. His sharp features – a strong jawline, determined hazel eyes, and close-cropped dark hair – gave him an air of quiet authority, while the faint scar above his right eyebrow hinted at a life spent in dangerous situations. He wore his tailored suit like armor, every button fastened, every crease perfect, a hint toward his meticulous nature.

Adrian's journey to the Vice President's security detail had been hard-earned. He had spent eight years as a Marine Corps officer, specializing in reconnaissance and counter-intelligence, followed by five years as a Special Agent with the Secret Service, where he distinguished himself during high-risk international assignments. Despite his outward calm, Adrian carried the quiet intensity of someone who had seen more than he would ever admit, and his reputation for quick thinking and unflinching loyalty made him a natural choice for the Vice President's inner circle.

Today, he was shadowing Alex King, a fifty-year-old Secret Service Agent who had been with the VP since the beginning. Back then, he had been assigned Hawthorne when he was still a Senator and Speaker of the House.

It was part of his induction.

This weekend nothing was booked on the VP's schedule. Consequently, Adrian was taking the time to learn more about the VP's habits, getting a firsthand walkthrough and mental map of the VP's residential address at One Observatory Circle, and overall way of doing things.

The day had passed uneventfully.

In other words, a good day in the world of a Protective Agent.

Most of the work the Secret Service performed was mundane. It was all about preparation, training, and getting ready for events that rarely eventuated.

In the distance, coming from the VP's private study, he heard a scream. But how? The walls had extensive sound dampening to prevent listening devices from eavesdropping on the VP's private conversations and deals.

Agent Adrian Shaw froze mid-step, his trained senses immediately honing in on the sound. It was faint, barely audible through the thick, wood-paneled walls of the Vice President's study. The sound was distorted, stripped of its sharp edges, but its urgency clawed its way through the otherwise quiet corridor.

In less than a second, he decided it was more a muffled wail than a clear scream.

Adrian's instincts, finely tuned by years of vigilance, latched onto the anomaly. His mind raced to decipher it: was it a cry for help? A burst of laughter that had lost its clarity? Or perhaps the echo of an old house settling in an unusual way?

He strained to pick apart the layers of sound dampening, leaning slightly toward the study door, his pulse quickening as he filtered through possibilities.

One and a half seconds after it began, the faint noise ceased, leaving behind an eerie silence. Adrian's hand hovered near his earpiece, ready to alert the team, but his gut told him to hold back for just a moment longer. He placed a hand on the study's doorframe, his jaw tightening as he listened harder, trying to make sense of the residual stillness and the barely-there vibrations that lingered in the air.

Something wasn't right.

Then it came again – sharper this time, though still muffled, like a desperate cry fighting to break free from a heavy veil. The sound carried a frantic, high-pitched edge, raw with terror, and it was unmistakable now: someone was in distress. Adrian's pulse surged as the scream climbed in intensity, the desperation in it clawing through the walls and igniting his instincts.

Adrian reached for his gun.

Alex King stopped him. "It's all right. This happens sometimes."

"What happens?" Adrian asked, still walking fast toward the VP's study, his hand still on his Glock.

"Agent Shaw! Stand down!" King said, his voice crisp and full of authority.

That triggered Adrian's training, and he stopped, turned to King, and asked, "If that scream isn't a threat, what is it?"

Agent King drew a breath. His sharp blue eyes watching Shaw with the weight of someone who had seen too much. His posture was relaxed, but there was a tension in his shoulders, the kind that came from years of carefully navigating the line between duty and disillusionment. He scratched at the stubble on his jaw, his voice low and measured, carrying the gravity of a mentor trying to prepare a rookie for the harsh realities of the job.

"Listen, we're not here to judge. Our job is just to protect them."

"What are you talking about?" Shaw asked.

Agent King sighed. "When the Second Lady is away the VP likes to play."

"Come again?"

"The Second Lady is riding horses on their farm in Connecticut for the weekend."

"So?"

"The VP likes to seek a certain type of entertainment."

A woman screamed out loud again. Agent Shaw cursed under his breath and took a step toward the door. The woman started to moan. There were more shrieks and cries of agony, blended in with intermittent sounds of pleasure.

Agent King said, "Listen, the VP likes to bring a certain class of women into Observatory One."

"And what, he likes to beat them?"

"Everyone has different methods of easing their stress…"

"There's laws in this country!" Agent Shaw was appalled. "I took an oath to protect the VP, but first I took an oath to serve the United States of America. In America beating a woman is illegal."

"It's just kinky sex," King assured him. "You know, BDSM with paddles, whips, and stuff. She's given signed consent so it's not illegal. The woman has been seeing him for years. From what I hear, she is compensated very well for the service. The VP pays for the rent on her apartment, health care, and exorbitant fees for her three kids' private school. Vanessa Ellis is more than happy with the arrangement."

"My God!" Agent Shaw couldn't hide the horror from his face. "This has been going on long enough that you know her name?"

"Of course," King said. "She's been heavily vetted by the Agency."

"Clearly." Taking a deep breath, Shaw regained some circumspection. He thought this through, looking at it more from his protective detail training perspective. "How does he keep Ms. Ellis secret?"

"There's a secret tunnel."

Agent Shaw made an incredulous, wry grin. "Really?"

"It was secretly commissioned by Admiral George W. Anderson Jr. – who served as the Chief of Naval Operations in 1961-63 during the Cuban Missile Crisis. He had it constructed under the guise of utility upgrades, but served as a means of escape if the worst should happen." Agent King paused, letting that sink in. "The mile-long passage was a masterpiece of clandestine engineering, blending seamlessly into the Naval Observatory's sprawling grounds. The exit leads to a walled garden. The entire place was filled in when Vice President Walter Mondale moved in during the seventies for security reasons."

"So how did Ms. Ellis come to use it?"

"The first thing all VPs tend to do when they move into Observatory One is commission their own works to the building. George H.W. Bush installed a basketball hoop for family recreation. Dan Quayle built a playground for his kids and undertook eco-friendly renovations, including energy-efficient lighting and recycling initiatives, reflecting Gore's commitment to environmental issues. Dick Cheney oversaw updates to the residence's security infrastructure post-9/11, and Vice President Daniel Hawthorne had that mile-long tunnel secretly excavated."

"How does it work?"

"Ms. Ellis drives her car – already on the approved list – into the outer grounds of the Naval Gardens. When she shows up, she parks at the garden entrance, the one near the old gazebo. Always at a specified time, never early, never late. Precision's part of the arrangement."

Shaw frowned slightly. "And then?"

King said, "She has her own pass for the outer tunnel door. Uses it to get in. From there, she walks the length of the tunnel."

"Couldn't anyone simply steal her pass?"

"No. It doesn't work that way. The pass needs to be used during a specified window, allotted by the VP on the day. That way, even if someone were to assault her and steal the security pass, it wouldn't work. What's more, the pass is designed to sound an alarm if it's used outside the preselected window on the day."

"Okay, then what happens?"

"There's a second major door just before it connects to the study. Reinforced, electronic, the works. She doesn't have access to that one."

"Only the VP does," Shaw guessed.

King nodded. "Exactly. There's a video feed in the study, hooked up to a discreet camera in the tunnel. Hawthorne checks it to confirm it's her and, more importantly, that she's alone. Once he's satisfied, he unlocks the inner tunnel door remotely from his study."

Shaw said, "There's no agents guarding the tunnel?"

"No, the VP expressly likes to keep some of his dealings secret."

"Even from his security detail?"

"Apparently."

"Seems risky."

"I think it's okay. Nothing's perfect. And VP Hawthorne uses it for more than just affairs. There are deals that need to be made. Every person who comes and goes from this building, or the White House, is documented. Some transactions can't be made in those arrangements, where all attendees are witnessed by the general public."

Shaw frowned. "I thought that was precisely why we have registers for the President and the VP."

Agent King was about to open his mouth to argue the way of the world, but another scream interrupted him.

This one seemed particularly brutal.

It was followed by a muffled moan of pleasure from the VP, and then silence.

King said, "Look, the VP's a good man. As I said, he just needs help to unwind sometimes..."

Agent Shaw frowned. "The VP's an asshole."

King grinned. "Yeah, I guess you're right on that account. But he's ours to protect and one of the most powerful men in the world right now. Just you watch him – his next stop will be in the Oval Office of the White House."

Shaw said, "He's making a bid for the White House?"

"Uh-huh. He'll announce next year."

"Will he get in?"

"Absolutely," King said, his voice emphatic.

"What makes you so sure?"

King shook his head knowingly. "If you only knew the powerful people who secretly come in through these doors."

Chapter Forty-Eight

Neft Daşları, Azerbaijan

It felt strange to be home.

It was the only house he'd actually owned his entire life, before he gave it away.

Paxton woke slowly, his senses stirring before his mind fully caught up. The steady thunk-thunk-thunk of an oil rig filled the room, a rhythmic beat that tugged at something deep in his memory. He blinked, taking in the faint outline of the bedroom, a place that felt familiar yet strange. The bed was firmer than he remembered, and the walls, though aged with cracks and faint water stains, had been repainted a lighter hue since his last time here. The dim morning light filtered through mismatched curtains, casting a soft glow over the scuffed wooden floor.

He placed a tentative hand on the other side of the bed to see if Leyla was still there. She wasn't. For a split second, he hoped she hadn't left him in the middle of the night.

Paxton closed his eyes and took a deep breath through his nostrils, letting the air fill his lungs. Scent, he recalled, was the strongest emotional sense, a direct line to memory like no other. Unlike sights or sounds, which passed through the brain's relay center, smells went straight to the limbic system – the seat of emotions and memory. That was why the faintest whiff of crude oil could pull him back to long nights on the rigs, or the aroma of tandir bread could summon the warmth of a family breakfast on a cold morning. It wasn't just memory, he realized, but the feelings entwined with it that made the experience so visceral, so inescapably real. The past wasn't just a thought: it was alive in the air around him, carried on the invisible threads of scent.

Well, that at least explained where Leyla had gone.

Paxton sat up, rubbing a hand over his face.

The sound of a distant rig and the clatter of pans from below grounded him in the moment, but there was a surreal quality to it all. The familiarity of the smells and sounds was a bridge between past and present, but something had shifted—subtle, intangible. This wasn't exactly the Neft Daşları he had known, but it was close enough to make his chest ache with a strange mix of nostalgia and unease.

Throwing his legs over the side of the bed, he let the mingling aromas and sounds wash over him. Downstairs, he could hear faint voices, muted and indistinct, the cadence of Azari words filtering up through the old floorboards. For a moment, he let himself sit there, caught in the liminal space between memory and reality, before finally pushing himself to his feet.

The air carried sharp scents so uniquely Neft Daşları that it was impossible to mistake it for anything else. The smell of the rigs, of the restless sea, of machinery working ceaselessly to draw wealth from the ocean's depths. But mingling with that industrial edge was something warmer and more inviting.

Mouthwatering aromas wafting up from the kitchen below.

Freshly baked tandir bread, and the smokiness of sizzling lamb sausage. The sweetness of black tea brewing in a samovar reached him. He imagined ripe tomatoes and freshly chopped herbs, breakfasts he'd grown up with. It was distinctly Azari, a taste of home that seemed out of place, yet oddly comforting.

The warmth inside the house was a welcome contrast to the biting cold outside. The old steam radiator hissed softly in the corner, fed by oil-powered pipes carrying hot water and steam throughout the building. The smell of breakfast drew Paxton downstairs, a smile tugging at his lips. The place felt lived-in, comfortable, and despite its simplicity, it felt like home.

When he reached the bottom of the stairs, he found Leyla standing by the stove, wearing blue flannel pajamas that looked as though they had faded over time. The fabric was soft and loose-fitting, reminding him of long, cozy winters. Her dark hair fell in waves over her shoulders, tousled from sleep, with strands catching the light and glinting like polished ebony.

Even in the simplicity of her attire, Leyla was beautiful. Her skin had a natural glow that didn't need enhancement. Her almond eyes, a deep and expressive brown, caught Paxton's. They sparkled with quiet amusement as she noticed him watching her.

A soft smile played at her lips, relaxed and genuine, as she turned back to the stove, her movements fluid and unhurried.

He went to her.

"Good morning, Paxton." She stood up on her tippy-toes to kiss his lips. "I made you breakfast. As I thought you might need your energy."

Chapter Forty-Nine

P axton sat down at the small wooden table opposite Leyla to eat. There was a veritable banquet in front of him, and he wondered why someone like Leyla would have kept so much food ready to go at a place like Neft Daşları.

The plate of food in front of him steamed with rich, familiar aromas.

It all felt very domestic.

A wedge of tandir bread, still warm from the oven, was piled high with soft scrambled eggs, tomatoes, and herbs. Next to it lay slices of lamb sausage, charred just enough to release their smoky, spiced flavor. Without hesitation, he grabbed the bread, scooping up the eggs and tomatoes in one fluid motion. The juices were soaking into the bread's crust as he bit down.

The first taste was enough to make him pause – a rush of flavors so vivid they felt like a memory brought to life. But nostalgia didn't slow him down. He worked through the meal with purpose, alternating bites of bread, eggs, and sausage, barely pausing to sip the strong black tea Leyla had poured. The tea was hot enough to sting his tongue, but he didn't care.

The lamb sausage was next, its smoky richness balanced by a hint of garlic and spices that lingered on his palate. Paxton cut the pieces smaller, almost as if to savor them, but they disappeared just as quickly. Within two minutes, the plate was empty, save for a few crumbs of bread. He leaned back in his chair, wiping his mouth with the back of his hand, and exhaled deeply, the warmth of the meal spreading through him.

He probably ate more calories in that one sitting than he had eaten in the previous week, as he made his journey from Siberia across the continent. And he had done it in under five minutes flat without saying a word.

Leyla raised an eyebrow from the stove, a knowing smile on her face. "Hungry?"

"Not anymore," Paxton said, with a big grin. "Thank you."

She suppressed a smile. "You haven't changed."

Paxton wasn't sure if that was meant to be a compliment or a complaint. So, he simply said, "Okay."

Leyla went about eating her breakfast, taking her time to enjoy it. "What are you going to do today?"

"I have to collect some things and start making plans." Paxton thought about that for a second. "Are you sure the stuff in my old room is still there?"

"You came back for whatever you have hidden in that room..." The realization dawned on her. "Not for me."

There was a subtle inference she was making, but Paxton wasn't built to make sense of subtleties, let alone have the time to deal with it either way.

"Yeah. Do you know if it's all still in there?"

She smiled, patiently, as though she had never expected him to take the hint. "Nobody's been in your room since you left. When you open the door, it looks like a bank vault, not that I've opened the door or been in there since you left. It's probably the only place in this building that's structurally sound."

He smiled stupidly and said, "That's good."

"It's not like you left me a key," she reminded him.

"Okay."

Paxton thanked her, got up, and made his way along the staircase, to the top level. The door to his true bolt hole was a constructional anomaly within the badly dilapidated building. Where the rest of the building was made of a mixed array of unmatching, recycled bricks, the top room was made from reinforced plate steel.

The thing looked like it could have withstood a direct hit from a bomb. It didn't belong in Neft Daşları.

Paxton studied the heavy door. A deep keyhole suggested that its locks weren't to be broken by amateur thieves with a lockpick. It was built into the solid, cast-iron, which made it near impossible for professional thieves to freeze the locks with liquid nitrogen and then break off.

He studied the mechanism. It looked intact. People could still have gotten in from the top, where little more than a glass skylight covered the entire ceiling.

But that was okay.

Anything of value inside couldn't be lifted up through the roof without knocking most of the building down. Given that the building was still standing, it meant what he needed was still there.

He left the door and took a few steps down the stairs.

Paxton stood beside the stairwell, his gaze fixed on the weathered brick wall. It was a patchwork of bricks – some red, others orange, yellow, or even faintly gray, each one telling its own story of reuse. His eyes narrowed as he scanned the surface, searching for a memory buried beneath the mortar.

Then he spotted them: two bricks, side by side, that were nearly identical in size and color. They stood out against the chaotic mosaic, the only pair that matched. A faint smile tugged at his lips.

The pointer bricks, he thought. Just like *Alpha Centauri* and *Beta Centauri* pointing to the constellation of the Southern Cross in the southern hemisphere.

His hand brushed the rough surface as he began counting.

One brick, then two, following the mental map he had left himself all those years ago. When he reached seventeen, he stopped, his finger resting on a brick slightly darker than its neighbors. For a moment, he observed, the past and present colliding in his mind. Then, he pulled a folding knife from his pocket and set to work.

The mortar was tough – tougher than he remembered – and his arms strained with the effort of chiseling it away. He'd done good work back then, sealing everything tightly, not knowing when or if it would ever be needed again. Sweat beaded on his brow as the blade scraped and chipped, the years of solid masonry resisting him at every turn. Finally, after what felt like all day, the brick loosened. With a grunt, Paxton wrenched it free, the piece of stone heavy in his hands.

He carried it downstairs to the basement, his boots echoing faintly on the wooden stairs.

Leyla, still finishing her breakfast, glanced at him carrying his brick. She gave a polite smile and said, "It's nice having you back, Paxton."

"Happy to be back," Paxton replied, giving her a brief kiss and grin, without offering any explanation for the brick.

He then made his way down to the basement, taking the steps three at a time.

Near the far wall, his old toolbox sat where he'd left it, the metal edges dented but still functional. From inside, he grabbed a hammer, its grip worn but familiar. Setting the brick on the concrete floor, he brought the hammer down with precision. The first strike sent a small crack spidering across the surface. The second blow deepened it. On the third, the brick split cleanly apart, fragments scattering across the floor.

Inside the broken shell lay his prize: a solid key, nestled snugly alongside a tiny battery and a computer chip. He picked it up, turning it over in his hands. The battery was long dead, its dull casing verifying the years that had passed. But the chip was intact, a marvel of engineering designed to provide more than just a physical key. The mechanism required a precise series of electrical impulses at an exact frequency to disable the magnetic locks it controlled.

A faint sense of satisfaction settled over Paxton. *It'll still work,* he thought, his fingers brushing the edges of the chip. *I just need a new battery.*

He exhaled, placing the key on the table in front of him. The weight of its significance pressed down on him, the object a reminder of the decisions he'd made all those years ago. Now, it was back in his hands, and he knew it was time to use it.

Next to the physical key was a flash drive.

It was surprisingly small, no bigger than a standard thumb drive, with a brushed metal casing that had dulled slightly over the years. The once-sleek finish was now speckled with faint scratches, likely from its long entombment within the brick. A faint engraving of a brand logo, partially obscured by time and grime, could just be made out on one side. The edges of the drive were slightly beveled, giving it an understated, utilitarian look.

What set it apart, though, was a tiny strip of translucent plastic along its spine – a status light that had long since gone dark without a power source. Paxton turned it over in his hand, his fingers brushing against a faint residue of mortar dust still clinging to the surface. The connection port was old, a USB 2.0 design that seemed antiquated now, but it had been cutting-edge at the time of its hiding.

He held the USB thumb drive up in his hand. It was hard to imagine that something so small contained the digital keys to an unimaginable wealth.

A digital vault, worth more than he could ever spend.

Bitcoins themselves were stored in a public blockchain, a decentralized ledger. Ownership of Bitcoins was controlled via cryptographic keys – specifically, a private key and a public key. The private key directed ownership of the Bitcoin, while the public key represented the location where the Bitcoin's blockchain ledger was stored. Each Bitcoin then had a public key that identified its location on the blockchain.

In Paxton's case, all of his public keys were stored under a Master Key known as a digital wallet.

To save the trouble of storing that code, Paxton had memorized his digital wallet's 64-character hexadecimal string.

His near photographic memory had served him well over the years.

Chapter Fifty

P axton thought about his newfound wealth. He hadn't bought it as a form of speculation. It was merely an untraceable method of moving and storing digital cash anywhere in the world.

There was no way he could have predicted in 2012 its monumental rise in value. He had purchased fifty-thousand dollars in 2012. Enough to start again with life if he had to.

He ran the numbers in his head.

Bitcoin had been a gamble back then, trading at around ten bucks a coin. That meant he'd bought about 5,000 bitcoins. His brow furrowed for a moment as he did the math, his lips moving silently. Five thousand bitcoins.

And now?

He exhaled sharply, the number flashing in his mind like a neon sign. Bitcoin was hovering at a hundred grand each these days. A hundred thousand times five thousand. His chest tightened as the figure clicked into place.

Five hundred million.

The number hit him like a jolt of electricity. He let out a low whistle, staring at the flash drive as if it had suddenly turned to gold in his palm. Half a billion dollars, sitting there, hidden in a brick for all these years. The enormity of it settled over him like a comforting blanket in the cold.

His pulse quickened at the realization, and he chuckled under his breath, shaking his head. "Rich," he murmured to himself. "Hell, I'm more than rich. I'm..." He trailed off, the words failing him as the scale of his fortune sank in. For a moment, he simply stood there, the quiet of the basement broken only by the faint clinking of the drive against his fingers. He wasn't just holding wealth – he was holding the key to a life he'd never thought possible.

Five hundred million dollars.

That was the sort of money that could buy him a kingdom. Paxton had never been driven by money. Still wasn't. He had no need for a kingdom.

He already knew what he was going to spend it on.

Some he would pay to make sure Rowena Vandyke and her kids were cared for as his friend had wanted. He would leave some for Leyla Rzayev. The money wouldn't make her happy, but it might buy her some freedoms she would otherwise struggle to afford.

There would be a lot left after that.

Paxton knew exactly what he would spend the remaining lion's share of the money on. Close to half a billion dollars could go a long way toward purchasing revenge...

Chapter Fifty-One

Labytnangi, Siberia

Umbra enjoyed hunting, yet this particular prey was like nothing he'd ever seen before. Paxton West had killed the rest of his team of Ghosts. All of them. Leaving just him, Umbra – AKA Vaughn Sinclair – ex US Army Ranger.

He'd tracked Paxton from Salekhard Airport, where an Interpol Red Notice had been flagged to the Russian passport he had been given for the mission. From there, he'd heard about the theft of the snowmobile and the discovery of a Buran 4T snowmobile at the Labytnangi train station. It was obvious – or at least likely – that he'd jumped a train.

But that's where the trail ended.

From Labytnangi he could have gone anywhere.

Frustrated, he picked up his satellite phone and called the number he'd been given.

Answering immediately, Peregrine growled, "Tell me you found him."

"Not yet, but I will."

"Then what are you calling me for?" Peregrine asked, not trying to conceal his rage and disappointment.

"I need to know more about Paxton West."

"What do you want to know?"

"You're the doctor. What do you think is relevant?"

Peregrine laughed. "You want to get inside the mind of Paxton West?"

"It might help me to find out where he's gone."

"The trail's run dry?"

"Only for the time being. I'll pick up his scent soon enough, just watch. I'm far more resilient than the rest of the Ghosts out there, and a much better hunter."

"I hope so."

"What can you tell me?"

"Paxton is the best operative the CIA has ever had."

"Thanks for the ego boost," Umbra said, his voice sarcastic.

"I'm not kidding. If the roles were reversed, you'd be dead inside that torpedo room in the *USS Indiana*."

Umbra didn't believe that for a split second.

But he hadn't called to have a pissing contest with Peregrine over who was a better operative. It was him against Paxton. Right now, Paxton had gone rogue, which made him no longer an operative, anyway.

"All right. Forget I asked." Umbra thought about it for a couple of seconds. "What can you tell me about Paxton's previous assignments?"

"He's been all over the world. He's got a brain disorder that affects the emotional parts of his brain. In fact, he's missing his orbital and ventromedial prefrontal cortices, which have a primary role in moral behavior, emotionally driving moral decisions and being involved in abnormal moral behavior.

"Oh, yeah?"

"The upshot is while he's an emotional void, the part of his brain that deals with languages is exceptional. It's picked up the slack."

"Great. So, in English, what does this actually mean?"

"Paxton learns languages faster than any other human alive."

"Great, I'll keep that in mind next time I go out with a pretty French girl and want to learn a few words to impress her." Umbra said, "Anything useful you can tell me?"

"I mean, he speaks a lot of languages and has traveled extensively throughout Eastern Europe."

"Wait. You said he's done a lot of traveling?"

"Yeah, why?"

"Anywhere in particular that he spent a lot of time?"

"Plenty. Why?"

"Let's go through them. Bring up his records."

"Sure. What are you looking for?"

"I'll tell you in a minute. It's just a hunch. What have you got for me?"

Peregrine said, "He spent three weeks in Paris in 2009, a month in Greece in 2010, eight weeks working on a boat in the Dead Sea, and nearly a year working on an oil rig in Neft Daşları in 2012..."

"Stop! That's it!"

"What's it?"

"I've got him!" Umbra nearly shouted into the satphone.

"Where?"

"Azerbaijan!" Umbra grinned like a kid at Christmas. "He's got a bolt hole in Neft Daşları!"

"What makes you so sure?"

"He spent a year there in 2012."

"Sure, but then he spent a year working on the oil rigs in Irkutsk in 2014."

"No, it's Neft Daşları! Trust me. I'm starting to see how he thinks and that's the place."

"Why?"

"When did he first become a Ghost operative?"

"In 2007."

"Right, but he spent nearly a year working on oil rigs in 2012?"

"That's right. It was intelligence gathering stuff and setting up contacts."

"Right. His first long term assignment." Umbra smiled. "Do you know the first thing Ghosts do when they're let out on their own, without the immediately watchful eyes of the CIA?"

"No."

"We set up bolt holes."

"You set up bolt holes," Peregrine corrected him.

"Wrong." Umbra smiled, ever more certain he had finally found Paxton. "Every Ghost does. We all know that the CIA doesn't have a retirement plan for its Ghosts. We're already dead. They just stop pretending otherwise. So, at the very first opportunity, when we're not being watched by the Agency, we set up a bolt hole, put aside some spare cash, put down roots for a fictional life. Maybe pay some taxes, buy property, and prepare for that day when the hand that feeds us decides we're not worth the trouble."

Peregrine laughed. "By God, I think you're right!"

"I'll get a ticket to Azerbaijan." Umbra grinned. "And this time, I'm not giving Rembrandt the slightest chance. I'm going to put a bullet in his head while he's asleep."

Chapter Fifty-Two

Paxton stepped upstairs, making his way back to Leyla. Still in the kitchen, she studied him as he arrived.

"Find what you were looking for?" she asked.

"Yeah."

"That's good."

Paxton said, "Do you have a computer I can use?"

"Of course. It's on my desk in the study. A laptop." She gave a little frown. "I don't suppose whatever you're going to try and do will get me flagged and then charged with treason and executed, will it?"

"To be honest, I don't know."

Leyla gave a quick choke of laughter. "My, Paxton. As usual, you're really selling this to me. What is it you want to do on the computer?"

Paxton brought her up to speed with what had happened to him and his team inside the alleged terrorist cell within the Cold War era nuclear silo. He then told her about Boris, and the fact that as he was dying, he'd handed him a USB flash drive, telling him the truth about Peregrine. He hoped everyone who had betrayed his country was all there on the drive.

"I see." Leyla nodded. "So, you need to have a look on that flash drive to see what this is all about?"

"Right."

"I'm sorry, Paxton. I can't help you."

"It shouldn't flag anything on the CIA. I can give you money to replace your laptop if it's a virus or something. I'll disconnect your computer from the internet. You'll be okay."

She smiled gently at him. "It's not that. I have a MacBook. You have a USB A flash drive."

"Your MacBook doesn't accept USB A?"

"No. It has an outlet for a standard USB C plug."

Paxton's eyes narrowed. "Can't you get an adaptor?"

"Sure, but I don't have one here."

"What about one of your neighbors?"

"Paxton, where do you think you are?" An incredulous grin spread across her animated face. "This is Neft Daşları for goodness' sake! The entire place is practically deserted, and those that are here, are unlikely to have adaptors to connect a Microsoft flash drive to an Apple adaptor."

"So what's the solution?"

"You want to get this thing as soon as possible?"

"I really need it. I could head back stateside and then sort it out, but I would much prefer to get access to the data on this flash drive and then at least find out who my enemies are before I step foot on US soil."

"I agree. Otherwise, you're running blindfolded through a mine field."

"Right." Paxton shot her an appreciative smile. "So what's the solution? Where's the nearest computer store?"

"Baku, in the republic of Azerbaijan."

"Great." Paxton said, "Let's go."

"When?"

"Now."

Incredulous, she asked, "You want to go right now?"

"Why not? Have you got something important going on today?"

Disappointed, she shook her head. "Not really."

"Great. Grab your laptop."

"Wait... why?"

"We're going to Baku to find out who was responsible for the attack and who I have to kill."

Leyla glared at him. "You see, Paxton, this is precisely why you and I can't be together."

"I know," Paxton agreed. "Now, what time's the ferry to Baku?"

Chapter Fifty-Three

Baku, Azerbaijan

The Yakovlev Yak-40 jet was buffeted by strong turbulence.

Vaughn Sinclair woke up from a restless sleep and glanced out the window. The Caspian Sea was far below, through intermittent cloud cover.

Vaughn's codename had been Umbra, yet after the last catastrophic mission, he had quit thinking of himself as Umbra. The name was tarnished with bad luck as his entire team was dead. On the plus side, he had been fortunate, as he was still breathing.

The Yakovlev Yak-40 broke through the gray winter clouds, its stubby, rugged form descending toward the icy runway. The tri-jet, with its compact fuselage and distinctive T-tail, seemed perfectly at home in the harsh, utilitarian landscape of the industrial section of Baku. Its silver-gray paint, dulled by years of service, reflected the muted light of the overcast sky, while faint streaks of grime on its belly hinted at a life spent ferrying passengers and cargo through equally unforgiving places.

The Yak-40 approached steadily, its wide, low wings and triple engines working in unison to keep the descent smooth despite the crosswinds that whipped across the barren terrain. A plume of vapor rose as the landing gear touched the frost-covered tarmac, the tires skidding slightly before gripping the rough surface with a squeal that echoed across the open space.

The aircraft taxied toward the terminal, its engines spooling down with a throaty rumble that reverberated through Vaughn's body. He adjusted the strap of his duffel bag as the plane came to a halt, its small set of stairs unfolding awkwardly from the fuselage. A handful of passengers began disembarking, their silhouettes sharp against the dull metal of the craft.

Vaughn stepped off the small jet into the biting wind. He pulled his coat tighter against the icy wind and inhaled the faint scent of the Caspian Sea. Vaughn moved through customs quickly, his duffel bag slung over one shoulder, blending into the small crowd. He quickly exited the airport, making his way to the ferry terminal.

The city of Baku sprawled beneath a leaden winter sky, a blend of ancient, industrial, and modern metropolis rising from the lowest point in the world. At 92 feet below sea level, the place seemed to fold into the Earth itself. Its architecture was a juxtaposition of crumbling stone facades and gleaming steel towers – a reminder of the city's oil-fueled prosperity layered over centuries of history.

The capital city of the Turkish Republic of Azerbaijan, Baku had a population of 6.5 million people, many of them middle-class or wealthy.

Vaughn figured the poor people were right here, surrounding him. Working hard to survive the winter.

The narrow streets were slick with half-frozen slush, the wheels of passing cars kicking up dirty sprays that splattered onto the edges of the sidewalk. Sinclair stepped around a deep puddle, his boots crunching against the coarse salt scattered over the pavement. The buildings around him were dark and weathered, their windows glowing faintly from dim lights inside. In the distance, the faint outline of the Flame Towers shimmered against the murky sky, a modern monolith overlooking the city's low-rise sprawl.

The climb began at the edge of the old quarter, where worn stone steps, slick with frost, wound upward toward the ferry terminal perched high above the city. Sinclair took the stairs two at a time, his breath forming white clouds in the frigid air. The effort warmed him slightly, but the cold clung to him like a second skin. As he ascended, the sounds of the city faded – the hum of traffic and the distant voices of street vendors receded into a muted backdrop.

Halfway up, he paused to look back.

From this height, Baku stretched out like a living map, its streets curling toward the distant oil fields and the horizon. The city seemed huddled against the cold, its lights flickering in defiance of the unforgiving winter. The knowledge that he stood below sea level, in a place shaped as much by its geography as its oil wealth, was an irony not lost on him.

Above him was the Caspian Sea – a force that had defined this region for centuries.

Reaching the top, Vaughn stepped onto the windswept plateau where the ferry terminal loomed against the backdrop of gray water. The sea churned restlessly, its dark waves reflecting the heavy sky. Workers bundled in heavy coats loaded crates onto the waiting ferries, their voices muffled by the wind. Sinclair adjusted the strap of his bag, his gaze scanning the scene with the calculated detachment of someone who left nothing to chance. He moved toward the ferry terminal with purpose, each step bringing him closer to the next leg of his journey.

Out there, beyond the mist-shrouded waters, lay Neft Daşları.

Baku in winter was a stark, unforgiving place. The city sprawled outward from its shallow harbor, a haphazard collection of Soviet-era concrete buildings, repurposed shipping containers, and narrow streets clogged with slush and grime. The skyline was dominated by skeletal cranes and oil rigs visible even from the airport, their towering frames wreathed in mist and smoke.

This was no tourist destination – it was a hub of necessity, where industry thrived despite the hostile weather.

He flagged down a battered taxi, its windshield frosted at the edges. The driver, wrapped in a thick scarf with only his eyes visible above a cigarette, nodded silently as Vaughn climbed in. The heater rattled and sputtered as they drove through the slushy streets, passing gray buildings and hunched figures hurrying through the cold.

The ferry terminal was little more than a concrete pier jutting into the freezing harbor. Vaughn paid the driver in crumpled bills and stepped out, the arctic wind cutting through his gloves as he gripped his bag. The air here was sharper, tinged with the smell of diesel. Workers in oil-streaked jackets loaded crates onto the ferry, their boots crunching on the icy dock, while a few passengers huddled on benches under heavy coats, speaking in low tones to conserve warmth.

The ferry was a rust-streaked workhorse of the Caspian Sea, its once-white hull now a patchwork of peeling paint and corrosion. A weather-beaten flag snapped sharply in the wind atop its mast, while thick ropes, coiled like sleeping serpents, lay piled on the deck. The vessel groaned as waves slapped against its side, its bulk swaying slightly as passengers and cargo were loaded. A large crack ran through the glass of the main cabin's forward window, spider-webbing out like frozen lightning – an unmistakable mark on an otherwise unremarkable vessel.

Etched into the side of the hull was the name of the ship: *Obadiah.*

Vaughn boarded the ferry into the mix of workers, engineers, and weary travelers huddled on the deck, bundled against the biting wind. He moved all the way to the forward section of the vessel. The ferry's deckhands worked with slow moving competence, securing crates and shouting over the mechanical rumble of the engines warming up.

Passengers chattered as they settled into worn wooden benches under the partial shelter of the deck's awning.

He stepped into a shadowed corner of the vessel near the loading crane, his gaze sweeping the deck as the ferry lurched slightly against its moorings. The crack in the forward window caught his eye again, reflecting the weak sunlight like fractured crystal. A small, inconsequential detail, perhaps, but one that stuck in his mind.

Vaughn, AKA Umbra, adjusted the collar of his coat and leaned back, the rhythmic thrum of the engines vibrating through the deck as the ferry prepared to depart.

Where to sit?

The boat was packed with people, and passengers were still boarding. It was likely that all of them were going to Neft Daşları for work on the oil rigs. Vaughn moved inside and walked all the way to the front. Then he settled back, waiting to depart.

With a smile on his face, he shut his eyes, and mentally prepared to kill Paxton West.

Chapter Fifty-Four

After finding the information he needed, Paxton and Layla left the ferry terminal in Baku, for the 34 miles trip back to Neft Daşları and her home.

The *Obadiah* was a cumbersome and slow workhorse ferry of the Caspian Sea, with a badly cracked windshield in its pilot house. Despite its namesake, which paid tribute to the once prosperous ruler of the Khazar Empire during its golden age in the 9th Century, the ferry appeared far from reliable. Its diesel engine, sounding long past its halcyon days, kept coughing and then cutting out.

The journey should have taken under two hours but ended up being nearly five. The slow and steady speed was typical of a Neft Daşları, no-need-to-rush pace.

Paxton didn't mind.

His mind drifted to thoughts of Azerbaijan, the unique country in which he'd spent more time than any other, living what he considered an almost normal sort of life. One where he labored during the day, spent time with a beautiful girl after work, bought a house, and enjoyed a happy domestic life. It had felt real and at the same time, much like acting in a play.

Yet these were things he'd never done stateside.

In his mind's eye, he pictured Neft Daşları. Such a complex and magnificent location. A place he had once called "home."

Azerbaijan was a nation which straddled the line between east and west. It borders Russia, Georgia, Armenia, Turkey, Iran, and the Caspian Sea. In 1949 it was a part of the Soviet Union and was called Azerbaijan SSR. As far back as the 3rd and 4th centuries there was evidence of the trade in petroleum.

Arabic and Persian scholars describe the trade frequently, as do later visitors to the area. In 1683, Secretary to the Swedish Embassy, Englebert Kaempfer, made a point of detailing the gaseous smell and fires emanating from fissures in the oil fields. Oil production sped up rapidly in the late 19th century, and by 1901, Baku – Azerbaijan's capital – was producing more than half of the entire world's oil supply, and it all came from wells that were within 6 miles of one another.

Unfortunately for them, the wealth couldn't last.

With the Russian Revolution in 1905 causing a drop in oil production and then further catastrophe during WWI, when oil production plummeted, Azerbaijan's independent government – which had only been in place from 1918-1920 – could not jumpstart it again on their own. The Bolsheviks had seized power in Azerbaijan and rerouted all oil to Russia. The country that was both east and west desperately needed innovation and power to restore their petroleum industry.

Enter the USSR.

In the late 1940's geologists had been busy surveying the area in the Caspian Sea, suspecting that there was an oil deposit. In 1949 they were proven correct, and construction began on creating the necessary infrastructure for people to work on water. In the beginning, Neft Daşları was built on seven sunken ships, including the very first oil tanker in the world. Yet this outpost, which was situated over a very rich oil deposit only 3,300 feet below the seabed, grew rapidly from its discovery in 1949 to the start of its drilling operation in 1951.

Soon more "islands" were built, mostly from soil and landfill.

Trestle bridges connected everything. They created a cramped and complicated system to get oil from the drilling sites back to land. They had built the world's first operational offshore oil rig and the floating city grew exponentially.

At its height, Neft Daşları had around 2,000 drilling platforms pulling from the underwater oilfields.

A staggering 160 miles of bridges were erected in the middle of the Caspian Sea with apartment blocks and buildings multiple stories high, bakeries, soccer fields, parks, cinemas, cafes, and cultural spaces. The residents began to cultivate soil from the mainland to grow their own fruits and vegetables.

Then, with the fall of the Soviet Union, its population dwindled. Without financial investment in the city's maintenance, sections quickly fell into disrepair and were claimed by the sea.

The *Obadiah* pulled up alongside a small harbor that formed the edge of Neft Daşları, and the crew tied off.

Paxton and Leyla stood up.

They were the first to leave.

Chapter Fifty-Five

Vaughn hated boats.

Always had.

There was a time in his youth when he'd considered joining the Navy, just so he could become a SEAL. He wanted to hunt and kill people in the name of protecting his nation. He had even passed the recruitment exams. Then, a friend from school whose dad had a fishing boat, took him out in the calm waters of Tampa Bay, Florida.

He had spent the day filled with such violent seasickness he vowed to never go to sea again. The next week, he saw the recruiting officer and switched his application from the Navy to the Army Rangers, becoming part of the elite Special Forces group instead.

Standing on board the *Obadiah* reminded him that he'd made the right choice all those years ago.

After being nearly the first passenger on the ferry, he ended up being the last to leave it. Who knew disembarkation was from aft of the boat? If he had known, he would never have chosen to make his way to the forward deck.

When everyone else had gone ashore, he approached the skipper, a wiry man in his sixties, with a leathery seaworn face. The official language of Azerbaijan was Azari, but more than half the population fluently spoke Russian.

Vaughn greeted the skipper in Russian and showed him a photo of Paxton. "I'm looking for my cousin. He works on the oil rigs here in Neft Daşları. He said he could find me work if I showed up. I'm here now, but I didn't realize just how big this water world really is. It might take me days to find him."

The skipper studied the photograph. "Tall guy. Big. I mean really big?"

"Yes, that's the one."

The skipper grinned. "You didn't see him? He was on the ferry! Sat right at the back with Leyla, a woman who runs the local bar."

Vaughn cursed his luck.

That would explain why, sitting inside up in front he'd never spotted Paxton. The man, he admitted, was certainly born under some kind of ridiculously lucky star. If there was a chance for him to get a break, he always managed it.

"I don't suppose you know where he lives?"

The skipper shook his head. "No, sorry. If you ask around, someone will be able to tell you where Leyla Rzayev lives though. She seemed to know your cousin. Leyla will be able to point you in the right direction."

"Thank you," Vaughn said, climbing off the boat.

"Good luck finding your cousin. There's plenty of work going for strong men, so I'm sure he'll find you a job."

"I hope so," Vaughn replied, knowing that killing Paxton was the only job he wanted.

Chapter Fifty-Six

L eyla unlocked the door to her house and Paxton followed her inside. In the study, she plugged her laptop into the power source and inserted the USB-C to USB-A adaptor into her MacBook.

She turned the laptop to face Paxton. "It's all yours."

"Thanks."

Leyla got up to leave and Paxton turned to her retreating back. "You don't want to see what's on this?"

"I didn't think I'd be allowed."

"I'm not with the CIA anymore. In fact, I'm fairly certain it was my boss who tried to take me out. So, I don't know. I figure after all that, the rules governing security clearance don't apply."

"You want me to read it?" she asked, edging closer to him. "Why?"

"I trust you." Paxton shrugged, "And I think you can help. Two sets of eyes are generally better than one."

To Leyla, confiding his trust in her was a compliment of the highest order. She smiled at that and took a seat right beside him. "All right. I'll stay."

Paxton slid the USB flash drive into the MacBook's port, the soft click barely audible over the hum of the room's air conditioning. The laptop recognized the drive instantly, and a single folder appeared on the screen, its name unassumingly titled: "Data."

His hand hovered over the trackpad for a moment before double-clicking the folder.

Inside was one lone file: an Excel spreadsheet labeled "*Inventory_ Transactions.xlsx.*" Paxton clicked it open, and the document filled the screen, revealing row upon row of information. Each line chronicled years of illicit activity – a damning ledger of weapons sales from ex-US Military stock, the payments going to, no doubt, already overstuffed personal pockets.

His eyes scanned the columns: descriptions, serial numbers, dates, buyers, and most damning of all, the prices.

Paxton scrolled through, viewing various entries:

M4A1 Carbine: $1,800/ 2000 units

FIM-92 Stinger MANPADS: $90,000/ 50 units

Javelin Anti-Tank Missile System: $120,000/1000 units

AN/PRC-117G Tactical Radios: $35,000/2500 units

General Atomics MQ-9 Reaper Drone (decommissioned): $1.2 million/ 120 units

Aegis Combat System Software License: $10 million/ 20 licenses

Standard Missile-6 (SM-6): $4 million/ 500 units

TOW Missile Launcher Systems: $80,000/300 units

Advanced Encryption Modules (for secure communications): $200,000/ 400 units

The pure audacity of the fraud staggered him. This wasn't small-time smuggling; this was systemic, industrial-scale theft and redistribution. The spreadsheet extended back over fifteen years, with the most recent entry dated just two weeks prior. Each sale was meticulously documented, suggesting a well-oiled machine of corruption.

Paxton scrolled lower, expecting more rows of transactions, but he found a second sheet labeled *"Key Personnel."* When he clicked on it, four names stared back at him in bold script, along with payments in equal quarters to match offshore accounts:

Sir Marcus Voss

Dr. Alan Kepler

Dylan Frost

Daniel Hawthorne

He leaned back in his chair, heart pounding.

Three of the names were familiar. Marcus Voss, CEO of Obsidian Sentinel Systems, had long been a shadowy figure in the world of military contracts. His company had secured major deals with the US government for decades. Dr. Alan Kepler, the man Paxton once trusted as his neurologist, had been revealed as Peregrine, the elusive CIA handler of the Ghosts. And then there was Daniel Hawthorne, now the Vice President of the United States – a man who had risen from the coal mines to one of the highest offices in the land.

But the fourth person, Dylan Frost, was a mystery.

The name stirred no memories, yet here it was, listed alongside some of the most powerful figures Paxton had ever encountered. He stared at the screen, his mind racing.

Who was Frost? Why was he tied to this operation? And what role did he play in this intricate web of theft, deceit, and betrayal?

Paxton's gut churned as he pieced it together.

This wasn't just a criminal syndicate; it was a cabal that spanned government, private industry, and clandestine operations. These weren't just deals gone bad; this was high treason on a monumental scale.

His fingers clenched into fists.

This spreadsheet was a ticking time bomb.

It was evidence that could bring down giants, but it also explained everything. Like why there was a target painted on his back. The wealthy and powerful men named here would stop at nothing to protect their secrets.

As Paxton's eyes returned to the screen, the weight of this discovery settled over him like a shroud. He needed to act – and fast. The question was: who could he trust?

Paxton scrolled further through the spreadsheet, his stomach twisting as he uncovered another layer of the conspiracy.

Among the inventory was a final chilling entry: Eight Davy Crockett nukes.

Miniature nuclear weapons, relics of the Cold War, were sold two years ago. Paxton's breath caught in his throat. That would explain how they had ended up in the missile silo beneath the Ural Mountains.

He examined the details in the adjacent columns. Most transactions included bank transfers from Boris to a private financial address registered to an offshore bank in the Cayman Islands. But the Davy Crockett nukes were different. There was no price listed.

Instead, under "Agreed Terms," there was a cryptic note: "Service to be Rendered."

Assassination. Had to be.

Paxton's eyes narrowed as he focused on the accompanying detail. Boris's team was tasked with an execution. A cold, professional hit. Like shuffling a deck of cards, his mind flipped through possibilities. But who was the target? There was a date – two weeks away. Unfortunately, the name of the intended victim was written in a secret code: Ironback.

"Ironback," Paxton muttered under his breath, feeling the phrase sink into his thoughts like a splinter. It was deliberately vague, intending to obscure the target's identity. Yet something about it nagged at him. He read further. The notes mentioned a public event involving the target. It was a meeting with Estonia's Minister of Digital Affairs, Aleksander Kiik, in Tallinn.

Leyla asked, "Any idea who Ironback is?"

"None." Paxton smiled. "But I intend to find out."

Paxton's pulse quickened as he connected the dots. Whoever Ironback was, Boris's team believed the assassination would spark a chain reaction. Perhaps even a geopolitical crisis that could lead to World War III.

His chest tightened as he leaned back, staring at the glowing screen. He needed to figure out who Ironback was, and fast.

Paxton reached for his phone and searched for recent schedules of high-profile figures. His thoughts circled around the cryptic title. "Speaker..." It could mean a politician. Iron? It suggested resilience or strength.

Then it clicked, like a thunderclap in his mind.

Vice President Daniel Hawthorne.

Hawthorne, known for his distinctive silver hair and his ability to command a room, had earned the nickname during his years as a lawyer. Paxton's blood ran cold as he recalled reading a news piece about Hawthorne's upcoming trip to Estonia. The VP was set to meet with Eero Talvik, his Estonian counterpart in Tallinn to discuss NATO's cybersecurity initiatives and the looming threat of Russian interference.

The timing matched perfectly.

"It's him," Paxton whispered, his voice barely audible.

His fingers trembled as he scrolled back to the spreadsheet, his eyes darting over the cryptic entries. If Hawthorne was the target, his death could be framed as a deliberate provocation by Russia against the United States and NATO.

The fallout would be catastrophic.

He thought of the four people on the list: Voss, Kepler, Frost, and VP Hawthorne.

"Could it be possible this is some sort of inner revolt?" Paxton asked. "Are Voss, Kepler, and Frost planning to have Hawthorne terminated?"

Chapter Fifty-Seven

Leyla frowned. "Didn't you tell me that Hawthorne was the man responsible for ordering Peregrine to have your team killed?"

"He most likely did."

"But why would he do that if he knew about that flash drive?"

"Because he didn't know. He only *thought* there might be a flash drive. We were ordered to terminate Boris as he knew details, and the VP feared Boris could pass on incriminating evidence of his treason. That's why he needed to shut down anyone who may have been able to reveal his secrets."

"Okay, that makes sense." Leyla thought about it some more. "Then it seems to me that the other three men would want him alive. They all shared the same offenses. Why would the others plan to have him killed?"

"I don't know."

Leyla said, "I thought you mentioned earlier that VP Hawthorne was a supporter of the Ghost program?"

"He was. I mean, it makes sense. He's in bed with a CEO of a high-tech weapons company who has been negotiating sales of US military hardware for years to terrorist organizations." Paxton shook his head. "What better way to keep control of the situation than to have a trained team of Ghosts capable of secretly executing anyone who is inconvenient or gets in your way?"

"Right." Leyla took it one step forward. "Again, why would his three partners in crime want to kill Hawthorne?"

"It depends." Paxton thought about that for a few seconds. "The real question is, what does Hawthorne currently bring to the cabal?"

"Influence, general and legal, also connections and power."

"The Vice Presidency."

"Oh."

"The incumbent is about to finish his second term."

"Meaning Hawthorne's political power is about to be lost?"

"Right, unless..."

Leyla's eyes went wide, she slapped the desk excitedly. "Hawthorne's making a play for Presidency!"

"Yes. I would think so."

Leyla said, "I don't keep up with a lot of US politics, but from what I've read, Hawthorne's quite popular on both sides of the political spectrum. He might just get it."

Paxton frowned. "Yeah, that's what worries me too."

"Why?"

"It doesn't make sense," Paxton said. "I mean, for the syndicate. They know Hawthorne is likely to become the next President. If that happens, their little syndicate can only get better because of his power. So why kill him?"

"Maybe they don't think he'll win?"

"Who cares. Even if they don't, why cut their losses now? I mean, it's like the gambler ripping up his ticket before the final fight. The card's already been played, they may as well wait and see how it lands."

Leyla thought about that for a minute. "Perhaps someone has something on Hawthorne?"

"Like what?"

"I don't know. Don't they say the worst skeletons in the cupboard only come out when they get on a national platform and journalists start really vetting their past? Everyone has secrets." She looked at Paxton and suppressed a smile. "Some people more than others."

"Well, yes, I think we can both agree that my options for running for an election are unlikely any time in the future." Paxton shook his head. "I suppose that's possible. Maybe Hawthorne has some sort of dark secret that will come out as soon as he's on the ticket?"

"Why doesn't Hathorne's enemy reveal his discreditable secrets now, to prevent him from running?"

"It doesn't work like that."

"Why not?"

"If, whoever has his secret is part of the opposition, they will rather have him battle it out among his own side. Wait until he's won the Democratic Nomination, before revealing his fatal piece of history making him unable to fight on the big stage."

"Then let the other party play catch up and nominate someone new."

Paxton said, "Exactly."

"All right, so let's say Hawthorne is about to lose. What does their nasty little crime syndicate do about it?"

Leyla said, "They look to see who could replace Hawthorne."

"Right, and what do they see?"

"I've no idea."

Paxton grinned. "I have an idea what they see…"

"What?"

"It all depends on the timing."

Leyla smiled, although she looked like he'd lost her. "Go on."

"They have nobody if the government is stable and the world is running on status quo."

"But?"

"If the VP gets assassinated and Eero Talvik dies in the explosion, then NATO gets brought into the war. The finger gets pointed at Russia. Russia denies its involvement, but nobody believes that. US citizens cry murder, an uproar breaks out, and they demand war. The Baltic countries would side with NATO."

"And then the election becomes a completely different event."

"The American people will be looking for a hawkish government. Who better to elect than a billionaire CEO of a defense company?"

"Marcus Voss!"

"Yes. He gets the nomination, and the world goes to war."

Leyla said, "What will you do?"

"I'm not sure." Paxton's lips formed a grim line. "First, I have to save my enemy's life to prevent World War III from erupting."

Chapter Fifty-Eight

P axton pushed to his feet. "I need to go."

Surprised, Leyla's brows shot up. "Right now?"

"Soon. I need to start making arrangements."

Paxton made his way to the hole in the wall where he'd removed the brick. He reached inside until his fingertips touched a small, plastic container. He fumbled with it for a minute, before his fingers caught, and he pulled. Paxton brought the plastic container back to the computer table.

He popped the lid open and withdrew a Swiss Passport. He'd spent years cultivating the identity on that passport. He rented an apartment in Zürich, paid taxes, even had a wife and two children, who went to an expensive private school, *Institut auf dem Rosenberg*. The kids had a dog named Kiri, and a cat named Leon.

Switzerland enjoyed a visa waiver program with the USA.

He would buy a business class ticket and explain that he was there in a professional capacity. He needed to find Rowena Vandyke and make sure that she and her girls were well funded and okay, before hopefully tracking down the members of the syndicate who plotted to kill the Vice President.

It would be hard work, but if he got lucky, he might manage to complete the task in time to stop the assassination. Or better yet, he might kill the VP himself?

Paxton smiled.

He liked that idea. Kill the four enemies responsible for the death of his team and prevent World War III from happening.

Not bad for a Ghost.

Paxton looked around, but Leyla was gone. "Hello?" he said, slightly confused. Leyla came back into the room with a small backpack.

"Are you joining me on my trip?" he asked.

She shook her head. "You know I can't be a part of this."

"I know." Paxton said with alacrity. "It would be too hard to travel to the US with short notice on an Azerbaijanian passport, and I don't have time to get you a fake one."

Leyla smiled a smile full of love and affection. This was precisely why she couldn't go with him, because of the way his mind worked. "No, Paxton. I'm not going to be part of your retribution. Murder is not for me."

"Oh. Okay..." Paxton smiled. "I mean, you don't have to do the killing personally. We could just go traveling together. Maybe on the days that I'm busy you could go see the sights. Washington, D.C. is interesting. The Smithsonian Institute is fantastic."

"Yeah, maybe one day. But I think I'll take a raincheck on that one."

Paxton paused. "You're really leaving?"

"Yes."

"Where will you go?"

"Listen, when you left the first time," Leyla said, "it took a long time to get over you. I know you're not built the way I am, and I know that our lives simply aren't meant to be together. I'm glad you came back. You sort of gave me the type of closure I didn't even realize I needed. But it's done now."

Paxton couldn't deny that. "I'm sorry."

"Yeah, me too." She handed him her keys back. "All the same, I need to get out of here."

"You don't need to go!" Paxton argued. "I mean, this house is technically yours any-way."

"Yeah, I do." Leyla gave an apologetic smile. "Whatever bad people are after you, they're going to find you. When they do, I don't want to be part of whatever happens."

That seemed fair. He said, "Where will you go?"

"I have money. I always wondered what happened to you. Now I know." She paused, thinking about it for a moment. "I'm going to travel for a bit. See some of the world to take in the sights, not to kill people!" She said the last bit with a laugh in her voice, but he could tell that his life-choices still made her uncomfortable.

"Okay."

She kissed him, her lips lingering on his. "Goodbye, Paxton."

He watched her go. In some areas, he knew he was incapable of making the right decisions. A voice in the back of his head, part of his gut instinct which he'd worked hard for years to ignore, said, *Don't lose Leyla again...*

Paxton said, "Hey Leyla..."

She stopped at the door, looked back at him with those eyes he loved more than any others in the world. "Yeah?"

"Do I have to never see you again?"

"What do you want?" she probed.

"I have to sort some things out. When I'm done, maybe we should do something together."

"I love you, Paxton. But I'm never going to marry you. Our paths are on two very different directions."

"But if I find you... in a time in another life?"

She made a bemused smile. "You mean, in a time when people aren't trying to kill you?"

Paxton turned his palms outward. "Yeah."

"I left you an email. You can contact me there. Drop me a line, and let's see where we're at." She stood on her toes and kissed his lips once more. "Bye, Paxton."

"You don't have to go now that I've come back," he tried to reassure her.

"You left here all those years ago because of some terrible threat." She gave him a soft, self-deprecating smile. "Whatever the danger is this time, it's going to follow you here again. I have no interest in being here when it does."

Her eyes locked on his, as if to challenge him to contradict her.

He couldn't. "Goodbye, Leyla."

Chapter Fifty-Nine

V aughn knocked on several apartment doors.

Few people were interested in opening their doors to a stranger. Particularly one who looked like he was a Russian hitman. The irony wasn't lost on him. He was, in fact, exactly what he appeared to be – albeit he was technically an American hitman. Yet he'd spent so many years living under cover in Russia that he's appearance and mannerisms were more Russian than American.

The pervasive scent of oil flooded everything on Neft Daşları. No wonder they once called the place "Oil Rocks." As he walked away from the main set of apartment buildings, a wrinkled woman who looked about a hundred years old, stepped outside. She had the appearance of someone who'd accepted they could die at any moment, and without any fear left in her world, she said, "Can I help you?"

"Hello. My cousin who has been staying with Leyla Rzayev said he could get me work on one of the oil rigs if I made my way here." Vaughn gave a humorless smile. "So I came here, but Paxton – that's my cousin – didn't give me his address. I pictured Neft Daşları as being a small offshore oil rig station. But I see now I was mistaken. It is very big."

She nodded. "Is your cousin dating Leyla?"

Vaughn didn't have a clue what Paxton's relationship was with the woman. He needed an easy out that worked no matter what their connection. "He mentioned he'd met the most beautiful woman in all the world, and that he hoped to one day marry her. I don't know if he's progressed with his romantic endeavors."

The old woman laughed. "If your cousin has even half a chance with Leyla, he's an incredibly lucky man."

"Ah, that is my cousin." Vaughn said, "Do you happen to know where Leyla lives?"

The woman gestured toward a large, three-story house, on a massive pontoon toward the end of a jetty.

Vaughn smiled politely. "Thank you so much for your help."

"You're welcome." She smiled. "Tell Leyla that Oksana sends her love."

"Will do."

Two minutes later, a strikingly beautiful woman walked past him from the direction of the house where Paxton had hopefully been staying. Vaughn smiled at her, and wished her a good day. In Russian. He didn't speak the local Azeri, but most people in Azerbaijan spoke Russian fluently, and those who didn't spoke enough to understand it.

Either way, his greeting was no surprise to her.

He watched her walk past, admiring the sway of her hips.

He had to admit, Paxton had good taste. It would appear he had good luck in that area too. Another five hundred or so feet, and he'd found the house at the end of the jetty.

It looked like it had probably once been separated into apartments. Somewhere along the line – most likely as the population dropped at Neft Daşları and real estate became cheap and available, a new owner had converted it into one large house.

It was late in the afternoon. Not quite dark yet, but not far from sunset. Vaughn had no intention of making the mistake of underestimating Paxton this time around. Better that he should heed Peregrine's advice and kill him while he slept.

Vaughn made a mental note to return in the middle of the night.

2 a.m. was good.

Most people – even someone like Paxton – would likely be in a deep sleep at that point of the night. It was the deepest part of the sleep cycle and occurs during Stage 3 of Non-Rapid Eye Movement, known as NREM sleep. At this point, Vaughn would have the highest likelihood of taking Paxton unaware.

Yes, that's what he would do. He was about to turn around, and walk away before Paxton caught a glimpse of him when the door to the house opened.

Paxton stepped out with his Glock aimed straight at him.

Vaughn reached for his weapon, but it was impossible to draw a weapon faster than a trained professional could simply squeeze the trigger of their already aimed pistol.

Paxton didn't say a word. He simply aimed and squeezed off three shots in a row. Every single one of them formed a tight grouping in the middle of Vaughn's heart.

Pain seared Vaughn's chest. He staggered and fell backward.

Chapter Sixty

Paxton kept his Glock pointed at his attacker.

He never forgot a face, and this asshole was the same man who shot some of his team and tried to kill him on board the submarine. Paxton's eyes swept the rest of the area. Neft Daşları was a big place – some 180 miles of floating roads and decks, but it was also very flat. He'd specifically bought this place because it was built at the end of its own jetty, meaning if any attackers ever did come, they would be easy to spot.

There was nothing and no one was there.

Only him and this Ghost.

It made him wonder if his team had killed the rest of the Ghosts on board the submarine. It made him question whether the mission to terminate Boris in the Ural Mountains had single-handedly destroyed all the CIA's Ghosts, thereby shutting the program down permanently.

Paxton stepped closer to the dead Ghost.

He walked calmly toward the man on the ground, ready to perform the *Coup de grâce,* known as the mercy bullet into the head. It was the only way to be certain he was dead. In Paxton's experience, nobody ever lived after being shot in the back of the head.

A split second later, the Ghost rolled over and fired a short burst from his Israeli Uzi.

Paxton swore, and jumped back, running toward the house.

The Ghost rose like some sort of super villain from the old Terminator franchise. Only, there was nothing supernatural about it. The guy had been wearing Kevlar body armor. Paxton cursed himself for not taking the time to make a head shot.

Firing his submachine gun, the Ghost started running toward him.

Paxton darted back into the house as bullets shredded the walls and splintered the furniture behind him. The rapid staccato of the Uzi's fire echoed like thunder in his ears, followed by the unnerving click of Umbra reloading. Paxton knew the rhythm – reload, fire, reload. He'd counted three magazines already.

Taking the stairs two at a time, Paxton reached the second story, his breath controlled despite the adrenaline coursing through his veins. He crouched near a shattered window, his eyes flicking toward the shimmering water below. The pontoon beneath the house creaked under the strain of its precarious design. This had been a temporary hideout, nothing more.

Now, it was a trap.

The gunfire resumed, and Paxton's sharp ears picked up the crunch of boots over broken glass. Umbra had entered the house. He was bold, confident, and no doubt arrogant as hell. Paxton crouched lower, his hand moving to the small device in his pocket. He pulled it out, the weight of the detonator solid in his palm.

His thumb hovered over the button as he took one last deep breath.

Then he saw him – the one the other Ghosts had called Umbra, a dark silhouette framed against the chaos of the downstairs wreckage. His predatory gaze swept the room.

Their eyes locked.

Umbra smirked, his hand tightening around the Uzi.

Paxton gave him a hard look, one filled with the kind of cold, calculated resolve that only years of hardship and survival could forge. No words were exchanged. None were needed.

With deliberate calm, Paxton raised the detonator, and his thumb pressed the button.

The explosion was instantaneous.

It ripped through the structure beneath the house in a deafening chain reaction. Paxton barely flinched as the floor beneath Umbra disintegrated. The pontoon imploded with a sickening groan, swallowing the house's foundation in an instant.

For a split second it seemed as though the house was going to hold.

And then it began its journey to the bottom of the Caspian Sea...

Chapter Sixty-One

U mbra hit the floor hard.

The crazy bastard had rigged the entire pontoon upon which the house had been built to explode. One by one, they were going off, and the entire three-story house was rapidly sinking into the Caspian Sea.

The explosion began with a hollow, reverberating thud that Umbra felt more than heard. The pontoon beneath the house collapsed inward, folding like a crushed tin can. A shockwave rippled through the water, followed by a cacophony of groaning wood and splintering beams.

Umbra's gaze snapped upward as he steadied himself against the rocking floor, getting back up on his feet. He caught sight of Paxton sprinting up the stairs, his silhouette stark against the flickering light from the chaos below.

He's heading for the rooftop, he thought.

Umbra gave chase, his Uzi snapping up to fire. He emptied the magazine as he ran, his rounds splintering wooden railings and peppering the stairwell. Paxton's figure disappeared around the next landing, and Umbra swore under his breath.

The house tilted further, throwing him off balance for a split second, but he pressed forward.

The sound of rushing water filled the air – a deep, guttural roar that came from everywhere at once. Umbra paused for a heartbeat, glancing down. A frothing white torrent surged through the lower level, crashing into walls and sweeping away furniture in its relentless ascent. Within seconds, the water breached the stairwell, racing upward like a marauder in pursuit.

Umbra's boots splashed as he bounded up the stairs two at a time, the icy water nipping at his heels. His pulse thundered in his ears, matching the rhythm of the cascading flood. The stairwell became a torrent, the current threatening to drag him backward.

He shoved forward, a determined and relentless hunter.

This time, he would not lose his prey.

At the very top, Umbra reached what looked like an attic bedroom. Paxton darted inside and slammed a solid iron-plated door shut behind him. Umbra didn't hesitate, slamming his shoulder into it, then stepping back to deliver a powerful kick. The door didn't budge. He fired a burst of rounds into the metal, but it was futile. The sound of rushing water grew deafening, drowning out even the Uzi's report.

In the next instant, the flood reached the ceiling. Umbra barely had time to take a breath as the stairwell filled completely. The freezing water surged around him, disorienting and blinding, forcing him to hold his breath.

The entire house groaned ominously. Then sank beneath the surface, the pressure squeezing the air out through shattered windows.

Umbra swam hard, clawing his way through the swirling debris and the chaos of rising bubbles. His lungs burned, the cold searing his muscles. His world turned dark, and he began to genuinely fear drowning.

Then a giant suction drew him out of a broken window and into the open sea.

Once outside the sinking building, he kicked as hard as he could against the current. Eventually, he broke the icy surface, gasping for breath and coughing as he treaded water.

The dark outline of the jetty loomed nearby. Umbra swam for it, each stroke powerful and purposeful, until he dragged himself onto the slick wooden planks. He lay there for a moment, his chest heaving, his soaked clothing clinging to his skin.

When the water around him settled, Umbra pushed himself to his feet, scanning the waves. The Caspian Sea was eerily calm now, its surface reflecting the starlight as though nothing had happened.

He waited, his sharp eyes trained on the water.

It was deadly still.

Umbra frowned. He didn't like to leave things uncertain, yet there was no sign of Paxton on the surface. It had been nearly three minutes since the explosion. Brain death started to occur around the three-minute mark.

He grinned.

Was it possible the great Paxton West had drowned? Umbra rifled thought his backpack, took out his satellite phone, and hit the call button.

Peregrine answered right away. "Is it done?"

Umbra said, "I think so."

"What do you mean you think so?"

"Paxton detonated the pontoon that held his house afloat. The entire thing sunk within seconds. I was lucky to get sucked out a broken window. I don't know if Paxton was so lucky, but I'm staring at the still water, and there's no sign of him." Umbra felt the response was weak, even when he said it. "It's more than six hundred feet here. Too deep for me to dive, but given the location and all the oil rigs, I'm sure I can find some commercial divers who I can pay to go retrieve the body."

"Forget it. You're wasting your time. Paxton's too good to get killed by his own stupidity. The commercial divers won't find anything."

Umbra glared at the icy cold water that had nearly ended his life. He couldn't imagine how Paxton had survived, but he wasn't going to get into that argument with Peregrine. Instead, he asked, "What do you want me to do?"

"Come back stateside. You need to get ready," The tone of Peregrine's voice turned hard. "You have a Vice President to assassinate."

Umbra said, "Everything is already prepared in Estonia."

"Regrettably," Peregrine said. "There's been a change of plans."

"Really?"

"Yes. We can't wait that long. Estonia's too risky now."

"What then?"

"We're going to move the timeline for the assassination up another week."

"Where will the target be?"

"Harvard University." Peregrine said, "The VP is giving a talk to a delegation of Taiwanese and Chinese college students on exchange."

"You think it will work?" Umbra asked.

"Why not?" Peregrine answered. "The match you strike will be from a different venue, but the fire of World War III will still burn hot."

Chapter Sixty-Two

Paxton locked the heavy iron-plated door behind him with a firm twist of the wheel, sealing himself inside the large chamber. The room was dark except for the weak, gray light filtering through the skylight above. The sound of groaning metal and splintering wood echoed through the structure as the house continued its slow descent into the abyss.

At the center of the room was a small, white submarine.

He climbed into the cramped cockpit of the single-person Sports Sub. The vessel smelled faintly of oil and saltwater, and its interior was just large enough for him to maneuver. He pulled the hatch shut above him with a metallic clank and turned the locking wheel until it clicked.

Outside he heard the banging on the iron plated door, where Umbra appeared to be doing his best to break inside. The thought made Paxton smile. The man could do that all day and not get through that door.

The house shook some more, moving faster toward the bottom of the abyss. He thought to himself, that Umbra didn't have all day.

A moment later, everything went dark.

The skylight above vanished beneath the swirling water, the last vestiges of daylight swallowed whole. The eerie silence of the sinking house was replaced by the muffled roar of water flooding the chamber. Paxton took a deep breath, steadying his nerves. His fingers hovered over the controls before he flicked the switch.

The submarine was built in 1998, but it used simple technology and tended to work perfectly well forever. He'd bought it for a song from an oil company that had used it for geological research in the Caspian Sea, and then wanted to get rid of it, after discovering the machine wasn't rated for its depths.

The submarine hummed to life, the soft glow of its dashboard casting him in pale light. Indicators blinked green. He gripped the controls tightly, feeling the vibrations of the machine through his hands. Overhead, the skylight shattered with a deafening crack, and seawater poured in like a hungry beast.

The submarine rocked as the chamber filled, but Paxton remained focused. He toggled the thrusters, and the sub responded immediately, propelling him forward just as the weight of the water crushed through the remnants of the room.

Within seconds, he was clear of the sinking house, the water's turbulence giving way to the eerie stillness of open ocean. The submarine glided smoothly, its thrusters carving through the deep blue.

Paxton exhaled slowly, listening to his rapid heartbeat in his ears. His hands shook, his chest tightened with adrenaline. He checked the depth gauge and carefully adjusted his heading. Then he disappeared into the shadows of the sea, leaving the remnants of the house to vanish into the dark below.

He set a course northeast toward Astrakhan, Russia.

Chapter Sixty-Three

P hiladelphia, Pennsylvania – USA.

It felt good to be stateside again.

The Uber pulled away from the curb, leaving Paxton standing in front of a modest house in a quiet residential neighborhood in Philadelphia. The house was small but tidy, with pale blue siding that had seen a few seasons but wasn't peeling or faded. The lawn was patchy in spots but well-kept, bordered by a short, uneven picket fence that looked more decorative than functional. A weathered porch swing swayed slightly in the evening breeze, creaking faintly.

Paxton climbed the two concrete steps to the front door and gave a firm knock. Moments later, the door opened to reveal a blonde woman in her mid-thirties. She was attractive in a wholesome, understated way, her golden hair loosely pulled back into a simple ponytail. Her blue eyes were sharp but warm as they settled on him. Paxton immediately recognized her as Rowena Vandyke.

Rowena crossed her arms and leaned against the doorframe, studying him. "You're Cole's friend, aren't you?" she asked, her tone more curious than accusatory.

"Yes, ma'am," Paxton replied.

"What are you doing here?" she asked, curiosity in her voice, rather than any misgivings. If she was concerned about a big guy like Paxton turning up unannounced at her house, she wasn't showing it.

Before Paxton could answer, two young girls, identical twins with bouncing blonde curls and matching yellow t-shirts, came rushing up to the door. Their excitement was palpable as they peeked around their mother, trying to get a better look at the visitor.

"Mommy! Is it them?" one of the girls asked breathlessly.

"No, sweetie," Rowena said with a soft laugh, looking down at them. "Grandma and Grandpa aren't here yet. They're still on their way."

The girls' faces fell slightly but only for a moment before their boundless energy returned. They whispered to each other, giggling and occasionally glancing up at Paxton with shy, yet open curiosity. Rowena gave Paxton an apologetic smile as she ushered the girls back into the house.

"They're just excited. My parents are taking them for the night." She glanced over her shoulder before looking back at Paxton. "So, what can I do for you?"

"It's about Cole, actually."

Her eyes narrowed, and the blood drained from her face. "What about Cole?"

"In addition to the Navy's regular insurance package, Cole took out his own private life insurance because he wanted to make sure you and your girls were going to be okay."

One of the girls piped up with, "My dad was in the Navy."

Paxton squatted right down to his knees. He was still twice the girl's height and several times her size. "That's right. Your dad was in the Navy. He was a hero. The best man I have ever known."

The girl squealed. "That's my dad."

The second girl's voice took on a melancholy tone. "I wish I got to meet him."

Paxton nodded. "I'm sure he wished he got to meet you, too. I'll bet he would have been super proud of you both."

"You think?" the first girl asked.

"I know it," Paxton replied, picturing the way Cole spoke when he said he'd do anything in the world – including betray his best friend – for the opportunity to leave the Ghosts and spend the rest of his days with his wonderful girls. "I'm Paxton by the way. What are your names?"

"I'm Ruby," the first girl said. Then, looking at the second girl, she said, "And that's Lisa, but she doesn't talk much – especially to strangers."

"I do so talk!" Lisa said. "Besides, Paxton used to work with my daddy so he's not a stranger."

"Well, I'm pleased to meet you both," Paxton said, offering his hand to shake.

Lisa went up to him and with all the maturity she could muster, she shook his giant hand with infinite enthusiasm. "Nice to meet you Mr. Paxton." She then smiled, revealing a big gap in her teeth. "See, I do talk."

"I never doubted it," Paxton said with a smile.

Not to be outdone, Ruby then used two hands to shake his hand. "Pleased to meet you, Mr. Paxton."

"Look at these manners! True ladies, both of you." Paxton laughed. "It's okay. Just Paxton will do. And yes, it's really nice to meet you both."

Rowena said, "You want to come inside?"

"Sure." Paxton paused. "Only if I'm not intruding? I can come back if this is a bad time, and you need to get the girls ready for their grandparents."

"No, it's fine." She gestured him through to the kitchen and put on the kettle. Then, to the girls, she said, "You want me to put on Moana?"

Both girls seemed to cheer at the idea.

Rowena found it on Disney Plus and pressed play. She exchanged a quick glance at Paxton, and said, "They're going through a phase. We've watched it many times, but it will keep them entertained and we can talk in private."

"It's a good one, Moana," Paxton said. "I mean, if you're going to have to watch something on repeat that is."

"Yeah, it's not bad," Rowena agreed.

Paxton took in the house. It appeared well lived in, but livable. Probably not much worse, and not much better than most people who have kids. There were dishes in the sink, but they looked like they were there from today and not the past three weeks. He wondered how she seemed to get by so well on her own.

Rowena said, "Can I grab you a coffee?"

"Yes please," he said. "If you're going to have one?"

"Yeah, I'll join you." She gestured toward the couch. "Take a seat."

Paxton sat down, shifting a mixture of toys and laundry to make room. Rowena poured the pot of coffee and took a seat opposite Paxton. She folded her legs over one another and looked at him.

"So what's this all about, Paxton?"

"There's some money for you and your girls. It doesn't make up for Cole's death, but it will hopefully make things a little easier for you. Help pay for the girl's education. Maybe you'll get some help around the house. It would be just one less thing for you to worry about."

She stared at him. Her face unreadable, and then she broke out in a suppressed laugh. "Seriously?"

"Cole was crazy about you and wanted to make sure you were okay."

Rowena met his gaze. She pressed her lips together, and said, "I don't believe you."

Paxton smiled. "This isn't a scam. I don't want your bank details. I have a check for you from his private life insurance policy, and he always wanted me to deliver it personally if anything should happen to him. I'm sorry it's taken this long to deliver it, but I've been away for a very long time."

"For someone who works for some secret spy department at the CIA, NSA, FBI, NRO, or any of the other government three-digit acronyms with massive budgets and nobody speaks about..." she said. "You sure are a bad liar."

Paxton laughed and wondered how she would feel if she had any idea how close she was to the truth. "I'm not lying."

"Okay, you're not lying. Hand me my money and leave."

"Ma'am, I'm really sorry about Cole. I meant what I said before. He was the best man I've known and when he was dying all he said to me was that he wanted me to find you and make sure you and the girls were going to be okay." Paxton took a check from his pocket and handed it to her. "That's all I'm doing here. I'm sorry to have taken so much of your time, I'll leave now."

Rowena's expression softened. Her eyes clouded over. She took the check. Swallowed and said, "Five million dollars!"

Paxton stood up to leave. "I told you Cole wanted to make sure you were okay."

"Sit down, Paxton."

"It's okay," Paxton said. "You're angry. You feel like you've been lied to all this time, and you didn't need me to stir up a whole heap of unwanted emotions."

"No, it's not that." Rowena said, "I'm not mad at you. It's just... I don't know how I feel about everything."

Paxton said, "That's okay."

She looked at the check again. "Is this for real?"

Paxton met her gaze. "Yes."

"It's a lot of money."

"It is."

"Are there any sort of rules with what I do with it?"

Paxton seemed confused. "Rules?"

She looked at him. "Yeah, like some sort of clauses or stipulation about what the funds should be spent on?"

"No, he only said I should make sure Rowena gets it." Paxton shrugged. "It's your money. I'm sure he figured you knew a hell of a lot more than he did about what you and the kids need. Personally, I wouldn't spend it at the casino, but you're entirely welcome to if that's what you want."

Chuckling, she shook her head. It was the sort of money that would change her life.

Rowena drew a breath. "Thank you."

"You're welcome," Paxton replied, although he didn't see what he had particularly done to earn her appreciation.

Then, meeting his gaze, she said, "Do you mind telling me how Cole really died?"

Chapter Sixty-Four

Paxton said, "It was an IED in Afghanistan."

Rowena put her hand on his massive arm, she looked up at him, and there was a somber truth in her eyes. "I know he didn't die nearly six years ago by an Improvised Explosive Device."

Paxton opened his mouth to argue the point, but she stopped him.

"I know he wasn't dead a couple months ago. So just cut the crap and tell me the truth. He's dead now. I can hear it in your voice."

Perplexed, Paxton frowned.

For someone who was almost entirely emotionally inadequate, he was having a hard time lying to two women recently.

First Leyla.

Now Rowena.

Paxton's immediate instinct was to dissemble. Yet he couldn't. Call it honor or duty to his friend, but he decided to tell her the truth. "He was killed somewhere in the Kara Sea off the coast of Siberia, when a mission we were on went badly south."

"I know this wasn't five years ago. So when was it?"

"Two weeks ago."

She closed her eyes and exhaled.

When she opened them, she gave Paxton one of those winning smiles. The sort Paxton could imagine any man happily falling in love with in an instant. "Thank you for being honest to me. You're the first one."

"You're welcome." Paxton said, "How did you know?"

"I began sensing he was nearby recently. At first, I just assumed it was a nightmare or whatever... then I began seeing him everywhere. There would be long dry periods, and I would dismiss it, but then he would be back. I couldn't always see him, but I just felt his presence. Does that sound crazy?"

"No." Paxton suppressed a smile. "Besides, after time working in the field, he could smell pretty bad!"

She laughed and pushed his chest playfully with her hand. "Give it a break Paxton. I'm serious."

He laughed. "So was I."

"In the end, I convinced myself that there was a mix up. That Cole hadn't died. He didn't break my goddamned heart. He'd found something so important that he couldn't help but go do it. He was always so damned duty bound, that I imagined he was off fighting some sort of wrongs on all ends of the earth. Then I began to picture him coming back here to watch me. Because, somewhere, deep in that kind recess of his heart, despite all that duty, he had unconditional, passionate love for me."

Paxton nodded. "You have no idea how right you were."

"I know I'm right. I've always known. It was the only reason Cole would have left." She smiled, as tears streamed down here face. "I just wished this once, he'd forgotten his honor and his duty, and instead, chosen love. I wish he'd gotten the chance to meet his kids."

She stopped talking mid-sentence.

"What is it?" Paxton asked.

"Cole came back to check on me, didn't he?"

"Yes."

"He saw the kids."

"Yes."

Rowena said, "That's why everything changed. That's why he started visiting. Everything was different. The equation – his equation – changed. It was no longer about saving the world. He had children. Everything changes when you have kids. They are the most important thing in your world."

Paxton nodded. "Yes."

"Cole would have seen this. He wanted to come home and make it work somehow."

"That was his plan."

"Why didn't he?"

Paxton frowned, but didn't say anything.

Rowena covered her mouth with her hand. "He tried, didn't he?"

"Yes. The department we worked for didn't really have a retirement plan. We were Ghosts. Our true lives and all those we knew beforehand were gone. If we quit, it became a security problem for everyone."

"What happened?"

"Cole made a deal with the director of the organization, a man named Dr. Alan Kepler. Thanks to the pact he made, he was granted approval to quit the program and come home to you."

"What did he have to do?"

"Betray me."

"Seriously?" Rowena's eyes looked horrified.

"It's okay." Paxton shrugged. "Like you said, priorities change when you have a family. I get that."

"You do? Do you have children?"

"No. The team I worked with, including Cole?" He cleared his throat, which suddenly felt tight. "Well, the Ghosts were my family."

"Oh." Rowena tilted her head, not sure what to make of that. "If Cole had the approval to come home to us, then why isn't he here?"

"Because the mission went wrong and Kepler, along with the treacherous people he works with, decided my team knew too much. All of us, all the Ghosts, needed to be silenced."

"Is that a euphemism for killed?"

"It is."

"Oh. My. God." Her eyes widened with shock. "I'm so sorry."

Paxton nodded but said nothing.

"So now what?" she asked.

Paxton shrugged. "Now, I'm going to go back to Kepler, and some of the other powerful men we worked with. Then I'm going to show them where *my* priorities lie when someone kills *my* family."

Chapter Sixty-Five

Paxton watched as Rowena hugged her kids and put them in her parent's car. They waited until the car was gone.

"I should go," he said.

"No, please don't," Rowena replied.

"It's okay. I'm sure you've got plans for your child-free evening. I'll leave you to it."

"I really don't. Have plans, I mean. I'm fortunate my parents are retired and they live only two blocks from here. My girls love them, and they love the girls. It's a win/win situation for everyone involved. And sometimes..." she drew a breath. "Sometimes I just want to eat junk food and watch what I want to watch, and not have to worry about someone fighting in the background."

"Okay, so should I leave you to that?"

"No." She shook her head. "Let's go to dinner."

"All right."

"Yeah?" She smiled, and Paxton could see just how easy it had been for Cole to fall in love with her. "Just like that, you'll come have dinner with me?"

"Of course."

Ten minutes later, they drove out, using her car. They ate a relaxed dinner at a simple low-key Thai restaurant.

They chatted about Cole and about life in general. They each told anecdotes and laughed. Then they talked about life in the SEALs. About chasing dreams that were always just out of one's grasp. Paxton told her the story about Cole teaching him to swim during the original assessment phase of the SEAL application process. She laughed at the thought of someone like Paxton applying for the SEALs without first learning to swim.

Paxton decided he liked the way she laughed. It was a nice, genuine laugh. Throaty and unguarded. It was one of those sounds he could easily get used to hearing.

They finished dinner and she drove them back to her house. Parking the car out in front of the house, she switched off the ignition and looked his way.

He said, "I should go."

"Where are you going?" she asked, not making a move to get out of the car.

"I'll get a motel or something for the night before I head home tomorrow."

"Don't be ridiculous. You can sleep here."

"That's okay," Paxton said. "It wouldn't feel right."

Her eyes narrowed. "What are you, a guilty teenager? How old are you, thirty-five?"

"Forty," Paxton corrected her.

"And you're worried about sleepovers?"

"No."

"Then what?" she asked. "Is it because I was Cole's girl?"

"No. I'm concerned because I can see how easily it must have been for Cole to fall for you."

She pulled a strand of hair behind her ear, looked at him slowly as though really seeing him the first time today. A grin spread across her parted lips, the tip of her tongue just touching the spacing between her white teeth, teasing him.

"Would that be so bad?"

"Yes," he replied, a little too emphatically. "I'm sorry, I didn't mean it the way you may have taken it. It's just... trust me. I come with a certain level of baggage that surpasses most people."

"You mean, because you kill people for a living?"

"Well, yes... that's one of my issues." He regarded her, a smile in his eyes. "And to be honest, it was kind of a deal breaker for the last girl I really liked."

Her fingers found his arms, then made their way along his forearm down to his hand. "What else have you got?"

"I am missing the part of my brain that regulates emotions, morals, and ethics."

"Really?"

"Yeah."

"It's funny. I feel like I can trust you, and quite frankly, I'm a good judge of character." She said, "Am I wrong?"

"No."

"So how does that work?"

"Well, you know how you have that inner voice, or that sort of gut instinct to tell you right from wrong?"

"Sure."

"Mine lies to me. In fact, my brain simply can't make sense of emotions."

"Nobody's brain can. We're all just a bunch of blithering messes."

"Sure, but in my case, I have an anatomical fault in my brain that guarantees my ineptness."

"Wow! I don't think I've ever had a boy make such perfect sense to me before. Normally they just act stupid."

Paxton chuckled. "I can do that too."

She said, "Yet, we've chatting all night and you seem to get me more than any other man I've talked to in a really long time. It's actually just been really nice having dinner with you."

"Look. When I was four years old, I beat a kid nearly to death." Paxton spread his hands apologetically. "He was a bully and was going to probably kill me if I didn't act first. Not that I'm making excuses. I'm purely okay with my decision to inflict damage on him before he got to me."

"Why are you telling me this?"

"The neurologist who saw me discovered I was missing the part of my brain that regulated emotions, morals, and ethics. That's what he told me, at any rate. He taught me to ignore that inner voice, and then set about teaching me a sort of code – a way to govern rights from wrongs. Consequently, I make decisions based more on logic than emotions, but that doesn't mean I don't have emotions running wild inside me."

"That neurologist saved your life."

"Yes."

"He saw your potential and helped you become a better person. Yet at the end of the day, it sounds like you made a choice to become the man you are."

"Maybe. Then again, maybe not."

"What does that mean?"

"Dr. Alan Kepler was that neurologist, and I was a four-year-old orphan. You know the guy who decided my team had to be eliminated? What I didn't mention was that he worked for DARPA – the Defense Advanced Research Projects Agency, and he investigated me, because of my unique neurological anomaly."

"Why?"

"Because he wanted to see if I could be directed to learn to fight, and instructed in such a way that I would grow up and want to serve my country."

"What are you saying?"

Paxton shrugged. "Before I was even old enough to go to school, Dr. Kepler chose me for an experiment. He wanted to experiment. To study me. To discover if someone with my neurological deficits could be guided into becoming the best possible CIA Ghost, that is, a government sanctioned killer."

"That's a terrible story, Paxton."

"Yeah. We go through life thinking we have it all set. We're in control. We make the choices, the decisions to be who we want to be and become what we want. But in my life, I was born, dropped off at a local orphanage at birth, and when I was four, someone decided they want me to become a killer. Their very own perfect weapon."

"That's only part of the story, Paxton."

"You think?"

"Yes."

"What's the rest of the story?"

Rowena leaned in close to him. "I've always believed that your life can be whatever you make it."

Paxton shook his head. "And what if I don't know what I want to be?"

"Then that makes you human. Most people have no idea. They just bumble along, trying to get by on a day-to-day basis." She smiled at him. "What do you like doing?"

He thought about it for a minute. "I enjoy helping people. Some of that comes from the programing I had to serve my country, but it's more than that. I know what it's like to help someone in need. It's a good feeling."

"That's great. So maybe you'll become a paramedic or something."

Paxton doubted that very much. In fact, he had never been a fan of blood in general. But instead, he said, "Maybe."

She unclipped her seatbelt and got out of the car. "Stay with me tonight."

Paxton said, "I shouldn't."

Rowena leaned in and kissed him on the lips. "Yes, Paxton you should. I haven't been Cole's girl for nearly six years. We loved each other, but we never managed to make it work, and that's okay. I'm not asking you to marry me. I'm just saying you should stay the night with me tonight."

He told her he probably shouldn't...

... and then he followed her inside.

Chapter Sixty-Six

Paxton stirred slowly.

The faint light of dawn was filtering through the heavy curtains. He felt the warmth of Rowena's lithe body wrapped languidly around his, her head resting on his chest. Her arm was casually draped across him and her leg hooked over his thigh. Her skin was smooth against his own, and he was happy to listen to her steady, rhythmic breathing all morning.

For a long moment, he lay still, savoring the quiet intimacy.

She was just shy of six foot tall, but compared to him, she felt small. As he shifted slightly, Rowena murmured softly, her body instinctively curling closer to his. As she stirred, her long, toned limbs stretched against him in a slow, feline motion. A sleepy smile touched her lips, and her eyes fluttered open, catching his in the dim light.

"Hello," she whispered, and he kissed her.

"Good morning," he replied, his voice low.

He brushed a strand of her blonde hair away from her face, marveling at how stunning she looked, even in the first light of the day.

He kissed her again, briefly. It was supposed to be a gentle, affectionate kiss, but she opened her mouth, and the kiss quickly became enamored. They lay together for a while, half asleep, kissing now and again.

She traced her hand in lazy circles on his muscular chest.

Then, without saying a word, she draped her legs across his hips, and they began to make love again languorously.

Paxton smiled as he gazed up at her.

She stared back at him, her blue eyes alive and animated, her wide mouth sensual. They gently kissed, reveling in each other's pleasure.

Afterward, they clung together in each other's arms for a few minutes, before Paxton got up and had a shower.

When he got out, Rowena propped herself up on one elbow, a playful glint in her eye as she watched Paxton emerge from the bathroom, a towel slung low on his hips.

"You know what we need?" she said, her voice light and teasing.

He raised an eyebrow, curious. "Enlighten me."

"Pancakes. Blueberry pancakes," she said with a grin, sitting up and swinging her legs over the side of the bed. Her lithe movements were as effortless as they were graceful. "Come on. Let's make some."

Paxton chuckled, shaking his head but unable to resist the infectious energy she brought into even the simplest moments. "Blueberry pancakes, huh? All right. Lead the way."

Moments later, they were in the kitchen, the cool tile underfoot a stark contrast to the warmth of the morning sun streaming through the windows. Rowena had already pulled her hair into a loose knot, an apron tied around her waist. She rummaged through the cupboards with casual confidence, pulling out a mixing bowl, flour, and sugar.

Paxton leaned against the counter, watching her with a faint smile as she worked. "You've done this before," he observed.

"Don't sound so surprised," she shot back with a smirk, tossing him a bag of blueberries. "Start rinsing these."

He caught it easily, turning to the sink. The sound of running water filled the kitchen as he washed the berries, glancing over his shoulder occasionally to see Rowena cracking eggs and whisking them into a frothy mixture. There was something oddly soothing about the simplicity of the task, a rare pocket of normalcy in his otherwise unpredictable life.

"All right, flour's in," Rowena announced. "Now for the milk." She handed him the whisk, her fingers brushing his briefly. "Your turn."

Paxton took over, mixing the batter with smooth, deliberate strokes. He could feel her eyes on him, her amusement unspoken but palpable. "What?" he asked, glancing at her sideways.

"Nothing," she said with a laugh, her voice light. "You just don't strike me as the pancake-making type."

"Everyone's a pancake type. We all have hidden talents," he said with mock seriousness, making her laugh even harder.

Together, they folded in the blueberries and ladled the batter onto a hot skillet. The aroma of sizzling pancakes soon filled the kitchen, mingling with their laughter as they teased each other about who was the best pancake flipper.

When the first batch was done, Rowena popped a bite into her mouth, sighing dramatically. "Perfect," she declared, handing Paxton a forkful.

He tasted it, nodding in agreement. "Not bad. I guess you're not the only one with pancake skills."

"What are your plans?" she asked between mouthfuls.

"Today or in life in general?" he asked, cautiously.

"Just today."

"I have to go to Washington, D.C. and start devising and strategizing. I need to work out how I'm going to make all of this right."

"With revenge?" she asked

He shook his head. "I'm calling it justice."

"Is that what you do?" Rowena asked, seriously. "You're like little kids. You just go around murdering each other until justice is served?"

Paxton thought about that. He wanted to say he was better than that, he was very good at the killing part, but it didn't seem appropriate.

Instead, he said, "The Vice President was involved in this. He's the one responsible for Cole's death."

Incredulous and shocked, her mouth dropped. "You're going to attempt to kill the VP?"

"No." Paxton shrugged. "Not yet anyway."

"Oh? Why not?" She met his gaze with a mixture of wonder and defiance.

Paxton said, "Someone's going to try and assassinate the VP when he visits Estonia in two weeks' time. If they're successful, it will lead to a chain reaction of events. The dominos falling will be like what happened in World War I after Archduke Franz Ferdinand of Austria was shot. The superpowers of the world, including Russia, China, and us, will struggle to prevent an escalation into World War III…"

Her face lost a bit of color. "This isn't a joke, is it?"

"No."

"This is the sort of work Cole was involved in. This was what he thought was so important. I guess it is important."

"Yeah, well, now you can kind of see why my mind is sometimes elsewhere. I don't have long to work out how I can stop this. Even just the logistical efforts of moving weaponry into Estonia and recruiting other professionals to help…"

"Wait, did you say this assassination was going to take place in Estonia?"

"Yeah."

"But the VP's not going to Estonia!"

"Yes, he is. In two weeks."

"He's not." Rowena said. "Not anymore."

"What are you talking about?" Paxton asked. "I've seen the plans for his assassination. It's meant to drag Europe and Nato into war with Russia and China."

"The VP has altered his itinerary," Rowena said, "What his new plans are, I haven't a clue, but his trip to Estonia was canceled two days ago."

Paxton swore. "This changes everything."

"Does this mean we have a reprieve from World War III?"

"I doubt it." Paxton shook his head. "The men who are pulling the strings will be looking for another opportunity."

"What does that look like?"

"All I know is that the VP must be at a very public event. The people there will have to be connected to certain countries, so that an assassination of the VP will result in finger pointing. It could cause the spark that leads to global war." Paxton said, "Do you have any idea what the VP's schedule is for the next few weeks?"

"Yeah, sure… because I keep it on my calendar…"

"You do?"

"Sarcasm, Paxton. That was a joke." She grabbed her phone and typed in the VP's public events into Google. "Here I've got it." She started reading his itinerary out one by one. A state dinner, a meeting with the PM of Australia, and a billionaire from Saudi having a Q & A on green energy of the future…"

"I don't see any of those events triggering World War III," Paxton said. "Anything else?"

"On Friday, the Vice President is scheduled to give a talk at his alma mater, the University of Notre Dame, to a group of Taiwanese and Chinese Foreign Exchange students."

Paxton said, "That's it!"

Rowena pursed her lips. "I think you're right. If the VP gets killed by a bomb, there's going to be massive collateral damage. Both the Taiwanese and the Chinese will feel attacked. It would be very easy to imagine how this could… er, blow up, so to speak."

Paxton abruptly pushed to his feet. "I have to go."

She asked, "Where?"

"To Washington, D.C. to work out how I'm going to save my enemy's life, prevent World War III, and to find out how far nearly half a billion dollars goes toward getting revenge against some of the most powerful people on earth."

"Okay, good idea," Rowena said, a mischievous wry grin on her parted lips. "I have to pick my kids up today anyway."

Paxton took a step back and kissed her on the lips.

When she pulled back, Paxton said, "Thanks. I had a really good time with you."

She smiled. "Yeah, me too."

Chapter Sixty-Seven

Washington, D.C. – **Thursday**

Marcus Voss felt nervous. He and the rest of the group had been summoned to meet the VP. One more day and the man would be dead. The very first life would be sacrificed to the cause, and the US would be slowly, inextricably, pulled into World War III.

When that happened, its people would look for someone powerful to guide them.

That someone would be Voss. Smiling at the thought, Voss accelerated his Bentley Bentayga EWB Mulliner. God, he loved this car.

Like him, it was rich, powerful, and in complete control on the road. It exuded luxury and supremacy as it prowled through the streets of Washington, D.C. The extended wheelbase SUV was painted in a deep Midnight Sapphire, its shimmering metallic finish catching the dim glow of streetlights. Chrome accents adorned its sleek contours, and its imposing grille was crowned with the iconic "Flying B" emblem.

Inside, the cabin was an oasis of opulence, featuring diamond-quilted leather seats in a creamy linen shade, a polished walnut dashboard, and ambient lighting that bathed the interior in a soothing glow. The car's cutting-edge infotainment system, complete with voice-activated controls, complemented its whisper-quiet cabin, a result of triple-glazed windows and meticulous sound proofing.

Sadly, despite the serene environment, Voss was anything but calm. His knuckles were white as they gripped the hand-stitched leather steering wheel. The Vice President's sudden summons had left him uneasy, and his phone call with Dr. Alan Kepler only heightened his anxiety.

"Keep it together for one more day," Kepler had said, his tone clipped. "We can't afford to ignore him now."

"What am I supposed to say to him?"

"Nothing." Kepler laughed. "Besides, at least you're not the one responsible for Paxton getting away."

"No, that was Vaughn's fault."

"Yes, but Hawthorne will blame me for it."

"Hell, I blame you for it, too."

"Don't worry about it. Vaughn is here now, and he has the dirty bomb. Everything is set for tomorrow... so don't stress. Everything will work out fine, Mr. President."

Mr. President...

Voss liked the way that sounded.

"Just keep your eyes on the ball and we'll win this game," Kepler added.

"All right," Voss said. "I'll see you there in half an hour. I'm on my way."

Kepler ended the call from his end without saying another word. When the call disconnected, Voss barely had a chance to take a steadying breath before the car phone chimed again.

He accepted the call, his voice sharp. "What?"

"Marcus Voss," came a low, calm voice. "I know the truth about you, Kepler, and the Vice President."

Voss stiffened, his heartbeat thundering in his ears. "Who is this?"

"Paxton West," the voice replied. "But you can call me Rembrandt. I don't care about you – yet. But I do care about Dylan Frost. Who is he?"

Voss hesitated. "You're wasting your time. I don't know who you think you are..."

"Don't lie to me," Paxton interrupted. His tone was mild, but the threat was unmistakable.

They sparred verbally for a few moments before Voss's temper frayed. "Get stuffed," he barked, slamming his hand on the steering wheel.

The Bentayga jolted sharply to the left, scraping the metal guardrail lining the road. Voss swore, fighting to correct the wheel, but the SUV didn't respond. Instead, it veered once more, the screech of tearing metal filling the cabin as the side of the vehicle slammed into the rail again.

"What the hell?" Voss shouted, panic rising.

"I told you not to lie," Paxton said, his voice chillingly even. "Now, you're going to listen."

"I'll talk!" Voss yelled, his breath ragged. "I'll give you Frost's details – just stop!"

The car straightened out briefly, and Voss's lungs heaved in relief. "It's..." Voss gave a name and a location, rattling the details off in desperation.

There was silence on the other end of the line, except for the faint tapping of keys. Then Paxton spoke again. "You lied to me, Marcus. I told you there would be consequences."

"No! I..."

The Bentayga surged forward, accelerating without Voss's input. It barreled down the road, ignoring his frantic attempts to brake or steer. Ahead, a bridge loomed, its span arching over the dark waters of the Potomac River.

"No! Please! No!" Voss screamed as the car swerved violently, crashing through the guardrail and sailing into the void. Time seemed to slow as the Bentayga twisted in midair, its headlights slicing through the darkness, before plunging into the icy depths of the river below.

Chapter Sixty-Eight

The icy waters of the Potomac rushed into the Bentley.

Marcus Voss's panic escalated to sheer terror. The water rose quickly, swirling around his ankles, then his knees. He reached for the driver's door handle, yanking on it desperately, but the locks had clicked into place – controlled remotely.

"No, no, no!" Voss shouted, his voice shaking as he scrambled for the controls. He pressed the button for the driver's window, and it began to lower. For a brief, hopeful moment, the air rushed with cold outside as the water level stabilized. Then the window halted – five or six inches down – and to his horror, it reversed course, sliding back up.

"Come on!" he yelled, slamming his fists against the controls.

The water crept higher, the window opposite him on the passenger side began to descend on its own.

Voss's heart leaped.

He unclipped his seatbelt in one frantic motion, his fingers fumbling in his desperation. Sloshing through the freezing water now up to his waist, he lunged toward the opening, shoving aside debris as he clambered across the seats.

But just as he reached the passenger side, the window slid shut with an audible click. He pounded on the glass, screaming, but the dark water outside muffled the sound. The Bentley, its pristine interior now a chaotic mix of rising water and floating debris, sank further into the depths.

The dashboard's touchscreen flickered to life, bathing the cabin in an eerie glow.

For a moment, it displayed the Bentley's logo, pristine and sharp, before the screen switched to a live video feed. Voss froze, his breath hitching. A man's face appeared: Calm, composed, and unmistakable.

Voss recognized the man from a CIA photograph.

Paxton West.

"Now, Marcus Voss," Paxton said, his voice amplified through the car's surround sound system. It was smooth, almost conversational, as though they were meeting for coffee rather than communicating into a sinking vehicle. "Do I have your attention?"

Chapter Sixty-Nine

Voss's entire world had been taken from him in a matter of seconds. "Okay Paxton, you win." He said, trying not to let the fear he felt show in his voice. "I'll give you anything you want if you get me out of this!"

"Good answer," Paxton said...

Voss said, "What do you want?"

Paxton tilted his head slightly, his expression unreadable. "I want the truth, Marcus. And I want to know how far you're willing to go to save yourself."

The water reached Voss's shoulders. His teeth chattered, and his mind frantically battled with what he should say. He banged his hands against the dashboard, his raw fear and desperation transforming into fury. "I'll give you what you want, damn it! Just let me out!"

Paxton leaned closer to the camera, his eyes narrowing. "You've already lied once, Marcus. Let's hope that this time, you're smarter."

The car plunged deeper, the screen dimmed slightly, but Paxton's image remained clear. Voss had never felt more powerless.

"Yes, I'll give it to you..."

Paxton said, "Good. I want you to think really hard. Are you thinking hard?" he asked. "Yes!"

"Good. Now tell me the names, and the details of everyone involved in assassinating the VP. I also want to know how it's going to happen."

"Yes, I'll give it to... for God's sake just get me out of here!"

Paxton said, "All right. Just do everything exactly as I..."

The electricals in the car shorted as water flooded the vehicle's interior... Voss hysterically stared at the video display. It was totally black.

He slammed it with his hand. "Work damn you!"

The Bentley sank deeper into the frigid blackness of the Potomac, its once-vibrant interior was reduced to a murky, claustrophobic tomb. The luxurious features that had once been Marcus Voss's pride now seemed to mock him – silent, useless, and utterly inescapable. The water pressed in from every side, and the cabin was almost completely submerged. The last remnants of air bubbled up from his mouth and nostrils, mingling with the cold flood.

The car's electrics gave a final, sputtering death throe.

The dashboard screen flickered, then went dark. The once-bright lights of the cabin extinguished, leaving Voss in complete darkness. Panic clawed at his mind as he banged uselessly against the doors, his fists scraping on the cold, unyielding surfaces. He pushed on the windows, his chest heaving as he tried to keep the last gasp of air in his lungs.

Then his car struck the bottom of the river. Voss found himself sliding forward into the dash, like one would in a head-on car crash.

The crushing weight of the water bore down on him.

His ears popped painfully as the pressure increased. His thoughts became sluggish as oxygen deprivation took hold. His body moved on autopilot, clawing at the unyielding door one last time before his strength began to fail.

Then, from the corner of his vision, a light appeared. It was bright, otherworldly, and disorienting. His oxygen-starved brain struggled to process it.

Was this real?

A hallucination?

A cruel trick of his dying mind?

The light grew stronger, cutting through the murky water with an almost ethereal clarity. Voss felt himself slipping away, his mind and body succumbing to the cold and the lack of air. He barely registered the sudden jolt as the door was forced open.

Strong hands grabbed him, yanking him free from the sinking car. A dark figure loomed before him, silhouetted against the light. The figure shoved something into his face, and Voss instinctively opened his mouth, feeling the rubber of a SCUBA regulator pressed between his lips. Fresh, life-giving oxygen flooded into his lungs, burning as it met his deprived body.

He coughed violently, sucking in deep, desperate breaths.

And a moment later, he drifted into peaceful unconsciousness...

Chapter Seventy

Cabin John Aqueduct System, Washington, D.C.

Paxton hauled Marcus Voss through the narrow underwater entrance, his SCUBA tank scraping against the rough stone. The tunnel was part of an abandoned section of Washington, D.C.'s Cabin John Aqueduct System, a relic of the city's 19th-century infrastructure. Originally built to carry water from the Potomac River to the city, it had long since been decommissioned and forgotten, its purpose superseded by modern plumbing and electrical systems. Hidden beneath decades of urban development, its crumbling masonry now served as a ghostly, damp labyrinth.

One of its many entrances, was straight up from the Potomac.

The narrow passage opened into a larger chamber, lit by the soft, flickering glow of battery-powered LED lamps Paxton had placed there earlier. The air was cool and damp, carrying the faint metallic tang of rust and algae. A trickle of water dripped continuously from the vaulted ceiling, pooling in shallow depressions along the uneven stone floor.

In the center of the chamber, a single metal chair sat bolted to the ground, the remains of some long-forgotten maintenance crew. It was rusted, its paint peeling in jagged strips, but sturdy enough to hold Marcus Voss, who was slumped over, still coughing up water.

Paxton dropped his gear bag onto the floor with a thud and pulled off his SCUBA mask. He shook out his damp hair, his movements precise and efficient. His laptop was already set up on a folding table nearby, its screen glowing faintly in the dim space. Paxton moved toward it, opening it with a practiced flick. The device hummed softly, a beacon of modernity in the otherwise archaic surroundings.

Voss groaned, his breaths wheezing as he struggled to sit upright.

Paxton glanced at him, his expression cold and analytical. He let the man recover for a moment, deliberately taking his time as he tapped on the keyboard, bringing up files and live feeds.

"Welcome back to the land of the living," Paxton said, his tone flat, almost bored. "Or, more accurately, the land of the barely breathing. You should thank me. If it weren't for me, you'd still be part of the Potomac's scenery."

Voss's head snapped up, his face pale and slick with water. His eyes darted around the chamber, taking in the grim surroundings before settling on Paxton. "What... what is this place?" he croaked.

"Does it matter?" Paxton replied, his fingers never pausing on the keys. "You're here because I need information, and you're going to give it to me."

Marcus shook his head. "You're right. I'll give you anything you want. Thank you for getting me out of there."

"You're welcome." Paxton shot him a humorless smile. "Happy to help."

He stepped closer, his presence looming over Voss. "Now, you and I both know that you've lied to me once. Let me assure you, I'm not feeling generous enough to let it happen again. And with the assassination happening tomorrow, I just don't have time to keep checking up on your answers. Do you understand that?"

"Yes."

"Good. Because one mistake from you, I'll put you back in that car and move on to the next person on Boris's list. Do you understand?"

Voss glared at him, his chest heaving as he fought to maintain a shred of defiance. But the out-of-control terror of having his car taken over, then the trauma of his car crashing into the river, followed by nearly drowning, defeated him. He was trembling from adrenaline, or the cold, damp air and darkness of this place. To top it all off, Paxton's unrelenting stare seemed to sap his strength.

"I understand." He slumped back in the chair. His head lowering in defeat, Voss gave up.

"Good." Paxton leaned in, his voice dropping to a low, dangerous whisper. "Now, let us begin."

Chapter Seventy-One

P axton was amazed by Marcus Voss' transformation.

The once arrogant, self-centered billionaire had crumbled, shifting from smug and tight-lipped to eagerly divulging every sordid detail. Voss outlined the entire assassination plot, sparing no detail. He went from the precise location of the attack to the carefully orchestrated plans drawn up by Vaughn (better known as Umbra) who would carry out the killing.

He didn't stop there.

Voss laid bare everything Paxton wanted to know about Dylan Frost – his identity, where he lived, where he worked, and how to reach him. So much for any semblance of loyalty among immoral conspirators.

Honor among thieves was dead.

Voss even went as far as exposing the blackmail material the Republican Party held over Vice President Hawthorne.

Apparently, Hawthorne had a long history of inappropriate relationships with women who passed through his office at One Observatory Circle. As if that weren't scandalous enough, Voss revealed an even darker truth: Hawthorne liked to take his anger out on them, in the form of cruelty and brutality.

Paxton frowned, then a curious expression came across his face. "The VP enjoys beating women?"

"Yes. It's his only vice. He appreciates whiskey, but not to excess. He's not a gambler. He believes in his country and genuinely thinks he can make it better. Hell, I still believe he could have, if he'd been given a chance – but that's impossible now. You must understand, sometimes the stress of his job becomes too great for him. Like everyone else, he needs an outlet. Some turn to gambling, drugs, or alcohol. The VP likes to have affairs and hurt women."

"Why?"

"Why does anyone submit to their own vices?"

Paxton remained mystified. "I've worked pretty hard at this," he said, shaking his head. "But I don't think I'll ever understand people."

"Hey, don't you get on your damned high horse, Paxton, AKA Rembrandt. I've seen your record. You are the best assassin the CIA has ever produced. You can say you do it for your country, and for that service, we all thank you. Still, the fact is, you're just as guilty as the rest of us, only your vice is hunting people down and killing them."

Paxton thought about that.

It was a good line of thinking.

In many ways, it made sense.

Then he dismissed it.

"No," he said, certain of the fact. "I don't enjoy killing, I just happen to be good at it. But it doesn't give me pleasure and I don't miss it if I go without. I'm not addicted to hunting and eliminating enemies of the state. Murder doesn't ease my pain if I'm stressed. I simply kill because I'm ordered to, and it's what must be done."

Voss looked horrified. "You really are a psychopath, aren't you?"

Paxton nodded, a boyish grin on his lips. "Now, that's the first time you've spoken the absolute truth."

Voss's eyes darted toward the edge of the tunnel.

Quick as a cat faced with a dog, he jumped up, turned to run.

Paxton punched him hard in the head. It was a gentle hit but it carried the weight and momentum of Paxton's powerful right arm.

Voss was knocked out cold.

Paxton checked his watch. It was nearly 3 p.m., time to go. He had a lot of work to do, and he needed to get a move on.

Chapter Seventy-Two

Asleep, Voss was having a dream.

It was an incredibly bad one. A horrific nightmare.

He had been captured by that psychopath named Paxton West. Dr. Alan Kepler's pet project. The brain-damaged freak, who didn't have any emotions, and Kepler thought it was a good idea to make into a deadly assassin. The very tip of the spear used by the CIA to keep the world safe.

Some fucking world, hey?

Only now, Paxton had him. The crazed giant was going to kill him, that was certain. Adrenaline pumping, with a split-second decision, Voss got up and began running. Only, like all nightmares, he simply couldn't seem to run fast enough to escape the killer that was hunting him.

His arms and legs seemed to move in slow motion.

There was a burn in his chest, as his lungs worked hard to bring in enough air to provide oxygen to his overburdened muscles. His heart hammering in his chest, trying to pump blood to those muscles.

His breathing was hard.

It was like there just wasn't enough air to breathe. He tried to scream, but nothing would come out. Almost as though he were drowning.

Suddenly, Voss' eyes opened wide in abject terror.

He was back inside the Bentley.

Fully submerged in water.

His eyes searched frantically for the door latch. Somewhere, in the back of his primitive, lizard-brain, he recalled that a fully flooded car would have equal pressure inside and out. This would make it easy to open the doors.

Voss fumbled with the door handle.

Nothing happened.

He struggled to open the other one.

Frantically, he swam to the back and tried the other two doors.

Nothing.

He pressed the door unlock buttons, but the electronics no longer worked.

Then, he looked out the window.

Paxton West stared back at him. The psychopath had SCUBA gear, and a creepy grin full of interest, amusement, and curiosity. He spread his hands outward in an apologetic gesture, as if he would have liked to help.

Paxton held up a dive slate and a flashlight so Voss could see what was written on it.

Voss read the words: *Sorry. The doors are locked. I was never going to let you live. Here's the news: Defense CEO dies, trapped inside his vehicle after crashing into the Potomac.*

Still smiling, Paxton exaggeratedly waved bye bye...

Leaving Marcus Voss in complete darkness, to scream in absolute silence...

Chapter
Seventy-Three

Number One Observatory Circle, Washington, D.C.

"Has anyone heard from Marcus?" Vice President Hawthorne asked.

Dr. Kepler shook his head. "I spoke to him this morning. He said he was going to be here."

"I spoke to him yesterday," Dylan said. "He seemed spooked by the idea that Paxton might still be alive. If I know him, he's probably hiding somewhere, waiting for the three of us to make sure this threat blows over."

Back straight, shoulders back, Hawthorne growled, "When I ask for a meeting, it's not a request."

Kepler and Frost both nodded in understanding, like two grade schoolboys at a private institution.

The VP said, "All right, did you bring the man's file?"

Dr. Kepler nodded, handing him a dossier. "It's all there."

Hawthorne took it and began reading the high points out loud, "Orphaned at two, Paxton displayed many levels of physical and mental exceptionalism at an early age, yet equally disturbing traits of nihilism, opportunism, and psychopathy." Hawthorne frowned at Dr. Kepler. "What happened to his parents?"

"We don't know, sir. He was found by the staff at Washington Hospital."

"It says here that the CIA knows who his parents were, but that their lives have been entirely redacted. Why?"

"I don't know," Kepler said. "That happened before my time."

"And you didn't think to find this out?" Hawthorne was shocked. "Does this happen often?"

"No," Dylan said. "But sometimes operatives have babies."

Hawthorne frowned. "What?"

"CIA operatives, Ghosts, spies. They're like most people, Paxton West excluded. They make mistakes. They fall in love. They get drunk and sleep with someone. Babies are made. The last thing they want if they're in the middle of an assignment is to raise a baby. There's even a name for it – Phantom Protocol."

"This happens often enough that there's a name for it?" Hawthorne asked.

Dylan shrugged. "I guess so."

Hawthorne said, "So Paxton West might have two equally psychopathic parents out there helping him?"

"I doubt it." Dr. Kepler said, "Listen. We're getting sidetracked. It doesn't matter if Paxton parents are alive or not. They don't know anything about him. He was orphaned at 2 years of age and that's the end of it. What does matter is the man that he became. Read on."

Vice President Hawthorne leaned back in the leather chair of his study, the soft glow of the desk lamp casting a warm light on the thick dossier spread out before him. He adjusted his glasses and flipped through the pages, scanning each line with a growing sense of intrigue.

Paxton West's file was exhaustive, the kind of deep-dive dossier that only the CIA could assemble. It included everything from his academic performance in high school – 4.0 GPA, captain of the debate team, top scores in AP courses – to his time at Georgetown University, where he'd double-majored in Ancient History and Linguistics. Hawthorne skimmed over the glowing professor recommendations, noting phrases like "exceptionally gifted," "unparalleled analytical skills," and "a once-in-a-generation mind."

"He graduated summa cum laude," Hawthorne muttered, turning the page. "Full Navy sponsorship. And look at this – fluent in six languages, two of them dead." He pressed his lips together and his brow furrowed with a mix of confusion and amazement. "This guy's a genius!" Hawthorne smiled. "Why isn't he building rockets for us or something?"

Dr. Kepler, seated across the room, didn't bother to look up from his tablet. He scrolled through his own files with calm precision, his voice steady as he replied, "Because there are dozens of genius rocket builders in the world," Kepler said, setting the tablet down. He folded his hands and leaned forward, meeting Hawthorne's gaze with a sharp look. "But there's only one top-notch assassin like Paxton."

Hawthorne blinked, his smile fading. He glanced back at the dossier, now viewing the file in an entirely different light. The glowing academic record, the Navy training, the pristine behavioral reviews—all of it seemed to take on a darker edge.

"And that's what we need him for," Kepler added, his voice lowering. "Because when the problem isn't physics or engineering, but people – dangerous, complicated people – you don't call in a rocket scientist. You call in a Paxton West."

"What are his weaknesses?" Hawthorne asked.

Dr. Kepler said, "Paxton is missing parts of his Ventromedial Prefrontal Cortex."

"What does that mean?" Hawthorne asked.

Dr. Kepler said, "He has no way to regulate or make sense of emotions, morals, or ethics."

"He must have some way of governing them, otherwise he'd be in prison or most likely dead, right?"

"Exactly." Dr. Kepler said, "He's been trained to ignore his gut instinct and instead, be guided by a series of moral codes, which we've instilled in him since childhood."

Hawthorne swore and slammed his fist on the desk, his face twisting with frustration. "You've created the ultimate weapon – a man who is to modern warfare and assassination what Leonardo da Vinci was to the Renaissance. And now he's coming for me?"

"He won't get anywhere near you, sir," Dr. Kepler said. "Not now that that we've canceled your trip to Estonia. It would be impossible to believe that he could reach our shores and get within contact distance."

Hawthorne looked at Kepler. "Forgive me Alan, but so far, you've done nothing to instill trust. I don't think you have any control over Paxton West."

Chapter Seventy-Four

According to his watch, Dr. Alan Kepler's current "resting" heartrate was running at 135 beats a minute. He gripped the steering wheel of his 1989 Saab 900 Aero Turbo 16s tightly as he navigated the darkened streets of Washington, D.C. The car's turbocharged engine roared as he pushed it hard, weaving through traffic with the precision of a man who valued time above all else.

He pressed a small button on the car's dash, and ahead, a nondescript garage door began to rise. The light came on and it revealed a tidy, two-car garage attached to a modest yet elegant home.

The house was a classic colonial-style brick home, nestled in a quiet, affluent neighborhood. Its symmetrical facade featured white-framed windows and a dark blue door, illuminated by a single brass lantern on the porch. Inside, the decor was refined but understated – hardwood floors, a Persian rug in the entryway, and built-in bookshelves lining the walls of the living room, crammed with titles on history, science, and philosophy. A grandfather clock ticked softly in the corner, and the air carried the faint scent of leather and wood polish.

Kepler slammed the car door shut and hurried inside, his footsteps echoing on the polished floors. His hands trembled slightly as he made his way to a cabinet in the study. Pulling open the drawer with more force than necessary, he retrieved a SIG Sauer P226, its weight comforting in his palm.

He checked the magazine, his breathing quick but controlled. Fear was there, alright. It gnawed at him, making him feel vulnerable and defenseless. A highly trained predator was circling, and he was the prey. Yet when his hand tightly gripped the gun, it steadied him.

Kepler moved to the desk, picked up his cell phone and dialed Vaughn Sinclair's secure line. The call connected with a single click.

"Vaughn," Kepler said, his voice urgent, "Paxton's here. In the US."

A pause, then Vaughn's calm, gravelly voice came through. "How can you be sure?"

Kepler swallowed, his grip tightening on the pistol. "Marcus Voss failed to turn up to his meeting with Hawthorne with the rest of us. There's no way he'd blow the VP off. Paxton must have gotten to him."

Another pause, longer this time. "Understood," Vaughn said, his tone colder now. "Stay put. I'm nearly at your house."

"Good." Kepler ducked down at the back of his study, where he had a full view of the door, and his pistol aimed at it. He wasn't taking any chances with Paxton. "Drive quickly."

"I'm going as fast as I can." Vaughn said, "What about the VP?"

"What about him?"

"Do you still want me to go through with the assassination?" Vaughn said. "I mean, now that your next horse isn't likely to be alive to step up to the Presidential ticket?"

"Yes," Kepler said. "Don't worry about it. I'll find another candidate to put in his place. Frost and I can still make this work. We just need to get rid of Hawthorne. He's a liability that will sink us all."

"Copy that," Vaughn said. "I'm nearly at your house."

"Great. When you get here, I'd like to know how you're going to take care of Paxton West." Kepler ended the call, but kept the pistol aimed at the door.

Behind him, Paxton West put the barrel of a Glock 19 at the side of his head.

Kepler slowly turned.

"Nice." There was a big, playful grin on Paxton's cheerful lips. "I'd like to hear how you plan on taking care of me, too."

Chapter Seventy-Five

D r. Kepler said, "I didn't want it to end this way."

Paxton grinned. "I believe you."

"I mean, with you. You were like a son to me. The best operative I ever had."

"If I were your son, you would be in jail for the things you did to me. Your actions and your experimentation amounted to uniquely perverse and cruel child abuse, all in the name of psychology." Paxton shrugged. "You guided me into being the assassin I am today. You taught me that I wasn't good at anything else, but that I might redeem myself by learning to murder for my country."

"I tried my best."

"Perhaps you did, but it wasn't good enough. For forty years I've had to live with that." Paxton made a theatrical sigh. "Fortunately, I've had the good luck to spend some time with two smart women recently. I didn't quite understand the guidance from the first one, but the second one got through and gave me really good advice. Do you want to know what she told me?"

"What did she tell you?" Dr. Kepler asked, returning to his neurology training.

Paxton said, "She said my future isn't written down anywhere. I can change. There's no rule about having to commit to be a psychopathic killer for the rest of my life. I get to choose. Not you. Not the CIA or anyone else. And I'm choosing a new life."

"I'm proud of you, Paxton..."

The door opened in the living room.

Vaughn said, "I'm here Kepler, where are you?"

Paxton said, "I'd love to chat about my newfound life goals, but time's up doctor." He squeezed the trigger, and a 9mm parabellum ripped through Kepler's skull, remodeling his magnificent brain.

Vaughn approached with his silenced Sig Sauer.

He kicked open the door.

Paxton grabbed Dr. Kepler's corpse and used it as a shield. He backed away, through the hallway, shooting back at Vaughn. The shots missed, but it prevented his adversary from stepping out long enough to take proper aim.

Bodies made incredibly poor shields, but dragging Kepler around was better than nothing. Besides, he didn't intend to take any chances, so he wouldn't actually need the corpse. Vaughn showed part of his head, and Paxton took a shot at it.

The drywall exploded where the round landed.

Paxton backed up down the hallway toward the garage. He grabbed a set of car keys from their hook beside the door. Stepping through the internal garage door, he slid a large snow shovel into the door handle, to prevent it from being opened.

There were two cars there.

A modern Mercedes-Benz E-Class sedan – sleek and powerful.

Next to it, was a 1989 Saab 900 Aero Turbo 16s – a collector's item, quirky and cool.

He wished he'd grabbed the keys to the more reliable modern Mercedes and climbed into the Saab.

Extended the seat all the way back, as far as it would go.

Put the key where the ignition normally should been...

And frowned.

It wasn't there.

He definitely should have grabbed the keys to the modern Mercedes!

Vaughn started kicking the garage door. Paxton looked around the interior of the old, classic sports car.

The door slammed open.

Paxton took two shots at the man walking through it. The shots hit Vaughn in the middle of his chest. He twisted in pain but kept moving, raising his Sig Sauer to shoot back.

Paxton fumbled with the key, still looking for the damned ignition.

Then, his eyes landed on it. There it was! At the center console just below the gear stick.

Who the hell puts the ignition switch there?

Another shot fired.

What did they think the were doing, building an aircraft?

Paxton turned the key.

The 2.0 L 4-cylinder, 16-valve, turbocharged engine roared into life. Paxton pressed his foot on the clutch, shoved the gearstick into reverse, and planted his foot on the accelerator.

The Saab launched itself backward, smashing through the unopened garage door.

Paxton swung the wheel.

Shifted into first, and accelerated away hard...

The Saab's front wheels screeched under the sudden acceleration.

Chapter Seventy-Six

Paxton West's 1989 Saab 900 Aero Turbo 16s tore through the streets of Washington, D.C. The Saab's headlights illuminated the darkened streets ahead, but its angular design and compact frame made it feel like a relic in the face of Vaughn's hulking, modern off road pick-up truck.

Leave it to that Vaughn to find himself a high-performance Ford F-150 Raptor R, a supercharged V8 engine, damn him!

Paxton downshifted and floored the gas pedal, pushing the vintage Saab to its limits. The turbocharger whined as it spooled up, the distinctive sound building to a crescendo. But then came the dreaded turbo lag – a brief, maddening pause before the boost kicked in.

For a heartbeat, the engine felt sluggish. The Raptor R was closing in, its bright LED headlights flooding his mirrors.

Then the Saab's turbocharger screamed to life, delivering a surge of power that slammed Paxton back into the seat. The tires screeched as the Aero surged forward, weaving between cars. It felt like he was on a Star Wars speeder bike, slipping in through a crowded forest. The exhaust note barked sharply with each gear shift, accompanied by the signature hiss of the turbo's blow-off valve as Paxton pushed the car harder.

Behind him, Vaughn's F-150 Raptor R was relentless, its engine roaring like a beast. The truck's massive frame allowed it to bulldoze through obstacles, but its size was a liability in the tight urban streets. Paxton smiled when he noticed Vaughn wrestling with the wheel as he tried to keep up, the Raptor's tires squealing with the strain.

Paxton spotted an intersection ahead.

The traffic light glared red, and the cross street was alive with rushing vehicles. He assessed the gap – a narrow, nearly impossible margin – and clenched his teeth.

"Here we go," he muttered, yanking the wheel to line up perfectly with the opening.

The Saab darted through the intersection, a hair's breadth from disaster as cars honked and swerved around him. The turbocharger howled, propelling him out the other side unscathed.

Behind him, Vaughn also took his chances.

His massive Raptor R followed too closely, its size making it harder to navigate the chaos. A Peterbilt truck barreling through the cross street was unable to stop in time. The semi's horn blared as it slammed into the Raptor's rear quarter, spinning the truck violently into the curb. Metal crunched, and sparks flew as the pickup came to a shuddering halt.

Paxton glanced in the rearview mirror, catching a glimpse of the wreck.

A grim yet satisfied smile flickered across his face as he shifted gears and pressed on, the Saab's engine still singing with the raw energy of its turbocharged power.

Vaughn climbed out of the wreckage.

A passerby ran toward him to check if he was all right.

Ignoring the helpful bystander, Vaughn aimed the Sig Sauer. Then he started shooting round after round at the retreating sight of Paxton's Saab.

Chapter
Seventy-Seven

Friday – University of Notre Dame

The University of Notre Dame stretched out before Paxton. Known for its football team "the Fighting Irish," its academic programs, and its traditions. The university had an impressive campus. For a moment, he suffered a twinge of jealousy.

Its iconic architecture was bathed in the golden hues of the setting sun. From his vantage point on the roof of a nearby building, he saw the Golden Dome glinting in the light, its shimmering surface, a beacon of convention. The surrounding buildings, a mix of Gothic Revival and modern styles, framed the sprawling quads where students milled about, oblivious to the deadly game unfolding above them.

Beyond the campus, the quiet streets of South Bend seemed remarkably peaceful, a stark contrast to the tension thrumming in Paxton's chest.

Paxton lay prone on the rooftop, his McMillan TAC-50 sniper rifle resting securely on its bipod. Through the scope, he watched the entrance to the University of Notre Dame's main drive, his eyes narrowing as the VP's motorcade approached.

The procession was exactly what he'd expected – two black SUVs bracketing a sleek, armored Cadillac One, its polished surface gleaming under the streetlights. The convoy moved steadily; the faint hum of engines audible even from his perch. Secret Service agents flanked the vehicles on foot as they pulled through the main gates and onto campus.

Paxton tracked the cars through his scope, watching as they passed his position and continued toward a parking area near one of the larger lecture halls. The vehicles finally came to a stop, the agents moving swiftly to secure the perimeter.

He adjusted the scope on his TAC-50, the weight of the weapon resting solidly in his hands. Vaughn was supposed to arrive soon. Paxton didn't know what car his adversary would be driving now that his Ford F-150 Raptor R had been totaled, so he watched every vehicle approaching the VIP entrance with careful precision.

Black SUVs, luxury sedans, and even the occasional nondescript car passed through the checkpoint, each scrutinized by Paxton's unerring gaze. But Vaughn wasn't with any of them. His gut tightened.

Vaughn was too meticulous to be late. Was he already here?

Paxton leaned back slightly, his mind racing with possibilities. If Vaughn wasn't arriving in one of those vehicles, it meant he was already in position. His thoughts flashed to an image of Dr. Kepler's garage, to the second car parked there. Yes, it was a Mercedes-Benz E-Class sedan, modern and unobtrusive. Perfect for slipping past without drawing attention.

Paxton shifted his scope to the parking lot nearby. His heart sank when he spotted that the E-Class was already there. Vaughn had anticipated him. God, he really hated that.

Paxton exhaled slowly, his instincts sharpening.

If he were Vaughn, he wouldn't waste time joining the motorcade. He'd already be in place, set up somewhere high, with a clear line of sight to take the shot first.

Paxton tensed, his eyes darting away from the lot and scanning the skyline. He turned his scope toward the roof of another building behind him, just as a flicker of light – probably a reflection off a rifle scope – caught his attention.

There he was.

Vaughn Sinclair. AKA Umbra. His arch enemy. His constant opponent over a period of weeks. The fellow Ghost and assassin he just couldn't seem to get rid of.

Umbra...

The darkest part of a shadow, where the light source was, had changed. It was now completely blocked.

They were both locked on one another, staring down the barrels of their rifles, their scopes aligned as though part of some deadly mirror image. Paxton's pulse slowed, his focus narrowing to the moment.

Vaughn's face behind the scope was a mask of calm, but Paxton knew better than to hesitate. Automatically, he adjusted his aim ever so slightly, targeting Vaughn's head instead of his torso. He had learned from their previous encounters that Umbra wore a Kevlar vest.

This round had to count.

Paxton squeezed the trigger.

The TAC-50 roared, its recoil slamming into his shoulder. Through the scope, he saw the impact – a single, precise bullet that pierced Vaughn's skull. The man's brain turned to mush, and his body crumpled backward and out of view.

Head shot.

Huh. That was easy.

Paxton lowered the McMillan TAC-50 onto the rooftop, leaving it exactly where it lay. He moved swiftly but without panic to the edge of the building, his boots making barely a sound on the gravel-strewn roof. Crouching at the back corner, he peered over the edge. The alley below was empty, its dim light providing just enough visibility for him to gauge the height.

Swinging his legs over the side, he gripped the ledge tightly, his body hanging for a moment. Then, he let go, dropping the last ten feet to the ground. His knees bent slightly to absorb the impact, and he straightened immediately, brushing himself off as though it were any other step in his day.

Without looking back, Paxton casually walked toward the Saab.

He got inside, inserted the key in the center console ignition, and drove away. Paxton suddenly threw his head back and laughed aloud.

That persistent assassin had been damned difficult to kill.

But you know what?

Paxton decided that the third time really was a charm.

Chapter Seventy-Eight

Foggy Bottom, Washington, D.C.

Paxton watched Vanessa Ellis leave her house and approach her car. The woman had a two-week-old bruise on her face, tastefully covered up with makeup. At five foot two, she was short, with a slim figure and a pretty face. She was good looking, not model or stripper goodlooking, but nice in a wholesome kind of way. She was dressed in a nice summer dress.

Paxton stepped forward and approached her. In his hand, he held a small canvas duffel bag. A warm smile across his lips, he made his expression soft and gentle.

Their eyes met briefly.

She looked away, as though she was used to men noticing her, or perhaps questioning her about her injuries.

Paxton said, "I can make the beatings stop, ma'am."

There was a crisp, audible gasp. Kind of like the sound a woman makes when she meets a big man in a dark alley at night. Yet the woman collected herself quickly. Her eyes glanced over him from the ground up, before landing on his eyes. She pressed her lips together, thinking it through, and made her voice almost seductive. "A man your size... I bet you could make it stop."

"Would you like me to make that happen?" he said, a little too cheerfully.

She instantly shook her head, dismissing the idea without a thought. "No, please don't! You can't."

That surprised him. All these years. So many sessions with a therapist since childhood, so much study and observation of emotions, and yet humans still had this ability to completely shock him.

Maybe he would truly never understand why people did what they did? This woman had routinely taken a beating from an asshole for years, and now he was offering to make it all go away, and she was begging him not to? What the hell was the go with that?

He met her gaze with a sort of curiosity spread across his lips. "Why not?"

"You just can't." The woman straightened her dress up, she seemed relaxed, and almost pleased that there were still gentlemen in the world who might take one look at her and see the truth and want to put an end to it. She pressed her lips together, vying for time, trying to find the right way to explain her situation.

Eventually, she settled on, "Some things no one can prevent."

"I used to think that way," Paxton said. "But recently a good friend taught me that while there is life, there is hope. We can choose and change our path."

She sighed. "Yeah, well in my case there's no hope, and there's no other option for me."

"Oh..." that gave him paused.

"Some things can't be stopped." She forced a smile. "Thanks for trying. Really."

Paxton said, "But I bet I can stop it."

"Maybe," she agreed, taking in his sheer size once more. Then she shook her head, almost apologetically, as if she were the one at fault here. "Listen. I really need the money."

"Really?" Paxton asked, starting to see the problem.

"Yeah. I have three kids at home. All boys. Good boys. They're gonna grow up to be good men." She shook her head again, unable to quite meet his gaze. "They're never gonna be like this monster. They're smart. They have a real chance to have a better life than me. I want that for them. So, you see, I need this money."

"Is there anything else you can do?" he asked.

A hint of anger flashed in her eyes. "If there was, don't you think I would have done it by now?"

"Oh. You're right." Paxton nodded. "I'm sorry, I wasn't thinking. Please forgive me."

She put an understanding hand on his large shoulder. "Look. It's sweet that you want to fix my problems. But they're *my* problems. I've made plenty of mistakes in my time, and when that happens you have to pay the price. Just now, that price is for me to occasionally take a beating."

Paxton studied her. A different man than him, perhaps someone who had a clue, might have felt sympathy for her, or sadness, or something else, but he didn't feel any of that. He had suppressed that sensitive voice in the back of his head so much, that it no longer meant anything to him.

So, instead, he waited, and he listened.

"It's okay. If you're gonna take a beating, it may as well be from the next President of the United States." She drew a breath and sighed slowly. "Do you know I get paid five times as much to take a beating?"

"Honestly, I didn't know that was a thing," Paxton replied.

"Yeah, well, for him, beating on women is an addiction. It makes him feel powerful and in control." She shrugged. "You don't look like the kind of person that has that sick kind of need."

Paxton considered that. "I guess not."

"It's okay. There are plenty of strange people out there. For him, it's usually only superficial. Sometimes when he's drunk, he hits a bit too hard, but generally, the bruises go away in a week or so. If anything, I see myself as a service to other women out there. While he's paying for it, at least some other poor unsuspecting girl isn't getting hit."

Paxton nodded. "That is a good thing."

The woman laughed.

"What's so funny?"

"I didn't expect you to accept it all so well. I don't even know why I told you any of this, but once I started talking, I figured you'd get all high and mighty with me."

"I'm not one to judge." Paxton spread his hands. "I'm not perfect, and hey, it's your life to live as you think best."

Vanessa, checking out his size once more, smirked. "I bet you've never had trouble with a man wanting to beat on you."

Paxton thought about telling her that most people generally tried to stab or kill him but stopped himself. It hardly seemed like the right time.

"Listen." Paxton handed her the duffel bag. "Have this and then tell me I can't take your problems away."

"I'm kind of in a hurry." She pressed her lips together. "I'm on my way to see him now. There's a very exacting routine my client uses, and I can't even be a minute late."

"You have a few seconds. That's all it will take to just check out what is in there."

Vanessa unzipped it and looked inside. Without thinking she swore volubly at the sight. Tightly packed stacks of crisp hundred-dollar bills were all lined up. The scent of freshly printed cash wafted up, unmistakable and sharp. Vanessa's brows lifted slightly as she surveyed the contents, her mind already working.

Vanessa was good at arithmetic.

She took in the rows and columns of bundled notes, calculating quickly. Each stack was bound neatly with a bank strap marking $10,000, and there were rows upon rows of them. Her lips pressed into a thin line as she finished the mental math.

"Half a million," she breathed.

"Correct." Paxton smiled.

"I don't sell drugs," she said, the tone of her voice emphatic, like someone who'd already learned that lesson the hard way.

"I'm not asking you to."

"And I don't deal in underage women."

"No underage women," Paxton confirmed.

"Or boys."

Paxton pressed his lips together, making no attempt to hide his distaste. "I'm not interested in kids of either sex."

She looked greedily at the money. It was a life-changing amount of cash, but this had to be a trap. No one gives anyone anything for nothing. A disbelieving sneer curled her full lips. "Okay, what's the catch? What do you expect me to do?"

"Go and live that life you wished for as a kid. That's it. The money won't last forever, but it's a good start."

"That's it?" she asked, a combination of joy and incredulity shining like a beacon from her face. "You're giving me a half a million dollars?"

"That's it," he confirmed.

"There's nothing else I can do for you? Are you sure?" There was something almost seductive and expectant in her voice.

Paxton grinned. "As a matter of fact, there is just one thing. You can help me prevent a very bad man from hurting anyone ever again…"

Chapter Seventy-Nine

S**unday – Number One Observatory Circle, Washington, D.C.**

Vice President Hawthorne opened the door to his study, then looked up and down the hallway. Agent Shaw was on duty.

"Can I help you, Mr. Vice President?"

"You can call me 'sir,' son, when it's the weekend and I'm at the residence," Hawthorne said in a friendly tone.

"Yes, sir."

Hawthorne studied him. He was a good operator and a "by the book" rule follower. Very diligent and keen as they come. Perhaps a little overzealous, but that wasn't a bad habit for someone in his line of work. He said, "I'll be having a guest over for some private relaxation time for the next few hours, and I'm not to be disturbed."

"Yes sir."

Then, just to make sure, Hawthorne added, "The other agents have explained the situation to you?"

"Yes, sir." Agent Shaw said. "Agent King briefed me. I'll leave you alone but I'll be just at the end of the hallway if you need anything, sir."

"Very good, young man."

Hawthorne closed the door and poured himself a glass of whiskey.

It was rare for him to spend time with Vanessa on a Sunday. He practically had to tell his wife to go out for the evening. His wife hesitated and then decided that it was better to go to the farm anyway, when he was in 'a mood.' His wife knew the signs as well as he did when he was under a lot of tension due to the pressures of his job.

Sometimes, he wondered if she knew about his perverse desires. She was a good woman who would have kept quiet for the sake of the nation if she had known the truth. Then again, who could tell what a woman might do?

Either way, it didn't matter.

What's that old Shakespearean quote? *To thine own self be true...* What was it, Hamlet or something? He had long since forgotten. But he would always remember the point: *Don't lie to yourself.*

Hawthorne was under more stress than he had ever had at any other point in his life. He was certain Voss and Kepler were both dead. Only he and Dylan Frost had made it through this frightening week alive.

Hawthorne thought of Venessa's young, soft, skin. It reddened and bruised so easily. *So beautifully.*

He was glad he'd made the decision to see her.

Hawthorne felt he deserved a reward tonight. He drew a breath and reveled in the fact that it was all finally over. He'd received a report from the Director of the Secret Service. They had found and shot a man armed with a military grade, sniper rifle on top of the roof of his old alma mater at the University of Notre Dame building. They had also found a bomb in an E Class Mercedes in the parking lot, which the man had stolen from Dr. Alan Kepler, after presumably killing him in his own home.

The bomb was laced with uranium, in addition to traditional explosives. If it had been allowed to detonate, it would have caused devastating injuries, killing hundreds during the speech he had given to a class of Taiwanese and Chinese foreign students. Imagining what could have happened sent ice cold shivers down his spine. He could barely envision the repercussions such an attack would have had on the world. The Chinese would have blamed the Taiwan, and the Taiwanese would have blamed the Chinese. They would have gone to war, and Russia would have sided with China.

The American People would have been outraged.

The US would be forced to take the side of the Taiwanese.

NATO would have been brought in, and the globe would have been plunged into its darkest hours as World War III would have begun.

The CIA, FBI, NSA, Homeland Security were all trying to find out who the assassin was. So far, they had no leads, and Hawthorne doubted they ever would.

But he knew what the man's name was:

Paxton West.

Chapter Eighty

Hawthorne heard the secret tunnel's buzzer alarm. He checked the security screen, confirming it was Vanessa Ellis.

She was wearing a yellow summer dress that made her look lovely. Young. Vulnerable. Weak and defenseless. She was everything his wife wasn't. That wasn't to say he didn't love his wife. He did. It was simply that Vanessa attended to his needs in a way his wife never could.

Hawthorne laughed.

His wife would have him charged for assault if he were to ever lay a single finger on her. What did he expect when he had married a successful Harvard Lawyer?

No. Just spending quality time with Vanessa was perfect. Besides, no one person could be all things to him. He was a powerful man with many and various needs. Hawthorne smiled and pressed the release button behind his desk.

The secret door opened.

Vanessa looked furtive, much more scared today than usual. The look in her eyes was what he liked best. That and her screams and when she begged him to stop. Not that he would stop.

"Hello, sir," she greeted him, her terrified eyes quickly downcast.

Oh, he liked that.

Perhaps our last session together had finally put them on a different footing? Was that genuine respect and fear in her gaze?

The secret door closed automatically and locked.

It was just the two of them.

Hawthorne glared at her, pointing to the ground. Vanessa went to her knees. Then the VP gestured for her to come closer. He stayed seated in his chair, making her crawl to him as he always did.

Head down, she crawled very slowly, until she reached his chair.

"Kiss me," he commanded.

As ordered, Vanessa kissed him on the lips. It was long, and slow, and he savored the taste. He drew back, studied her, and then punched her in the mouth.

She screamed. Shock radiated from her pain-filled gaze which she quickly lowered.

He examined her mouth. The force of his blow had been strong enough to split her lip, and there was blood running freely down her face. He shook out his fist as his knuckles had been grazed by one of her teeth.

"Come closer," he demanded.

She swallowed hard, and hesitantly moved toward him, clearly terrified of what he might do to her next. He drew her toward him and kissed her hard. There was something about her bloody lip that drove him mad with desire. She seemed to lean into that feeling, kissing him hard, as though she too was inflamed.

A moment later, he felt one of her fingernails scratch his neck.

Hawthorne swore loudly and stood up, knocking her back to the floor. Vanessa quickly backed away, frightened of what he would do to her now.

And he knew exactly what he would do to her.

Hawthorne reached up to touch his neck and felt something wet. He glanced at his fingers. There was blood on them.

Just a drop.

But this was the first time she'd ever drawn his blood.

How had she done it?

From her nails?

He glared at her with vitriolic rage and knew he was going to really lose it this time. It wasn't even his fault. What did she expect he was going to do?

This time, he was going to beat her so hard he would nearly kill her. "You fucking bitch!" he screamed.

She edged back further, terror in her eyes.

He lifted his arm to punch her, but the entire limb seemed sluggish. Like it was glued down. He dropped back into the chair, feeling stuck. Trapped in his own body, unable to move... Hawthorne tried to scream for help, but his body no longer obeyed him.

His eyes looked up at her and he silently mouthed: *What did you do to me?*

Ignoring him, she quickly reached across his body and onto the desk, where the secret control to open the tunnel door was located. She pressed the button...

A giant of a man came in.

Hawthorne could now barely hold his head up on his own. His gaze locked on the monster of his nightmares. It was Paxton West! The ghost assassin was coming his way!

The huge mountain of a man walked toward him.

Hawthorne just stared at him, startled by the sunny smile on Paxton's face.

Chapter Eighty-One

Panicked, Hawthorne wanted to draw back, but he couldn't. His heart jolted with fear like nothing he had ever experienced.

The monster towered over him. The VP was a big guy, and in his youth, he had been an exceptional quarterback. Even then, he was never as large as Paxton. The man's dossier indicated he was a big guy, but nothing like this. He looked like a human bulldozer.

Paxton exchanged a quick glance with Vanessa. "Thanks, you can go. I assure you nobody wants to see what I'm going to do to the Vice President."

Her instant reaction was to look a little horrified.

Touching her split lip, she glanced at the VP, paralyzed in his chair. Then she gave a one shoulder shrug. It was a gesture that suggested he'd made this bed for himself, and now he could lay in it for all she cared.

"Alright." She nodded. "Thank you."

"No." He shot her a mischievous grin. "Thank you for your service to the country."

Nodding goodbye, Vanessa walked out through the secret door.

Hawthorne, trapped in his own body, tried to shake off his invisible shackles.

"Please, don't get up." Paxton smiled like the psychopath he was. "I'll come to you."

Hawthorne tried to fight the sickness that was preventing him from moving his body, but nothing happened. His body seemed slack and trembling, paralyzed. The psycho assassin crouched down beside him... to watch.

The VP's labored breathing echoed in the quiet room, his eyes wide with panic but unable to focus on anything except Paxton's calm and chilling expression.

Paxton smiled again like a child opening presents on Christmas day.

So much for this guy being entirely devoid of emotions.

Paxton said, "Vanessa nicked you with a pin tipped in the sap of Antiaris toxicaria – AKA the upas tree in Papua New Guinea."

Hawthorne struggled to keep his eyes open, much less respond.

Paxton kept talking as though they were engaged in a fascinating conversation. "Its sap has been used for centuries by hunters in Africa and Southeast Asia, and of course, Papua New Guinea. They coat their arrows with it – one scratch, and the hunt is over."

He paused, letting the words sink in. "You've been scratched, too. A tiny cut, just enough to introduce the toxin into your bloodstream. It doesn't take much. The sap contains a compound called cardiac glycoside, which acts on your heart and nervous system. Right now, it's coursing through your veins, disrupting the sodium-potassium pump in your cells. That's fancy science talk for your heart beating itself to death."

Hawthorne's eyes flickered, his mouth struggling to form words, but no sound came.

His heart pumped harder, and more erratic.

Paxton smirked. "Oh, you're feeling it already, aren't you? The nausea, the dizziness. Soon, you'll feel your chest tighten, like someone's crushing your heart in their fist. Your pulse will slow, erratic at first, and then..." He made a snapping motion with his fingers. "It stops."

"One of the best things about it," Paxton went on, "Is the drug is almost untraceable in your bloodstream. It's so rare in western society, and its symptoms mimic a heart attack so completely, that it's unlikely anyone will ever check."

Paxton studied him.

Frowned.

"Then again. People like to be given a certainty. Don't you think?" Paxton took out a small, blue tablet. "Always better to provide a sure thing. This is called sildenafil. Some know of it as Viagra. Nothing to be ashamed of..."

Hawthorne struggled, and a slight whimper came out of his mouth.

Paxton regarded him. "Oh no... don't get the wrong idea. This isn't some sort of weird perversion of mine. I'm not that kind of guy. Like you, I have my very own, peculiar vices, but mine don't have anything to do with beating women."

Paxton looked at him, expectantly.

When Hawthorne didn't say anything, Paxton said, "In fact, I don't feel very much of anything."

Paxton seemed to be enjoying himself, despite what he just voiced.

He smiled and cheerfully added, "It was your friend Dr. Alan Kepler who helped me with that. He taught me to suppress my emotions – to ignore that little voice in the back of our head that gives us some sort of moral compass. In my case, and I guess in yours too, it was wrong more often than not."

The slightest of moans escaped from his mouth.

"Hey, you're doing great. You really are battling this out, aren't you?" Paxton grinned. "The poison affects the muscles of the diaphragm last, and maybe because you're a big guy, maybe you can fight it?"

Paxton lifted the blue tablet. "Here, take this."

Hawthorne felt tears stream down his cheeks, but no sound came out.

"Oh, right... the paralyzed thing." Paxton lifted a hand in a kindly gesture, and said, "No problem. I'll help. These things dissolve in your mouth."

Hawthorne felt Paxton's giant paws open his mouth as easily as if he were a baby, and the tablet was candy.

He felt it dissolve. Could imagine his blood rushing through his veins.

"You know," Paxton said, "it's you who's probably helped me the most."

Hawthorne felt his head tilting to the side.

He couldn't stop it.

"Here let me get that for you." Paxton grabbed his head and re-righted it again.

Hawthorne stared at him through anguished eyes.

"You're welcome," Paxton said, as though he'd done him a great favor. "Where was I? Oh right, it was you who taught me to find joy in righting wrongs and being a defender of the weak."

Hawthorne felt dizzy. His head was going fuzzy too. A combination of Viagra and the poison was taking its toll on the natural electrical activity of his heart and his blood pressure. He could feel his heart sending out multiple aberrant beats.

"Isn't that good?" Paxton smiled. "I mean, after all these years of therapy, and help, and really truly working at it, I've discovered that one of the things that brings me true joy is to put things right again."

Hawthorne felt his world slipping away.

"Are you following me?"

He didn't wait for an answer.

Paxton went on, happy to talk to himself. "In this case, you committed the ultimate offence."

"I was doing what's right for the country," he tried to mouth, but it came out more as a dribble than actual words.

"Maybe." Paxton gave an indifferent shrug. "Look I don't want to get caught up in semantics. The fact is, you were given a choice between my team to kill, and any other team on the planet – and you chose wrong. You made the call to eliminate my team. My family, really."

Hawthorne tried to scream, but only a grunt came out.

"Murdering my family was the wrong call. But you made it, and we all make mistakes." Paxton continued. "It's just, in this case, you have to pay for that mistake. You don't get to live with it."

Hawthorne's breath came in short, rasps.

Paxton came closer and looked right into his eyes. "You know what you should never ever do when you take Viagra?"

Hawthorne wanted to scream so badly.

Where was that uppity follow the rules guy, Agent Shaw?

Paxton looked at a bottle of Anginine – also known as Glyceryl Trinitrate. "Look, it has your name on it and everything. Now, it even says not to take this if you've had Viagra. I wonder why that is?" Paxton grinned. "Let's find out, shall we?"

Paxton held the VP's head up once more, opening his mouth, and dropping a couple of tablets in the buccal mucosa – that highly vascular part beneath the tongue. That way the key ingredients would be quickly absorbed into his bloodstream.

Hawthorne's body was heavy. Useless. The muscle relaxant coursing through his veins had robbed him of any ability to move, yet his mind remained cruelly alert.

Hawthorne wanted to shout, to beg, to bargain, but his lips wouldn't move.

A sharp, bitter taste filled his mouth as Paxton slipped the GTN under his tongue.

Seconds later, he felt unnatural warmth spreading through his chest.

It started as a faint buzzing in his ears, a warning of the storm brewing within. A wave of heat flushed throughout his body, making his skin slick with sweat. His chest tightened, a dull ache that rapidly sharpened into a spear of pain. His vision blurred, the edges of the room swimming in and out of focus.

What's happening to me?

The question screamed in his mind, but his body refused to obey his desperate commands. His heart pounded wildly, erratically – a racing thrum that seemed to fill the room. He could feel each beat as if it were a hammer striking his ribs from the inside.

Suddenly, his pulse faltered, stumbling like a runner tripping over unseen obstacles. His breaths came in shallow gasps, each one more labored than the last. His limbs tingled, his fingers curling involuntarily as if trying to grasp something – anything – to anchor him.

The ache in his chest turned crushing, like an invisible vise clamping tighter and tighter. His head swam, and dark spots danced across his vision. He was dimly aware of Paxton standing over him, watching with clinical detachment. A scientist observing curious reactions to an experiment.

The erratic pounding in the VP's chest reached a crescendo, skipping wildly, then slowing... pausing... fluttering. A moment of stillness, then a final, desperate spasm. His entire body jerked once, violently, before falling limp.

The last sound Hawthorne heard was the deafening silence of his heart ceasing to beat.

Chapter Eighty-Two

The Vice President was dead.

Paxton walked out of the secret tunnel, through the garden, and climbed into the Saab. He put the key in its quirky center console and turned the ignition. The 2L engine came alive with a gravelly roar. The car was growing on him. He could finally see why Dr. Kepler had kept it all these years.

Satisfied with what he had achieved so far, he drove off. There was just one more stop to make. Paxton made the short drive to Georgetown.

He ran his eyes across the rows of historic buildings with ivy creeping up their facades, wrought iron balconies, and colorful shutters framing windows like picture frames. He continued, looking for what he was after.

A four-story Federal-style townhouse came into view.

Its brick exterior was darkened with age, the mortar between the bricks crumbling in places, lending it an air of timeless respectability. A small plaque near the door declared it to be "Kensington and Co. Law Offices."

He regarded the shuttered windows, each adorned with neatly trimmed flower boxes that were just a little too perfect. It was as though they were tended by someone more interested in appearances than flowers.

Slowing to a stop at the side alley next to the building, Paxton reached into the glovebox and pulled out a small, nondescript black beeper.

He pressed the button and waited.

A moment later, a faint mechanical whir broke through the quiet, and a section of the alley's brick wall slid aside, revealing the entrance to an underground parking garage. A red light above the entrance flickered, scanning the area, and a security camera swiveled toward the Saab.

Paxton leaned back in his seat, letting the system confirm the car's plates and his presence.

The light turned green, and the heavy steel door groaned open, the dimly lit ramp spiraling downward like the throat of some secretive beast.

Paxton shifted the Saab into gear and guided it inside.

Behind him, the door rumbled shut, sealing him off from the outside world.

Voss had told him the building was intentionally separated from the rest of the CIA at Langley, Virginia to serve as a cut-out between the Agency's spies and the people responsible for building their fictional lives. This included a social media presence, education work histories, and familial connections. These days, Ghosts triggered more alarm bells when their online presence was non-existent.

This is why the Kensington and Co. Law Offices existed. Internally, they were referred to as Paper Magicians.

And Dylan Frost, the last living member of the cabal, was the head of the department.

Kensington and Co. were independent of the Office of Technical Services at Langley who specialize in fake passports, identification documents, and other forged materials. They were capable of producing all of these too, but they mainly specialized in background and online histories.

Paxton parked the Saab, got out and stepped up the two flights of stairs into the main building.

Dylan Frost, working alone, came out to greet him. "Dr. Kepler! I've been worried sick..."

Seeing Paxton, he stopped just about as dead as he would be soon enough.

The man had long hair, tied loosely at the nape of his neck, and his wire-rimmed glasses gave him the look of a man who could have walked straight out of a tech startup – or a hacker movie.

Paxton smiled, pointing his Glock at the man. "You must be Dylan Frost."

Chapter Eighty-Three

"I swear I had nothing to do with it," Dylan said, all but confirming his guilt.

Paxton nodded. "I believe you."

Dylan's shoulder's slumped forward with relief. "Really?"

"Sure," Paxton smiled cheerfully. "You don't look like someone responsible for the deaths of all the people in the world who I hold so dear."

Dylan swallowed, not sure if he should take Paxton at his word or not.

Together, they stood in an awkward silence.

Paxton let it linger.

In his experience, it was always better to let the other person talk first. He had the gun, so as far as he was concerned, he had all day.

Dylan drew a breath. "So, what can I do for you Mr. West?"

He grinned stupidly. "Paxton will do fine. We're all alone here. No need for formalities."

"Okay, Paxton." Dylan mustered all the show of strength he could, and asked, "What can I do for you?"

"You're a Paper Magician?"

"Yes."

Paxton tilted his head, curiously. "And a digital architect?"

Dylan nodded, trying to see where this was going. "Yes."

"Up until recently, you were responsible for the digital lives of the Ghosts, crafting their fictional lives, including their relationships, children, careers, universities, social clubs, and volunteer work?"

"Yes," Dylan confirmed.

"So, if say… I wanted to start over, and I needed someone to produce a passport, social security numbers, and so on for me, you would be the guy to do it?"

Dylan exhaled, suddenly seeing why Paxton was there, and what he wanted. He hurriedly agreed. "Yes, I can do that for you, my man, Paxton. No problem."

"Great. Thank you."

"What name do you want to go with for your new life?"

"I've been thinking about this." Paxton smiled. "What do you think about Pax West?"

An incredulous grin formed on Dylan's lips. "You want to go by the name Pax?"

"Yeah."

"You know what that means in Latin, don't you?"

"Yes," Paxton smiled. "It means 'Peace.'"

"You want to be known as Peace?"

"Fitting, don't you think?"

"For someone who spent the first forty years of his life raging war on all ends of the earth?" Dylan pressed his lips together. "Yeah, a little ironic more like. Want to try again?"

Paxton shook his head. "I would have thought you would be more agreeable to the name, given I have a gun pointed at your head."

"Good point." Dylan typed the words: *Pax West* into his CIA database. "Right you are, Pax."

"Thank you," Paxton replied.

He watched as the digital architect worked his magic. Twenty minutes later, Dylan handed him a brand-new passport in the name: Pax West.

Paxton took it, looked at the photo. He smiled. He looked good.

Dylan then printed an outline of everything that was known by government officials about the man. Paxton ran his gaze across the sheet of paper. There was his social security number, and he was up to date with his tax returns. He'd gone to junior school at Riverdale, then Lake Oswego High, in Portland, Oregon. He had a GPA of 3.4, worked in a timber yard and had done so since leaving high school, and had a single speeding ticket.

Paxton pointed to the ticket. "What's that for? I'm usually a very careful driver."

"Sure. Paxton might have been, but on paper, Pax West has made a mistake and gotten caught once. That has to go in there."

"Why?"

"Otherwise, it's too clean. It flags another series of problems on government databases, and you might be spotted."

Paxton grinned. "You mean, another agency outside of the CIA might pick up that I'm a spy?"

Dylan turned the palms of his hands outward. "Bingo."

"Interesting."

"Yeah," Dylan agreed.

Paxton said, "So, this whole new alias is good to go?"

"Absolutely, man. You can catch a flight to Europe, Australia, Africa. Or just stay here and enjoy the good old US of A. Whatever you want, man."

"That's great." Paxton pocketed the passport and the sheet with his newfound identity details. "Thank you, Dylan. Of the four, you've been the most readily helpful. I appreciate that."

"You're welcome." Dylan turned to face him.

Paxton pointed the Glock at the man's face.

"Woah! Pax!" Dylan swore, lifting his hands in supplication. "I thought we had a deal? What happened to peace?"

Paxton gave an unapologetic smile. "Sometimes the fastest way to achieve peace is by making sure you kill every single one of your enemies. This is me, leaving nothing but Scorched Earth."

Dylan opened his mouth to protest.

Paxton didn't wait to hear what he had to say. He didn't care, and whatever it was, it couldn't change the fact that the man was the final chain in the loop who knew the truth. He did nothing to prevent someone killing his men.

He squeezed the trigger.

Two holes.

Right in the head.

The *Coup de Grâce*.

Plain and simple.

He looked at the passport photo again, his eyes narrowing in on the name: "Pax West."

Out loud, he said, "Peace. I like that. The new me."

Pax turned and walked away.

No reason to tidy up or organize a cleaning crew. After all, he was a Ghost. It's impossible to find a Ghost, and therefore impossible to prosecute one.

Chapter Eighty-Four

Agent Shaw said, "The VP hasn't left his study in hours."

"So?" Agent King asked. "Didn't he say he was going to be having some private time in there?"

"Yes."

"Well, you know what that means, don't you? It's a code, not much of euphemism. It simply means he'll be in there with Vanessa Ellis."

"That was four hours ago." Shaw shook his head. "The VP might have been an athlete in his youth, but he isn't that young anymore."

With a sigh, Agent King decided that Shaw had a point. At first, he phoned, but the VP didn't pick up. Then he knocked heavily on the VP's door.

No response.

When the two agents used their passkey to enter the VP's quarters, they were both stunned to find the VP appeared to be dead. He wasn't breathing, and his heart had stopped beating.

Agent Shaw called for an ambulance, and together, the team of Secret Service agents worked their hardest to save his life, providing the very best CPR that could be performed. An AED – Automatic External Defibrillator – was brought to him and the pads attached to the man's barrel chest.

The machine analyzed the VP's heart rhythm, but there was no longer any electrical activity whatsoever.

When the paramedics arrived, they kept working.

Nobody wants to call it when it's the Vice President of the United States of America, yet death didn't discriminate. It didn't care about those who had near absolute power. And despite everyone's best efforts, the VP was pronounced dead on arrival at Walter Reed National Military Medical Center.

Afterward, there would be an extensive investigation.

Agent Shaw didn't follow the VP to the hospital. His job was to secure the potential crime scene. Shaw found notes on Hawthorne's laptop. Talking points for the need to raise minimum wages to increase the wealth of all Americans.

It was tragic.

Hawthorne had died looking after the little guys, the average citizen of the United States.

Nearby was an open bottle of GTN, a common heart medication used to relieve the symptoms of angina, or a heart attack. On the packet, was a note that the medication was not to be taken in conjunction with Viagra.

Shaw thought about all the moans and screams he often heard radiating from the study. Hawthorne seemed like a pretty healthy guy, but he was in his sixties. Was it possible he might need some erectile assistance?

He found a locked drawer, the key sat on a hook next to the desk. Using the key, he unlocked it. There, sitting clear as day was a small packet of Viagra. Several tablets were already missing. Shaw closed the drawer.

He called Agent King over as he was in charge of the investigation. Then he showed him both medications. "Look what I found sir."

Agent King stared at the two medications. The implication would be obvious to all, including the VP's wife. Vice President Daniel Hawthorne had been having an affair.

The news would ruin his reputation.

Agent King said, "This doesn't leave this room."

Shaw said, "But this is evidence..."

"No," King said, his voice emphatic. "VP Hawthorne was a great man. No way am I letting this ruin his legacy. Do I make myself clear?"

"Yes, sir."

"I'll talk to the doctors at Walter Reed. Explain how things are. They'll sign off to say he had a massive heart attack. A sort of ticking time bomb that nobody could have predicted. Are you good with that?"

"Of course." Agent Shaw nodded. "I understand, sir."

"Good man."

Hawthorne had indeed suffered a heart attack, and Shaw didn't know how he felt about that. The man was an asshole of the first order. Apparently, the strain of beating a beautiful woman had stressed his unhealthy heart, and he couldn't take it...

In the end, his wicked vice had killed him.

But Agent King was right.

The man had been a great powerhouse in the Washington. There was no question in his mind, had he lived, he would have been America's next President.

Chapter Eighty-Five

Santorini, Greece

Leyla settled into a cushioned chair on the balcony of her boutique hotel, the soft fabric cool against her sun-warmed skin. The view before her was nothing short of magical – whitewashed buildings with cobalt blue domes clung to the jagged cliffs, cascading down toward the shimmering Aegean Sea below. The water stretched endlessly, a deep sapphire under the cloudless sky, its surface glittering like scattered diamonds in the afternoon sun.

The balcony was bordered by a low wall adorned with vibrant pink bougainvillea, their blossoms framing the vista like a postcard. Far below, the caldera's tranquil waters cradled a handful of small boats, their wakes forming gentle ripples that spread outward. In the distance, the faint silhouette of a volcanic island rose, shrouded in a light haze.

The air was tinged with salt from the sea, mingled with the faint aroma of lemon blossoms from the courtyard below. A warm breeze carried the sounds of the village—a mix of laughter, distant church bells, and the clatter of plates from a nearby taverna.

Leyla opened her laptop, the sleek device a sharp contrast to the natural beauty surrounding her. She connected to the hotel's Wi-Fi, the signal strong despite the remote charm of the location. Her inbox pinged to life, a stream of emails spilling onto the screen. Most were mundane – a reminder about her flight, an update from a friend, a promotional newsletter, and a whole bunch of spam.

Then her eyes landed on a single message from an unknown sender. "An Apology and a Gift – Paxton."

She clicked on the message.

The email was short, brevity being a classic trait of Paxton's.

*

Dear Leyla,

That year I spent with you in 2012 was the best year in my life.

I'm sorry that I couldn't be a better man for you. I hope I didn't take away the good life that you deserved, with another man.

A better one.

*

She didn't believe that for a minute.

Paxton had been good for her. They were just young kids, living life and having a fine time. In another life, they would have run away together. But they didn't. And that was okay.

Her eyes scrolled down to the end of the email.

*

I know you don't care much about money, but given that you're traveling now, a bit of spending money never hurt. Enjoy. Paxton. xx

*

She smiled.

Oh Paxton, you never hurt me...

There was a link to a bitcoin wallet.

She clicked it.

The wallet was stored at a bitcoin exchange. Paxton had set up an account in her name. All she had to do was move the funds into a bank account of her choosing.

She looked at the current value of the account.

It was just over a million US dollars.

Chapter Eighty-Six

Philadelphia, Pennsylvania

The twins were both jumping on their new trampoline. They were laughing, and giggling away, seeing who could make the other one jump the highest.

Rowena stepped outside. "Ruby, Lisa… it's bathtime! There's no more ten minutes left."

"Just one more…"

Rowena drew a breath.

She liked watching them play outside, but it was getting late. She was about to put her angry mommy voice on, and try and assert the issue, when her cell phone rang.

She glanced at it.

It was an unknown number.

She almost dismissed it, but something told her not to. She hit the accept button. "Hello."

"Hey, you," came a familiar voice.

"Paxton!" her heart leaped. "You're alive."

"Yeah. I was a little surprised about that, too."

She stepped inside, letting the girls play a little longer. "Is it over?"

"Yeah, it's all over now. Everyone involved is gone."

Gone.

Another euphemism for dead. And he says it just like one confirming he'd remembered to pick up some milk at the grocery store.

"That's good. I guess. I mean, that we're no longer at risk of starting World War III."

"Yeah, that's what I think."

"What will you do now?" she asked.

"I don't know."

Rowena said nothing, but she thought about it. Paxton sounded different. There was a calmness in his tone. A sort of relief. Maybe a newfound vigor. She knew all this from simply listening to his voice.

"But I think you're right," Paxton offered. "For the first time in my life, I don't have to follow my preplanned programming or idea that someone else set for me. I get to do what I want to do."

"Good for you, Paxton." She smiled. "I mean it. I don't care what you tell me, or what you think you are. I know you're a really good person."

"I don't know if that's true."

"It is." She smiled, her heart bursting inside. "It is. A 100 percent. It's true Paxton. You're a good person. You're kind, and loving, and honest..."

"It's not kindness. It's laziness."

"What?"

"It takes less effort in most situations to be nice. I'm fundamentally lazy. I think that's why I go out of my way to be kind. Takes a lot less effort. See?"

"I think the fact that you understand that, makes you a kind person."

"Okay," Paxton said.

"Where are you headed now?" she asked.

"Union Station."

"Really?" she said, "Where are you headed?"

"I don't know. A new beginning?" There was a sound, as though Paxton was in the grip of a powerful emotion, then he said, "A woman I once knew and loved, told me that I'd traveled extensively, but all of it was just to kill people. I've never really seen the world. You know, really seen it for all its beauty, and wonder, and joy."

"You think you might try viewing the world in a different light? Like you're starting again?"

"Yes. At least, I think I should try it. It might... I don't know, help with my development and personal growth. I don't know if it will work, but I think I should at least try."

"Good for you, Paxton. If you're ever in Philadelphia, give me a call. I'd love to hear how you're getting on with your new life."

"Thank you, Rowena. I will."

Chapter Eighty-Seven

Union Station, Washington, D.C.

Paxton had the freedom to go anywhere and be anyone.

He stepped up to the ticket counter at the interstate Amtrak terminal and asked for the next ticket out of town. He gave no thought about where it was going to go. After all, he had all the time in the world.

The woman behind the ticket counter said, "The next train leaves in five minutes."

Paxton said, "I'll take it."

"Don't you want to know where it's going?" she asked.

Paxton shrugged. "I'm not fussy. Every great journey starts with a single step. It may as well be wherever this train's going."

Her eyes narrowed. "How far do you want to go?"

Paxton shrugged. "I don't care. How far does this train go?"

She glanced at the map. "It terminates in Portland Oregon."

Paxton smiled.

"I'll take it all the way to Portland Oregon." It was a good omen. He may as well visit the places where he was supposed to have grown up, based on his new passport and fictional life. Good to check out the sights and see what his fictional childhood may have been like.

He handed her cash.

"Sure, it's your money." The woman accepted his cash and printed a ticket. "Enjoy."

"Thanks." Paxton looked at his ticket.

He picked up his ticket and walked over to the track, where his train was waiting for him. As he boarded, a train conductor asked for his ticket.

Paxton handed it to him.

The conductor looked at the ticket, then stamped it. "Welcome aboard, Mr. Pax West."

"Thank you."

Pax walked through the train, located his room. He'd paid the additional fare for a Private Suite. He figured it was worth it given the forty-one hours the train was expected to take to reach Portland Oregon. His eyes glanced at the bed. At six-foot-three in length, he would still need to bend his knees for it to accommodate his six-foot-six frame. He sat down. The room would serve its purpose nicely.

A few minutes later, the train gently made its departure.

The Amtrak train rumbled over the Long Bridge, and Pax stared out the window. Below, the Potomac River stretched wide and dark, its still surface fractured by shimmering reflections of amber and white city lights. His gaze caught the Washington Monument rising above the skyline, its alabaster spire glowing stark white against the blackness of the sky. A symbol of power, ideals, and the unyielding grip they had once held over his life.

Farther downriver, the Jefferson Memorial appeared, its dome bathed in a muted, golden glow, soft yet steadfast. It stirred a memory of a promise made long ago. To Pax, it felt less like a monument and more like a sentinel, quietly guarding the weight of history and the choices that had been forged in its shadow.

Pax rested his head against the side of the train.

Then he closed his eyes and drifted peacefully off to sleep.

The End

Made in the USA
Columbia, SC
22 December 2024

50493424R00167